The Black Ledger Billionaires

Rebekah Sinclair

This novel contains **mature themes, explicit content, and dark romance elements** that may be **disturbing or triggering** for some readers.

This book is **intended for adult audiences** and **reader discretion is strongly advised.** If any of these topics are sensitive for you, please proceed with caution.

- Sex Work / Escorting & Virginity Auction
- Transactional / Contract Dynamics & Power Imbalance
- Sexual Power Dynamics & BDSM Undertones
- Obsessiveness, Possessiveness, and Emotional Manipulation
- Stalking, Hacking, & Surveillance / Monitoring
- Coercion, Blackmail, Kidnapping / Confinement
- Physical Violence, Assault, and Threats
- Explicit Sexual Content (M/F, M/F/F, Voyeurism)

- Derogatory / Degrading & Explicit Language
- Serious Parental Illness & End-of-Life Stress (cancer), Family Conflict
- Animal Endangerment (horses threatened and roughly handled, no injury or death)

The Black Ledger

Welcome to The Black Ledger

An elite, highly exclusive escort service where billionaires strike discreet deals, and escorts set their own terms.

~ No complications.
~ No attachments.
~ Just business.

But desire is never that simple.

Here, control turns into obsession, rules are meant to be broken, and the one risk no one dares take—falling in love—may be the most dangerous deal of all.

Because at The Black Ledger,
contracts are final…

But hearts were never meant
to be part of the deal.

Each book is a **standalone** with interconnected characters. ***No cheating***, ***no cliffhangers***—just powerful men, the women who bring them to their knees, and spice that will leave you breathless.

**Thank you for choosing The Black Ledger
and we hope you enjoy your contract.**

Lucian Vale

To my brother, Jonathan:
You're a fucking dick.

SIX YEARS EARLIER

The frat house is loud before we even open the car doors. Bass shakes the windows. Voices spill into the street. The porch is already crowded with guys in jerseys and girls in barely-there dresses clinging to red cups like lifelines.

It's exactly what I expected.

And I'm *ready for it.*

Trey throws the car into park and turns around. "Bree. Final warning. No sneaking off, no drinking, no skinny dipping again—"

"That was once," Bree says sweetly, adjusting the neckline of her sparkly crop top. "And it was *tasteful.*"

They bicker. Like normal siblings. Loud, dramatic, annoyingly endearing.

I don't get that luxury.

Next to him, my brother Jonathan says nothing. He just stares at me in the passenger seat mirror. No humor, no warmth. Just a look that says:

Don't make me regret this.

Bree and I hatched this plan. She threatened her brother Trey if he didn't let her come to the party. Said she would show their mom where he hides his stash of Jim Beam. He agreed but only if she brought a friend with her —probably because of the skinny dipping he just grumbled about.

Bree gave my name and said he'd have to convince Jonathan and—here we are—two high school juniors going to a college frat party.

Bree has been before. Her brother doesn't hate her guts like mine does. He's brought her to an after-game party or summer bonfire.

Jonathan would rather chew glass than take me anywhere. He's only doing it because Trey asked as a favor. He doesn't give a shit about me.

But I don't care. I'm not here for him or to make out with some sports-crazed frat boy.

I'm here for one thing and *that* is Jaxon Kane.

It's been four years since I last saw him. He left when I was thirteen—off to college while the rest of us were still figuring out how to pass Algebra. Back then, he was all crooked smiles and cocky charm. Jonathan's best friend. The boy who used to tease me in the kitchen while his mom cleaned our house and cooked our meals.

He's a genius. Skipped several grades and left my brother behind quickly. Jonathan never did like that but everyone wanted to be Jax's friend so naturally that meant Jonathan had to be his best friend.

He and his mom never had much but you'd never know it. Jaxon always had this carefree air about him. His freshman year in high school he sold an app. I didn't pay attention to it at the time but now I know he made millions off it.

Bought a house for his mom. She quit work.

And the next year he was gone.

Passed right through high school in a summer and colleges nearly offered him to world to come to their school. But now he's back. Several degrees later, if the rumors are true and tonight, I'm going to make sure when he looks at me, he doesn't see Jonathan's kid sister anymore.

Jonathan heads into the open double doors first.

Trey turns around pointing his finger at us, moving back and forth between both of us. "No wandering off. No drinking. If you see a guy in a toga, turn around."

Bree rolls her eyes. "Oh my God, okay Dad!"

"I'm not kidding, Bree!" He calls back. His final threats drowned by the thumping music.

Bree is practically bouncing as we walk toward the house. "You ready for this?"

"I think I'm going to puke."

"Girl, you've got this." Bree slides her arm through mine, and we step up on the wide colonial style porch. My eyes bounce from face to face looking for that tousled dark hair and near-black eyes.

"You are going to make every guy in this place drool over you. Jaxon Kane can either take the bait or watch someone else do it." She bumps her shoulder into mine as we step into the house.

We step into a crowd of dancing bodies and chaotic laughter, and I feel it hit me all at once—heat, nerves, adrenaline.

The loud music beats against my chest. The smell of weed is saturating one set of closed doors and I scrunch my nose at it. Bree heads over and cracks the door open.

"Jesus." She closes the door, blinking. Tears beginning to glass over her eyes. "Talk about instant fucking contact high."

I pull my green dress down a bit further when a gaggle of guys turn to look at us at the same time. They look like prairie dogs popping up all at once and I snort a half-hearted laugh through my nose.

The stares don't stop.

Every time we move, a new cluster of guys turns to look —smirking, elbowing their friends, nudging each other like we're a new flavor on the menu.

Bree eats it up, already dancing to the beat with her hands in the air and a grin on her face.

I'm occupied scanning the room.

Every face. Every flicker of dark hair or tall frame that makes my heart lurch for half a second before disappointment slams it back down.

No Jaxon.

I make another slow pass through the living room, then the kitchen. Nothing. I circle back, check the hallway near the bathrooms. Still nothing.

It's all anyone has talked about all week and that he was

definitely coming tonight. But it's like the universe is playing chicken with my confidence—and I'm losing.

I lean against the wall near the keg station, trying not to look like a sulking teenager. Bree's across the room, fully in her element, laughing with some guy in a beanie and doing this slow, swaying dance that has his full attention.

Good for her.

I scan the top floor where a wide staircase curves up and a wrap-around hallway is the perfect place to watch the entire party below.

Just when I think about walking up there, I see my brother.

He's halfway down the hall, tangled up with some blonde I don't recognize. Her hands are in his hair, his lips on her shoulder dragging across toward her neck. She giggles and sits up, sniffing and tugging at his nose once before she tugs him toward one of the rooms and he follows.

But before he disappears behind the door, he turns. His eyes scanning his surroundings before he looks down.

Right at me.

His expression hardens like stone. Holding me there suspended a second, then two before he disappears behind the door.

I swallow hard and try not to show how my stomach twists.

It's not just that he's an asshole—he is, obviously. But something about my existence pulls the most hateful anger out of him. The kind of anger that ended up with me bruised and crying.

I learned a long time ago not to give him a reason.

But tonight was supposed to be *mine*. My chance.

And so far it's one giant disappointment.

I tap Bree on the shoulder and lean in. "I'm gonna head outside for a minute. It's hot."

She doesn't even slow down. "You good?"

"Yeah. Just need five."

She nods, already moving to the beat again, her eyes on the beanie guy, the music too loud for anything else.

I slip through the crowd, past the beer pong table and the sticky kitchen floor, out the back door and into the cooler night air.

The second I step out, I can finally breathe.

The music dulls behind me, thumping low through the walls. Out here, it's quiet. Still rowdy in the distance—laughter, the distant clatter of a dropped bottle—but the air is fresher. Cleaner.

Cool enough that the sudden change burns behind my eyes making me blink fast.

I *hate* that I cry when I get angry.

I bite my lip and turn toward the railing, gripping the edge with both hands. I tell myself to get it together. I didn't come out here to fall apart—I came out here to reset.

Then I feel a warmth at my back. A presence. A tingle down my neck that tells me someone else is here.

And then his voice, low, smooth and dark like velvet wraps around me.

"You wouldn't be looking for me, would you, Cricket?"

Every muscle in my body tightens. My heart stumbles.

That voice—deeper now, richer.

I smile slow, still giving him my back, while inside it's chaos.

He's actually here.

And just like that, every plan I made, every clever line I rehearsed, scatters like smoke.

I inhale, roll my shoulders back, and turn with all the fake indifference I can muster.

Cool. Detached. Unbothered.

It lasts two seconds.

Because the boy who left at sixteen is gone. In his place?

Holy. Shit.

Jaxon Kane is a man now—taller than Jonathan, broad and athletic. A black t-shirt clings to his chest, stretching over his shoulders and biceps like it was made for him.

He was always beautiful—dark eyes, sharp cheekbones, that crooked half-smile that made me stupid.

But this?

Greek god. Sin in human form.

His near-black eyes lock on mine, glinting with amusement, like he's already laughing at a joke he hasn't told yet. His hair's longer now, brushing his ears, messy in a way that shouldn't work but does.

And it's still him. Jaxon.

That crooked smile spreads as I realize—shit—I've been staring.

He whistles low. "Damn, let me get a look at you."

Before I can move, he takes my hand, warm and sure, and spins me like a ballerina.

His scent hits me like pine, leather, and danger.

"Looks like you're all grown up now, Cricket."

My mouth opens, something flirty half-formed, but the back door bursts open. Music blasts as the Jaxon Kane fan club floods out.

"Kane!"

"Jax! Buddy!"

They clap him on the back, drape arms around his shoulders like he's a soldier returning from war. Then his gaze cuts back to me.

And he winks.

"Don't get into too much trouble, Crick." Velvet-low, like the nickname never left his mouth.

Then he's gone.

I'm frozen, unsure whether to follow—or stay. Bree steps onto the porch, eyebrow arched. "So... wedding colors and baby names, or what?"

I scoff. "He didn't even let me say hi."

"What?"

"He came out, said my name, then got mobbed and walked off."

Her eyes go wide. "That's it?"

I nod, pulse still racing—now from irritation.

Bree growls. "Rude."

"No kidding." But her earlier words echo in my head: *Jaxon Kane can either take the bait or watch someone else do it.*

I glance at her, a sly smile tugging my lips. She grins back.

"Hell yes," she says, slinging an arm over my shoulders. "Make him regret leaving you alone for another wolf to piss a circle around you."

I snort. "Gross metaphor."

"Accurate."

"Painfully."

We laugh, my nerves burning off with each step toward the house.

If Jaxon wants to walk away mid-moment? Fine.

Let him watch someone else drool over me tonight.

Let him see exactly what he turned his back on.

Chapter 2
Cassidy

I t takes exactly two seconds once we're back inside to find some unknowing accomplices to our ploy. One guy spots us, nudges his friend who looks immediately. Bree giggles and pulls me toward them. A space opens in their circle without a word.

Bree slides in like she owns it, looping her arm around some guy and making him laugh hard enough to nearly spill his drink. I follow her lead, letting a small smile play at my mouth.

A guy I haven't seen yet—tall, tan, good posture—steps toward me with one of the cups, offering it like it's a rose on a silver platter. "You looked like you could use one," he says, grinning. I take the cup, fingers brushing his, and let my smile widen a little. "That obvious?"

"Just enough to be charming."

He's definitely an athlete. Baseball, I think—he's got the build for it. Strong shoulders, forearms that could probably crack a bat in half. His shirt clings a little from the heat, and there's a smear of something near his collarbone that suggests he's already survived one beer pong incident tonight.

He's not bad to look at. He's even better when he angles himself slightly toward me, giving me his full attention while the conversation swirls around us.

He'll do.

I laugh at something he says, tossing my hair back and resting my hand on his arm. My gaze isn't on him, though— it drifts toward the kitchen, where I know Jaxon is with Jonathan. I catch glimpses of him, but he never looks my way.

"You want to dance?" he asks.

I give Baseball Boy my best smile. "Sure."

The dance floor—or what passes for one—is crowded, hazy with the heat of too many bodies and the undercurrent of alcohol, perfume, and sweat. The lights flicker low and rhythmic, turning faces into silhouettes and shadows.

The music pulses in my chest, the beat vibrating up through my heels as Baseball wraps his arm casually around my waist and pulls me into the crush of the crowd.

It's not awkward. He knows how to move.

He's confident, smooth, pulling me close in a way that's intentional but not gross. His hand presses into the small of my back, just enough to guide me, and our hips fall into the rhythm of the song without too much effort.

Behind him, Bree is already dancing—somehow on beat and off the rails at the same time—and she flashes me a quick thumbs-up as she twirls.

I keep my eyes down. Let my body move. Let myself be pulled into the moment.

Then I feel it again.

That prickle. That pressure.

I glance toward the edge of the dance floor, back toward the kitchen—and this time, he's there.

Jaxon. He's standing in a loose circle of guys, drink still in hand, but he's facing *me*.

His eyes lift and like a magnet, he finds me. Instantly.

Like he already been watching. Already knew where I was.

Our eyes meet and for a long second, neither of us looks away.

He raises one brow, slowly.

And I don't even think—I just wink.

His lips curve, barely. Just a flicker. But it's there.

This just turned into a game and I know sure as shit neither of us wants to be the one to lose it.

Baseball slides his arms around my waist, securing me against him. He's warm, solid, moving in rhythm with the beat like its second nature.

I rest my hands on his shoulders, palms flat, fingers curling slightly in the fabric of his shirt. He leans in, mouth close to my ear, his breath warm against my skin.

"You having a good time?"

I smile—small, practiced—and nod. "Yeah."

He pulls back just enough to inhale, slow and deliberate. "You smell *really* good."

Then his lips press softly to the curve of my neck.

The first kiss is light. Testing.

The second is firmer. Lingering.

And for a second, I don't move.

It feels... nice.

Really nice.

I close my eyes. Let the sensation wash over me. Let my mind drift to the only place it wants to go. I pretend it's Jaxon's mouth on my skin. His breath warming my neck. His body surrounding mine.

And for that brief, indulgent moment, I sink into the fantasy. I exhale a moan and Baseball Boy takes that as encouragement to amp it up a bit.

He wraps one arm tighter around me, pulling me close, anchoring me there. The other hand slides lower—down the curve of my back until it finds the round of my ass.

He cups it, bold and unbothered, fingers flexing slightly as he pulls me against him.

That's when I feel the hard press of his erection against my hip, unmistakably eager.

My breath catches.

It's not that I didn't know where this was heading. It's that I didn't expect the spark of panic threading through the heat.

I've never done anything like this before.

Never kissed someone like this. Never danced with someone so close I could feel *everything.*

And the idea of doing it here, now... with a boy whose name I still don't know... while my long-time crush is standing thirty feet away—*watching*—

I open my eyes. "Um,"

"I'm sorry. You're just—so fucking beautiful." He adjusts

his arms around me and keeps swaying. "How about some fresh air?"

I nod, tapping Bree on the arm as he holds my hand, pulling me toward the backdoor. Bree and her pair of admirers follow.

The backyard is lit in pockets—strings of bulbs winding along the wooden fence and the occasional cell phone flashlight flickering on someone's face. The party has bled outside, groups scattered around in mismatched patio chairs and upturned milk crates, drinks in hand.

And Jaxon is out here too. Well this is kind of perfect.

He's across the yard, leaning against the railing of the back porch with one hand in his pocket, a red cup in the other. He's surrounded by a few guys, including my brother. And his eyes are right on me.

"Cass," Baseball Boy sits in one of the metal chairs surrounding a round table. He grins and pats the empty space on his lap, legs spread wide like he's just *daring* me to say no.

I hesitate just long enough for it to feel coy, then lower myself into the space like I was always meant to be there.

My tight green dress rides up like it knows we're putting on a show.

It was barely appropriate when I was standing. Now, seated sideways across his lap, one leg draped over his, it's a borderline scandal.

When I glance up, I swear Jaxon's jaw is tight.

Tense in a way that wasn't there five seconds ago.

My lips curve. Just slightly.

I turn toward Matt again, letting my fingers toy with the

edge of his collar, nails brushing his skin like a casual afterthought.

We look like an actual couple. His hand doesn't leave my thigh. He keeps talking, keeps laughing, keeps pulling me closer like I belong there. Every so often, he kisses my neck or my shoulder—soft, slow, casual. A little too comfortable.

And honestly?

He's cute. Really cute.

If I wasn't so hopelessly wrapped around the idea of Jaxon Kane, I'd probably fall for this one in a heartbeat.

Across the yard, Jaxon shifts.

He pulls his phone from his pocket, his brows pinching together as he taps something out.

And when he's done, he slides it back into his jeans and looks up.

His eyes find me instantly.

And this time, there's no teasing gleam or faint smile. Just something dark. Heavy. Like he's pissed.

I turn back toward Matt just as he finishes a story, and he looks at me—eyes moving from mine to my mouth.

"You wanna take a walk?" he asks.

My pulse stutters.

He must sense it, because he immediately adds, "Not far. Just a little loud over here, you know?"

He gestures with his head toward the far end of the yard. A patch of lawn lit only by the faint glow of fence lights.

"We won't go any further than that," he promises.

It's actually kind of sweet. He's been handsy, sure, but he's not pushed. And right now, I'm not even sure if I'm attracted to *him*. Of being *wanted*. Or of being *watched*. But everything happening in the backyard is really turning me on.

"Okay,"

He helps me to my feet and laces his fingers through mine like it's the most natural thing in the world.

As we walk across the lawn, someone calls out, "Hey Matt! You headed out?"

Oh thank God. That's his name.

I bite back a smirk and glance down, pretending to study the grass—because when that guy called his name, I *felt* Jaxon's head snap in our direction.

Matt laughs. "Nah. Just taking a walk."

We stop right where Matt said we would. He turns to face me, hands slipping into his pockets like he's suddenly nervous.

I kind of am, too.

"You look incredible," Matt says softly. His eyes are warm. Honest. "I mean it. That dress, your hair..." He smiles, a little bashful. "You're really something, Cassidy."

I exhale slowly and feel my cheeks burn. "Thanks."

He shifts closer, thumb brushing mine where our hands are still linked.

"Can I get your number?" he asks. "I'd love to talk to you again. Maybe take you out sometime?"

I hesitate, biting my lip, then nod. "Yeah. Okay."

His grin spreads wide across his face. He hands me his phone, and I type in my number, saving it as just *Cassidy*.

When I give it back, he wraps one arm around my waist again, slow and careful.

His voice drops, low and husky. "I really want to kiss you, Cass."

The air sticks in my throat.

I'm about to answer—one way or another—when the back door flies open.

"Matt!" someone yells, breathless. "Coach is on his way to inspect our dorms. We're dead if we're not in our rooms in ten!"

Matt's head jerks around. "Shit."

"I'm sorry," he says quickly, spinning back to me. "I've gotta go. Like, *right now.*"

Before I can say a word, he leans in and presses a quick kiss to my cheek. "I'll call you."

And in a second, he's gone.

Running back toward the house with two other guys trailing him, cutting across the yard and disappearing into the chaos.

Leaving me standing there.

Alone.

Again.

Chapter 3

Cassidy

Matt disappears into the rush of college boys sprinting to beat curfew, and the night air closes in. The beer's warm buzz lingers in my veins, but the cold still nips at every inch my dress doesn't cover.

I cross my arms, debating going back inside—until a familiar shoulder brushes mine.

"Your boyfriend ditch you?" Jaxon's voice is low, teasing, beer bottle in hand.

"Not my boyfriend," I say.

His mouth quirks. "Good thing the coach showed up. Looked like he was about to eat you alive."

I meet his gaze, steady. "Maybe I wanted him to."

The smirk fades, replaced with something tighter. A challenge. He nods toward a quiet corner of the yard. "Come on."

He leads me to a koi pond hidden behind hedges, where

the party's chaos is just a dull hum. A stone bench waits in front of the water.

"Your brother know you were about to suck face over there?"

"I don't need his permission. I'm not a little girl anymore." I shift just enough for the dress to dip lower in the moonlight.

His gaze drags down, slow, then back up. "Yeah. I can see that."

"Can I have a drink?" I ask, sugar in my tone.

"How much have you had?"

"Barely one beer."

He studies me, then hands it over. Our fingers brush. I sip, hand it back, and he finishes it.

"All those summers you came to our house," I say quietly, "I never thought we'd end up here. Sharing a beer."

He almost laughs. "Yeah. I used to steal Oreos from your pantry until your scary-ass nanny would chase me off."

"She wasn't a nanny—just mean."

"Still ratted me out."

"You always came back, though."

He doesn't answer right away, just stares at the pond. I tuck my hands under my thighs.

"You were always there," I murmur. "Then one day... you weren't. I missed that. I missed you."

His eyes flick to mine. "Yeah. I missed home too."

Not *you*. Just *home*.

It burns more than I want to admit, but I didn't come here for nostalgia. I came here to make him see me.

I shift closer, fingertips brushing the inside of his knee. "You know... I've always liked you."

His eyes drop to my mouth. I wet my lips.

"I'll be eighteen soon."

"You just turned seventeen, Cricket." His voice is rough now.

"Do you ever think about me?" My hand inches higher. "The way I think about you?"

"Cass—" He leans in, close enough for my pulse to roar in my ears. I tilt my head, certain my first kiss is coming—

But his mouth brushes past mine, to my ear. "Go home, little Cricket."

The words hit like a slap. He walks away, leaving me alone on the cold bench, dress too high, heart in my throat.

Humiliation curdles to heat in my chest. I stand, heels biting into the grass as I pass him without a glance.

My brother's at the door, leaning in the frame, eyes flicking past me to Jaxon, then back again like he's piecing it together.

I don't explain. I don't hide the flush in my cheeks or the tight set of my shoulders. I brush past him into the heat of the party, the door closing on the sound of my brother's voice:

"Got a second, Jax?"

I don't wait to hear the answer. I just find Bree, ready to pretend I never came looking for Jaxon Kane at all.

"Yeah, *fuck* that guy," Bree declares, her voice a little too loud, a little too echo-y in the weed room.

The windows are cracked open now, letting some of the smoke curl out into the night, but the scent still clings to everything—pillows, posters, the back of my throat.

We didn't smoke anything, but we're definitely buzzing. Two more beers between us, and one tragic cinnamon-flavored shot that burned like cheap soap and bad decisions.

"Yeah," I echo, slumped beside her on the sagging couch, my knees pulled up and my hair slightly frizzed from the night air. "Fuck Jaxon Kane."

A girl across the room looks up—college of course, probably a junior—her eyes sweeping over us with a mixture of judgment and disinterest. She leans back toward her friend like we're nothing but background noise.

Maybe we are.

We're definitely too loud.

But I don't care.

"I'm totally hot," I say, mostly to myself, but Bree nods enthusiastically like it's gospel.

"Absolutely," she says. "A full-on goddess."

"I'm smart."

"Top of our class," she confirms.

"I'm a catch. Like, objectively."

Bree leans in. "Like, if I were into girls, I'd be obsessed with you."

I keep going. "And that guy—Matt—*he* wants to kiss me. He wanted to kiss me all night. Next time, I'm letting him."

"*Yeah,*" Bree agrees, swaying a little. "He was totally hot."

"I'm *so* over Jaxon Kane."

She nods solemnly. "Preach."

I sit up straighter, summoning whatever remnants of dignity I can. "In fact... I'm going to tell him."

Bree's head snaps toward me. "Wait, what?"

I push myself up from the couch, a little wobbly on my feet, my dress tugging awkwardly as I get my balance. "I am. I'm going to tell him that I don't need him to kiss me anymore. Because someone *else* already did. Or... will. Soon."

"You *should.*" Bree slaps the couch for emphasis. "You go give that cocky bastard a piece of your mind."

I nod, determined and fully committed to this plan that I probably would not commit to if I were sober.

I start to walk out of the room, brushing my fingers along the doorframe like that'll steady me, when the girl from earlier—the one who looked annoyed—steps into my path.

Her smirk is lazy and unimpressed. "Looking for Jax?"

"Yes," I say, trying to sound mature. And... not drunk.

I think I nail it.

She doesn't agree. The corner of her mouth quirks up just slightly, like she finds me amusing.

"He's upstairs," she says. "Second door on the left."

I expected her to be catty but she's surprisingly helpful. "Thank you."

She doesn't answer—just turns back to her friend, laughter already spilling between them before I'm even out of earshot.

Each stair creaks under my heels, my hand trailing along the banister. My pulse hammers in my ears, my mouth dry. I feel both too heavy and too light, like gravity can't decide what to do with me.

But I keep climbing.

He doesn't get to ruin tonight. Not after the way he looked at me. Made me believe—if only for a second—that maybe I wasn't the only one who felt it.

Second door on the left.

My hand hesitates on the knob, just for a heartbeat. Then I turn it.

The door swings open, light spilling in from the hall.

At first, the shapes don't make sense—just a tangle of limbs, skin, hair. Disjointed. Abstract.

Then it sharpens.

Jaxon sits sprawled on a couch, a massive bed behind him. Shirtless. Pants unzipped. His cock thick in one woman's hand while another kisses the tip, both of them naked and laughing like they've done this before.

One leans in, moaning around him. The other strokes him lazily, eyes fixed on his face like they're sharing a private joke. Then they kiss over him—tongues, wet sounds —before trading places, one swallowing him down while the other licks at the base.

My stomach drops. The warmth of the beer evaporates, leaving me cold and clear-headed in the worst way.

Jaxon hasn't noticed me yet. His arms stretch across the back of the cushions, his head tipped back, enjoying the two women on their knees like a shared prize.

Then he lifts his head.

His eyes are bloodshot, unfocused but not unaware. He sees me standing there and doesn't even look surprised.

He raises his drink to his lips and takes a slow pull, the motion lazy, while one of the girls continues working him in her mouth and the other trails kisses along his thigh.

His hand finds the crown of the girl's head, fingers tangling in her hair as she bobs up and down on his cock.

"Isn't it past your bedtime?" His voice is lazy, almost bored. One of the girls looks back at me and laughs. "Close the door on your way out, little girl."

The words don't hit all at once—they slide in like ice water, slow and numbing.

Something in me shifts. Not a dramatic shatter—just a clean, precise break.

He's a fucking asshole.

This is who he is. This is his world—older, confident women who know exactly how to please him. Compared to them, I'm just a kid playing dress-up.

God, I'm such a fool.

My throat tightens. A single tear escapes before I can stop it.

"I hate you."

It came out a soft whisper. Not a scream or a huff. Just a silently spoken truth.

I turn, pulling the door closed without checking if it latches. I just need to get out.

Down the stairs, every step a fight to keep from splintering apart. The music and laughter swell around me, a party still in full swing, but for me, something's ended.

The girls laugh again from upstairs, sharp and careless.

Bree calls my name from somewhere behind me, concern threading her voice, but I keep moving not looking back.

Because I know—in my bones, in my blood—that I will never want anything to do with Jaxon Kane again.

SIX YEARS LATER

The tires crunch over the gravel as I turn off the main road and onto the long, winding drive I've known since before I even understood what roads were.

The Hayes estate always did feel like more than someone else's home—it was part of my childhood. My second backyard. My second kitchen. My second family.

The horse pastures stretch out on either side of the drive, wide and open, dotted with fences that seem to go on forever. Late summer sun bathes the fields in gold, and like always, a few of the horses trot up to the fence to race me in.

Retired racers, still full of fire.

One of them breaks into a full gallop just for the hell of it, and I can't help but grin as I downshift and keep pace.

Fitting.

This place has always been about speed. Strength. Power you can't bottle.

I roll to a stop in front of the house, just outside the wide double doors, and kill the engine.

The silence afterward feels heavier than it should.

I swing a leg off the bike and pull off my gloves, tucking them into the side compartment before unhooking my helmet. My hair sticks to my forehead, sweat and heat pressing down after the ride, and I swipe a hand through it before turning toward the house.

My gaze lifts automatically to the second story window on the right—the one where the curtains were always drawn back.

Always occupied.

It's empty. Has been for years now yet I still look.

I pull my backpack off, unzip it, and take out the bouquet—bright, obnoxiously colorful wildflowers that look like they were picked in a field by someone with no taste.

I balance them on the seat of my bike while I shrug off my jacket. The leather's still warm from the road, and I sling it over my forearm before grabbing the flowers again.

"Hey, Ben!" I call out, raising my voice over the breeze as I spot the oversized caretaker leading a horse toward the stables.

Big Ben lifts a hand in acknowledgment, pausing just long enough for me to catch the familiar gleam of Dominion's coat—the prize of the farm. All black, sleek as oil, with a stride that still looks like it could break records.

The fourteenth horse to win the Triple Crown, he's a living legend.

I nod to both of them, then head toward the front door, twisting the handle and stepping inside without knocking.

"Honey, I'm home," I call out, already knowing where they'll be.

Sure enough, I hear the answer from the back room, Jonathan's voice echoing down the hallway. "We're in here, dickhead."

A beat later, I hear Mrs. Hayes's soft, familiar scolding—too quiet to make out the words, but I don't need to.

Jonathan's response is louder. "Sorry, Ma."

I smile and shake my head, letting the door close behind me as the smell of vanilla and old wood settles into my chest.

I pause in the doorway of the library.

She's right where she always is.

Lilly May Hayes.

Seated in her wheelchair by the tall arched window, blanket tucked neatly across her legs, posture proud even when her body refuses to be.

She looks smaller than the last time I saw her. More fragile. Her cheekbones sharper, her hands thinner, but her eyes—still sharp. Still hers.

It punches something right in the center of my chest.

I take a breath and throw on a grin, the kind I used to use to get out of trouble when I broke a lamp in this house.

"Well, *Miss Lilly May Hayes*," I say, laying it on thick with my worst Southern drawl as I step inside. "Still the prettiest lily in the bunch."

Her lips curve faintly. Not much, but enough.

I kneel down beside her and hold out the bouquet, bright and messy, with a few pink lilies tucked in on purpose.

She places one thin hand on my cheek and pats it softly.

"Thank you for bringing the horses with you, Jackie."

I follow her gaze to the window, where three of the mares still linger at the fence line, swishing their tails and sniffing the air like they're waiting for a treat.

"Anything for my best girl," I murmur, giving her a wink as I rise to my feet.

Heavy footsteps accompanied by the unmistakable clink of a tray announces the arrival of my biggest fan.

Cassidy Hayes enters carrying soup like it's a weapon and her eyes lock on me the second she crosses the threshold.

She doesn't say anything at first, just lifts her brows and offers me a spectacularly exaggerated eye roll—classic Cassidy, the human embodiment of *unimpressed.*

She places the tray in front of her mother with practiced precision, adding a glass of water and a tiny cup of pills like it's a ritual.

"Mom," she says gently, "please try to eat something, okay?"

She plucks the flowers from her mother's lap without acknowledging me further and walks to the far cabinet to grab a vase.

I lean against the bookshelf, arms crossed. "So... you're still using that 'resting bitch face' as a full-time personality trait, huh?"

She turns just enough to look at me, her eyes flat. "You still pretending you're charming?"

"Ouch." I press a hand to my chest. "You wound me."

"Not nearly enough." she fires back, plucking the stems and snipping the ends like she's imagining it's my neck instead.

"I have a pair of scissors in my hand, Jaxon."

I hold up my hands in surrender, laughing as I take a step back.

Before she can say something sharper, Jonathan pushes through the opposite door at the far end of the library, flipping through some papers in a dark blue leather ledger.

"I figured I'd find you two in a standoff."

"Three guesses who started it," I'm talking to him but keeping my eyes on her.

Cassidy snips the shears at me like a threat. I wink back.

"Don't need three," he mutters, coming to a stop. "She eat anything yet?" He nods toward his mother.

Cassidy shakes her head, returning her attention to the flowers. "Not yet."

We all fall quiet, the kind of silence that never really settles—just hangs heavy between the walls like smoke.

When someone you love is dying slowly, silence stops being peaceful. It becomes a place where all the unspoken things sit. The thank-you's you haven't said. The apologies you keep telling yourself you'll get to. The grief you haven't earned yet but feel anyway.

Jonathan clears his throat. The sound is short, clipped.

"Make sure she does."

His voice is flat—curt—like he's giving a directive to one

of his junior associates and not his sister. Not the woman who wakes up in the middle of the night to adjust their mother's blankets, who learned how to change IV lines off YouTube and heartbreak.

Cassidy doesn't flinch.

She just nods once and keeps arranging the flowers.

Jonathan looks at me next, all steel and tension in his stance. "Come on. I need to talk to you."

He's already heading toward the other side of the library, toward the room that used to be their dad's study and now doubles as Jonathan's home office whenever he's here.

I offer Cassidy a slow, mocking kiss from the air—fingers to lips, hand tossed wide like I'm onstage—and her eye roll is sharp enough to draw blood.

Worth it.

I follow Jonathan through the arched doorway, stepping into the cool quiet of the study.

He leaves the door mostly shut but not fully, as if that keeps things less serious somehow. Like cracked doors can soften hard conversations.

The room's barely changed. Dark paneled walls. Over-filled bookshelves. The smell of scotch soaked into the floorboards.

Their dad died two years ago. Massive heart attack. Dropped right in his study chair, if I remember right. No warning. No second chance. One minute he was pouring bourbon, the next, gone.

Now their mother is slipping too, but slower—piece by piece.

Whether it's the cancer or the chemo, no one can really say. The doctors go in circles while Lilly May fights tooth and nail with a soft smile and bones that look like they might splinter in a strong wind.

Jonathan takes a seat behind the desk and gestures toward the chair across from him.

I drop into it, sprawling like I own the place. "So, what's the emergency? You finally need a tech guy to fix your printer?"

Jonathan doesn't rise to it.

"I'm headed to the UK in a few days. Might be gone a few weeks."

"Fancy CEO shit?" I ask, propping one ankle over my knee.

"London arbitration."

"Sounds miserable."

"It is."

He opens a drawer and pulls out a stack of paperwork, sets it aside, and then finally looks at me.

"I need you to keep an eye on the house—on Cassidy while I'm gone."

"Excuse me?"

Jonathan's gaze stays fixed on the decanter as he pours himself a drink. Doesn't even bother looking at me when he says, "Cassidy. Keep an eye on her while I'm gone."

"No, I heard you." I narrow my eyes. "Just trying to figure out why you think your grown sister needs a babysitter?"

"She's been getting... reckless."

I huff a laugh. "Cassidy?"

"She's acting out," he continues, voice flat. "Showing up late. Picking fights. Getting mouthy with people who don't deserve it."

I lean against the wall, arms crossed. "So... like she always has?"

Jonathan finally looks up at me, his expression unreadable. "I don't want this stress falling on Mom. She doesn't need any more of it."

"And what exactly do you think I'm going to do? Ground her?"

"She listens to you more than she does me."

I bark a short laugh. "She also can't stand the sight of me. So if this is your plan for peace and quiet, you've officially lost it."

Jonathan just takes another sip like he's already somewhere else.

"She respects you," he says flatly. "Even when she's pissed."

"That's generous. She growls when I breathe too loud." I lean against the doorframe, arms crossed. "So what's this really about? You scared she's going to throw a rager while you're gone?"

He cuts me a look over the rim of his glass. "I'm asking you to keep an eye on her. Stop by and check on mom and the house a few times. That's all."

"But why?" I press, my voice light, curious. "She's not a kid. She's a grown woman. Doesn't exactly need a leash."

I narrow my eyes, straightening off the wall. "She's not stupid, Jonathan."

"I didn't say she was." His tone sharpens just enough to

warn me off. "I said she's being impulsive. And that's a risk I won't leave unattended—not with Mom in the condition she's in."

I let the silence stretch a beat too long, then shrug. "Fine. I'll babysit. But when she figures it out, I'm not stepping in when she starts swinging."

"I trust you'll manage."

Oh, I will. *And I plan on enjoying every second of it.*

He turns away, back to whatever paperwork he's pretending to read.

I pause at the door. "You sure there's nothing else I should know?"

His pen doesn't stop moving. "Just keep her in line, Jaxon. That's all I'm asking."

Chapter 5
Cassidy

I watch him from the kitchen window.

Jaxon moves with the same cocky swagger he's had since we were kids. Arrogant. Infuriating. The kind of man who's always had too many girls, too much charm, and not nearly enough accountability.

He hasn't changed a bit.

Six-four with shoulders build to rest your legs on them. His body is carved from stone and he's always wearing that smirk that's probably trademarked by now. He's not just some kid who came to our house with his mom when we were little. He's *Jaxon fucking Kane*. Master of his own tech domain, and girls who clearly don't care about being discarded the next morning.

I scoff and toss yesterday's tabloid in the trash. Face down, so I don't have to look at Jaxon with yet another picture-perfect model on the cover. I swear he has a life goal to never be seen with the same woman twice.

And yet...

As he swings one leg over the seat of his bike and leans forward to fire up the engine, I wonder—just for a second—what it would feel like to climb on behind him. To wrap my arms around his waist, press my face against the back of his leather jacket, and feel the hum of the road vibrate through my bones.

Jesus.

I shake the thought out like it's poison, disgusted with myself.

God knows how many other girls have sat on that seat. It probably needs to be bleached.

You'd think I'd be over him by now. It's been six years since he humiliated me. Six years since he shattered whatever leftover feelings I had into dust and ash. I told myself I was done that night—done with him, with everything he stood for. I've stuck to that.

Mostly.

Except for when he shows up here like nothing ever happened, like he didn't twist the knife in my gut and smile while he did it.

Still. That doesn't stop me from watching him leave. Doesn't stop me from feeling something warm in my chest when he looks up at my bedroom window. The one I used to sit at and draw.

He straps his helmet on and guns the engine, kicking up gravel as he disappears down the drive. Popping a wheelie while several of the horses dart after him, racing down the fence line.

God, I hate him.

But I hate myself more for remembering how much I used to love him. Or at least thought I did.

The sound of the kitchen side door opening jolts me out of the thought.

Shanae steps in, balancing two cloth tote bags on her arms and kicking the door shut with her heel. "Got your oat milk, fresh ginger, and those weird probiotic gummies she likes."

"Thanks," I say, moving to help her unload. "She managed a few bites of soup earlier. Kept it down."

Shanae hums, setting the bags on the counter. "Then tonight's mission is orange marmalade. I'm thinking hot biscuits, maybe a little bone broth to sip with it. Sweet and savory—she won't be able to resist."

"She might," I murmur. "She didn't sleep much last night. She's tired."

Shanae pauses, watching me carefully. "Which is exactly why *you* should take the night off. Go be twenty-three. Go be a little reckless. Put on something short and make bad decisions."

I let out a weak laugh. "You are such a bad influence."

"You need one. Otherwise you'll shrivel into an old crone before your time."

I smile at her teasing and turn to the bread drawer to make myself a quick sandwich—but the smile drops the second I see what's hidden inside.

Wedged behind a half-empty bag of rye, is a stack of unopened envelopes. The one on top I recognize. The results from my doctor's exam.

The other's, the return address reads *Delancey Mortgage Services.*

My stomach drops.

We don't *have* a mortgage.

This house—this land—was paid off decades ago. Dad built it from the ground up for my mom after they got married. She sketched the dream on a napkin in a diner booth—the wraparound porch, the floor to ceiling windows overlooking the pasture, a kitchen big enough to feed half the county and smell like cinnamon every morning.

And he made it real. Poured the foundation with his own hands. Framed the bones of the house like it was a living thing, meant to hold generations of Hayes'.

I glance at the framed napkin on the wall. It still hangs under the photo of Mom and Dad in his truck, both of them grinning like love-struck fools.

Mom hasn't smiled like that in years.

With shaking hands, I pull the envelopes free, and rip open the first. Then, the second. By the time I get to the third, I can't feel my hands.

Notice of Default.

Notice of Intent to Foreclose.

Property Scheduled for Public Auction – Friday at 9:00 AM.

Oh my God.

I flip through the papers like if I move fast enough, the words will change. Like I'll find some fine print that makes it all go away. But it's there in black and white, over and over again.

This house. *Our* house. It's going to be taken. Sold. Stripped from us like it was never ours to begin with.

The horses.

I can't breathe.

What will we do with the horses?

"Cassidy?" Shanae's voice is soft behind me.

I don't respond. I can't. The walls feel like they're pressing in. My vision swims.

"Cass?" she asks again, gentler now. "What's wrong?"

"Nothing," I say too fast. My voice cracks halfway through the lie. "Just... just mail."

She knows it's bullshit but she doesn't press.

I force a tight smile, press the papers flat, and slide them back into the envelopes.

"I'm gonna see how Jonathan's packing is coming along," I say, my voice robotic.

Shanae watches me, but she doesn't stop me.

Jonathan took over everything after Dad died. The business, the finances, the estate. We never talked about it. I didn't think we had to. I always thought—no, *trusted*—that he'd honor what this house meant. That he'd protect it, protect Mom.

And now I know the truth.

He's been hiding this. Letting it all collapse.

And I don't know what hurts more—the betrayal or the realization that, maybe, I never should have trusted him to begin with.

Jonathan's bedroom door is open.

Of course it is. He's never needed boundaries—never once respected mine.

The sight of him packing punches me in the gut. Polished slacks folded with military precision, dress shirts lined up like he's inspecting his troops. His silver Rolex ticks softly with every motion. Calm. Unbothered.

The envelope edges bite into my fingers as I watch him, rage climbing up my throat like acid.

He's really doing it. He's leaving.

Not just the country—he's leaving while the house gets auctioned off. While strangers walk the halls of our childhood, bid on our mother's dream.

And he was never going to say a word.

I cross the threshold without thinking.

"When were you going to tell us?"

His back stiffens, but he doesn't turn. Doesn't stop folding his navy suit into the suitcase like I'm just a breeze passing through.

He looks over his shoulder a moment later, the flicker of recognition passing across his face like a shadow. Then it's gone. He clocks the envelopes in my hand. The crumpled edges. My shaking grip.

But still, no apology. No shame. Just mild irritation—like I've interrupted something more important.

"You weren't, were you?" I say quietly. "You were just going to leave."

My voice wavers, and I hate the way it cracks. But I press forward anyway, because if I don't say this now, I'll never get another chance.

"You were going to run off to London while Mom's house—*our* house—is handed over to the highest bidder. And you weren't even going to tell her. Or me."

He stops folding.

A long breath leaves his chest, slow and heavy. Like I'm the one exhausting him.

"Looks like Daddy's little princess finally figured out the world isn't all sunshine and roses."

I see red.

"No," I snap, stepping into the room. "I'm just realizing how much of a coward you really are."

That gets his attention. He turns, slowly, a sick sort of calm tightening his features.

"You want to say that again?" he asks, stepping forward.

I take a reflexive step back. My heel hits the edge of the doorframe.

He smirks. "That's what I thought."

My pulse hammers, but I have to hold my ground, even as my fists tremble around the papers.

"You think this is handling it?" I throw the stack of notices into the room. "You think hiding foreclosure notices behind a loaf of bread is leadership?"

He glances down at the papers as they scatter across the floor, then back up at me with a shrug.

"You want the truth?" he says, moving back to his suit-case. "We're liquidating non-essential assets to protect the core. It's strategic. Temporary."

"This is our *home*," I bite out. "The place Mom brought

me to after I was born. The place Dad built with his own hands—"

"And she won't be needing it much longer."

The words don't hit all at once.

They slither in. Curl around my ribs.

I stare at him, stunned. My stomach flips, then drops into nothing.

"You don't mean that."

His face gives nothing away. "She'd want us to save the company. She's not stupid."

I shake my head, tears burning behind my eyes now. "She's dying, Jonathan. And you'll stripped away everything she ever loved. Her house. Her legacy. Her horses—"

"Those horses don't feed anyone," he snaps.

"Those horses are her heart and soul!" I can't help the tears streaming down my face now. "She and I took those horses to races and made them champions and you're just going to—"

"Oh, give me a fucking break, Cassidy. You've never worked a day in your prim little life of delusion and sketch books." He slams a drawer harder than necessary. "Anyone can tell a horse to run."

"She's not just anyone," I cry. "She's our *mother*."

The final thread holding my voice together snaps, but I don't care.

"I'm the one that came home from college to take care of her. I have watched her fight every day to live. To smile through pain. To hold on for us. While you ruin everything you touch."

Like a storm breaking free of its restraints, he turns and

surges toward me. I don't even have time to flinch before his hand snaps out.

He grabs my face, his fingers crushing my cheeks, forcing my gaze to his.

"You want to play hero?" he hisses. "You think you've got what it takes to fix this?"

My back hits the wall hard, breath catching as his grip tightens.

"Then *fix it*, Cassidy. Go on. Save the fucking house."

He lets go with a sharp shove, and I stumble sideways. My shoulder slams into the doorframe. The pain flashes down my arm, but I don't cry out.

I won't give him the satisfaction.

He sneers down at me, pure ice in his eyes. "Do something useful for once in your life."

I press my hand to the wall to steady myself.

He adjusts the cuffs on his shirt like nothing happened.

Then he nods toward the hallway. "Now get the fuck out of my sight."

I don't move. Can't. My feet are rooted, chest heaving, heart crashing against my ribs like it's trying to break free. I want to scream, to fight, to make him understand what he's doing—but the words catch behind the burn in my throat.

But I stay standing because fuck him.

Someone has to say it.

My voice shakes, but I make sure it's loud enough to carry. "You don't deserve this family."

Jonathan's eyes narrow before he's on me in a blink.

"I said, get the fuck out of my face," he growls, stepping forward again. "Before I put you on the auction block too."

His hand shoves hard into my shoulder. My feet slip out from under me, and I crash to the ground just outside the threshold, my hip catching the edge of the hallway runner. Pain flares sharp and hot, but before I can do more than gasp, the door slams shut behind me.

The sound is deafening.

Final.

I lie there for a breath. Then another.

The hallway is silent now—no footsteps, no apologies. Just me and the echo of everything I didn't say.

I push myself up, one palm braced to the floor, the other gripping my ribs.

He's really going to let it happen.

He's going to let strangers strip this house bare. Let Mom's dreams turn to dust. Let her die without the only place that's ever felt like home.

Unless I stop him.

And I will.

No matter what I have to do, I won't let her lose this place.

I have officially become the most bored tech genius billionaire to ever walk the face of this earth. Possibly the universe. And I'm not being dramatic. This is totally legit.

All my companies are running like oiled machines.

Data centers are operational and stable.

I finished a prototype schematic for a robotic AI assistant with full environmental and spatial AI awareness this morning. You know—just because I had nothing else to do.

I should've been proud of it, but I yawned through the whole thing.

Even got into my motorcycle cosplay—leather pants, no shirt, helmet confidence and that whole "is he a criminal or a Calvin Klein model?" aesthetic—and filmed a dozen thirst trap videos for my socials. Nothing fancy. Just brooding helmet-eye contact and flexing in various lighting conditions while my bike purred beneath me like the damn slut she is.

My scripts will post them over the next two weeks, my bots automatically interacting with comments and feeding the fanbase their daily dose of digital wet dreams. I have nearly five hundred million followers. Most of them think I'm an enigma. Mysterious. Brooding.

I'm just really fucking bored.

Maybe I'll fire off the robot specs to my top teams. Tell them the first team to get a working prototype before I do gets an all-expenses-paid cruise. First-class. Unlimited liquor. Full spa package.

I might even go into the office and challenge them to a build-off. Give the interns heart palpitations.

But even that sounds... meh.

So, I flick on the TV. Open Snapchat on the big screen. Pull up the map just to people-watch. It's Friday night. Everyone's out doing stupid shit they'll regret by morning. Maybe I'll find some inspiration in an underground fight I can join for shits and gigs.

One avatar specifically screams at me in an instant.

"And what do we have here?"

Cassidy Hayes' adorable little avatar is bouncing along in a car like she has somewhere important to be.

I narrow my eyes.

"Well, well. Where's my little chargee off to?"

Because yes—I'm babysitting her.

No—I didn't ask for this.

Yes—I'm going to have way too much fun with it.

Her avatar stops moving, settling at a restaurant I don't recognize from the bird's eye view, so I zoom in.

Liotta.

"Oh, for fuck's sake."

Trendy spot. Pretentious name. The kind of place that serves radish foam and thinks charging twenty bucks for "heritage carrots" is revolutionary cuisine.

I grin as my boredom gives way to intrigue.

"Let's have some fun, shall we?"

It takes me less than thirty seconds to crack their camera feed. They're running the same third-party system I've seen a hundred times. I punch a hole through the shit-excuse for a firewall and scroll through their camera screens like I'm flipping TV channels.

And... bingo.

Cassidy Hayes is following the hostess through the space to a table for two.

And damn.

She's a vision. Even in grainy black and white, there's no mistaking her—long raven-black hair tumbling over one bare shoulder, her features sharp, elegant, *fierce*. The camera doesn't do her justice, but it tries.

Her raven hair has volume for days and is just screaming for someone to run their fingers through the strands and pull.

I tilt my head, squinting a little.

"Damn. Could you wear a shorter fucking dress, Cass?"

Can't tell the color. Their feeds are outdated and grayscale. But I know it will be on her Instagram story. Not that I look at it every day to know she always posts her outfit before going anywhere.

And there it is.

A full-length mirror selfie. Phone held to cover her face. She's kneeling, back straight. Round ass fucking screaming at me in the deep purple mini that makes her skin glow.

The woman's a work of art—and for reasons I can't quite explain, I feel like punching a wall.

No, that's bullshit, I know the reason and it's the asswipe sitting across from her.

Button-up shirt, lazy smirk, and the kind of energy that screams *I peaked in college.*

Naturally, I hate his fucking guts.

So, I do what any rational, calm, definitely-not-jealous person would do.

I take a screenshot of his face and drag it into the CIA's facial recognition software.

Yes. I have access.

Yes. It's illegal.

No. I don't care.

Their system is garbage. If they didn't want me poking around, they should've made it harder.

While that processes, I flip back to the feed and start rerouting the restaurant's cameras.

One by one, I rotate each lens until all fifteen of them are pointed at Cassidy's table.

Fifteen different angles.

Fifteen goddamn Cassidy's.

I could make a collage.

She's laughing now. Leaning forward like she's actually

interested in whatever Discount Wall Street is saying. She's *smiling* at this piece of garbage.

Nope. Don't like that either.

I grab my phone, pull up her contact, and hover for a second thinking of what to send. Something subtle. Just enough to make her squirm.

> JAXON: So... what cha doin?

A few seconds pass.

On screen, her phone lights up against the table. She glances down discreetly, just long enough to catch the preview. Doesn't even open it. Just turns it over.

Face down.

Harsh.

"Mkay... so we're gonna play hard to get." *That's my favorite fucking game, Cricket.*

I stretch out on the couch, crack my neck, and type again.

> JAXON: Oh that sounds like fun.
>
> Me, you ask?
>
> Nothing much. Just... hanging out. Watching something interesting.

Still nothing.

She's nodding along now like this guy invented Bitcoin and didn't major in fraternity keg stands.

I drum my fingers once, grin wide.

> JAXON: Are you out?

Nothing.

> JAXON: With friends?

I know her phone is buzzing every few seconds with my texts.

Her hand reaches for her wine, jaw tight.

She picks up her phone again. Glances at the screen. Taps out a reply with her thumb.

> CASSIDY: Why are you texting me?

I can *hear* the irritation in those four words.
I respond immediately.

> JAXON: I don't know. Thought we were bonding.

Don't you feel this emotional connection?

> CASSIDY: No.

> JAXON: Ouch.

> That's cold, Cricket.

> Like... ice bath in the Arctic cold.

> You're lucky I'm into emotional unavailability.

She rolls her eyes so hard on screen it's a miracle

they stay in her skull. She says something to her date —laughs again—and it grates like nails on a chalkboard.

> JAXON: I sure could go for some fried goat cheese with fig jam right about now.

She freezes.

Head tilts. Eyes narrow. She glances at the plate that just hit their table.

> CASSIDY: Are you here?

> JAXON: 👀

She starts scanning the room like she's about to start flipping tables. My head falls back as my laugh bounces around my empty penthouse.

"God, this is better than cable."

She texts again, fingers flying.

> CASSIDY: Are you spying on me??

> Jaxon: I prefer the term vigilant admirer.
>
> Or if we're being formal—light stalker.
>
> Definitely not spying. That implies clearance.
>
> This is more of a… rogue operation.

On-screen, she looks around once more—slower this time. Like she's *really* considering it.

Then she types something, slams her phone facedown.

CASSIDY: UNBELIEVABLE.

I shift one of the camera feeds, zoom in tight on the dude's face.

"What a fucking cocksucker."

He's a very animated talker. I take a series of world-class screenshots, catching him in perfectly ridiculous expressions that look like he's both constipated and holding in a sneeze.

"Ew!" I squint and lean closer to the screen like it will help. "What the fuck is that?"

I zoom in. And this couldn't get any better than if I were scripting it.

Tooth spinach.

Big ol' leaf wedged in his front teeth like he's pre-gaming for a Jurassic Park audition.

JAXON: You should tell him he's got something in his teeth.

Like, half the produce aisle.

Her lips twitch. Almost a smile but she schools it fast.

CASSIDY: I will not tell him.

Now leave me alone.

JAXON: Can't.

I've got a job to do. 😇

CASSIDY: Stalking me isn't a job.

JAXON: A little light monitoring.. if anything.

Her nostrils flare. I zoom in, frame it and hit the screenshot. That's art.

She types again, stabbing the screen.

CASSIDY: Where are you sitting?

I'd like to slam that flambé in your smug face.

JAXON: Mmm, I love foreplay.

You look unbelievable tonight.

I attach the screenshot and hit send.

On-screen, she blinks. Sees it. And if looks could kill, I'd be a smoking crater in the middle of Manhattan.

She's livid.

God, I love it.

Without moving her head, her eyes lift—straight up.

Right at the camera I'm watching her through.

My grin kicks up a notch. I lift my beer in salute like she can see me.

I snag another screenshot and send it to her.

JAXON: Hey, beautiful.

Right then, the corner of my screen lights up with a notification the facial recognition results just hit.

Finance Douche is now identified, and I immediately initiate a full background check.

Pings come back faster than a Red Bull-fueled coder during a hackathon.

My jaw tightens. "My, my. What a colorful history we have here."

CASSIDY: Don't call me that.

JAXON: He doesn't deserve that dress.

I stand, grabbing my phone, heading to the closet.

JAXON: I mean look at this guy…

I fire off the screenshots I've been collecting like trading cards.

One of him mid-bite—mouth wide fucking open. Eyes rolled back into his head.

JAXON: It's giving "I identify as a Sea Bass" energy.

Cassidy lifts her napkin to her mouth, trying—*failing*—to hide her smile.

Gotcha.

She quickly sobers, glancing around at more cameras. Guilty. Slightly paranoid.

JAXON: Yes, Cricket.

Every camera in the place is watching you right now.

I tug on a pair of dark jeans, black tee hugging my chest, cologne spritzed at my neck.

CASSIDY: This is quite concerning.

I'm sure the police would be interested in this information.

I think I'll give them a call.

As I lace my boots, I chuckle low in my throat.

"Oh, Crick. You're playing into this too perfectly."

You just don't even know.

JAXON: You should.

In fact, I'll do it for you. 

CASSIDY: Why are you really texting me?

Well... she'd figure it out sooner or later so might as well let the cat out of the bag now.

JAXON: Jonathan asked me to keep an eye on you.

The house.

Whatever. Same thing.

There's that eye roll again. I feel honored I can evoke it from her so easily.

CASSIDY: Good night Jaxon.

She clicks the side button, and the screen goes black.

She turned it off. She actually turned the fucking phone off.

Oh.

Hell.

No.

You wanna play games, little Cricket?

I'm in. I'm so fucking in, you have no idea.

Chapter 7
Cassidy

If there is one person in this world who can get under my skin, twist me up, and light my entire nervous system on fire with nothing but a smirk...

It's Jaxon Kane.

I shouldn't be surprised.

Of course he hacked the security cameras. Of course he's watching me like some smug, overbearing bat perched in a billion-dollar cave.

This is exactly what he would do.

Still—knowing I'm under surveillance from every angle?

It does something to me.

I sit a little straighter.

Take smaller, more graceful bites.

I laugh a little too loudly at something Brad says—something he probably found on Reddit six months ago—but he beams like he's charming the hell out of me.

I hope Jaxon hates it.

The appetizers come and go, replaced by salads. Brad

tells me about his firm's expansion plans and his daily meditation practice. He's not a bad guy. But he's not what I'm looking for, either.

Too polished. Too performative.

And I can't shake the feeling that if I peeled off his designer button-down, I'd find a motivational quote tattooed across his ribcage in cursive.

I'm halfway through my salad when a woman in an all-black uniform approaches our table.

"Miss Hayes?"

I glance up. "Yes?"

"There's... a phone call for you."

She's holding a cordless phone. Like we're in a hotel lobby in 1998.

You've got to be fucking kidding me.

I take the receiver slowly, bring it to my ear. "Hello?"

I don't even get the word fully out.

"Cricket."

Jaxon's voice is low and firm, and it slides across my skin like warm silk dipped in warning.

He's pissed.

I'm thrilled.

"Turn your phone back on."

"Mr. Kane," I reply with matching venom. "Kindly get bent."

"Cassidy, I'm not kidding."

"Neither am I."

I move to press the button to end the call, but he speaks again—sharper this time.

"End the date, Cassidy—"

Click.

Whatever else he was about to say is lost to the dial tone.

I give the phone back to the hostess and glance at Brad, who's currently trying to eat his salad like it owes him money.

He chews with his mouth open—loud, wet, aggressive.

"Everything okay?" he asks, a shredded carrot clinging to the corner of his lip.

"Yeah," I say, forcing a smile. "Just... work."

We move on. Kind of.

I sip my wine. He tells another story. Something about venture capital and kombucha.

My phone sits face-down next to me, practically vibrating with repressed chaos. I don't dare turn it back on. I'm not giving Jaxon the satisfaction.

Brad reaches across the table suddenly and takes my hand.

"I'm really glad you agreed to meet me tonight, Cassidy."

"Thanks, Brad. I'm having a great time."

I'm not.

I was.

Until I turned off my phone.

But no. I refuse to go there. Jaxon Kane is a closed door. Boarded up. Chained shut. Padlocked and buried.

"I was thinking, after dinner maybe you could come back to—"

The restaurant explodes into chaos.

Cops pour in from the front and side doors, shouting

commands and flashing badges. Diners gasp. Chairs scrape and I'm frozen.

Two officers rush toward our table.

"Don't move!" one barks.

The other grabs Brad, wrenching his arm behind his back and slamming him—*slamming him*—face-first into the table.

"What the hell?!" I yelp, jerking away, pressing myself back into the leather bench.

"Bradley Mercer," the officer shouts. "You're under arrest!"

They cuff him like he's a violent fugitive and haul him toward the exit, ignoring his protests. Half the restaurant is filming. The other half is staring at me like I'm Bonnie to his Wall Street Clyde.

My face burns.

My chest is tight.

And right beneath the panic, another emotion builds.

Rage.

Rage at Jaxon. Fucking. Kane.

This has him written all over it in bold font and flaming italics.

I snatch my phone off the floor—victim of the flailing arrest scene—and grab my purse, storming out before someone hands me another ancient telephone or slaps me with a search warrant.

My phone boots back up as I hit the doors.

Pings and dings explode across the screen.

The last one from Jaxon.

JAXON: I'll be outside.

That asshole.

Sure enough, as I shove the door open, there he is.

Leaning against a matte black McLaren like it's part of his wardrobe. All black—jeans, shirt, boots. Messy hair. Muscles folded beneath his crossed arms like he's the goddamn final boss in a dating sim.

And he's *smiling*.

The kind of smug, self-satisfied smirk that makes my blood boil. Like this is all a joke. Like watching my date get hauled off in handcuffs was some kind of prime-time entertainment.

I march right up to him and jab a finger into his chest.

"You arrogant, egotistical, morally-bankrupt *asshole*. How *dare* you?"

He doesn't even flinch. Just stands there, looking down at me like I'm a mildly amusing weather event.

"Careful, Cricket. You're poking the bear."

"Are you *insane?*" I hiss. "You got my *date* arrested!"

"Technically," he says, shifting his weight lazily, "your date did that himself."

"You tipped them off!"

He lifts a shoulder. "Not my fault the guy had a warrant out for his arrest."

I gape. "You're—"

"Though," he adds with a thoughtful squint, "telling them he had a kilo of coke shoved up his ass was *probably* a little overboard."

My mouth drops open.

"I can't believe this."

"I know," he says. "He is going to be quite pissed when he gets to booking and they go on a *treasure hunt*."

I spin on my heel, my hands clenched into fists at my sides, ready to walk straight into traffic before I spend another second near this man. But of course—because he's the devil in a designer tee—he falls into step beside me.

"Where are you going?" he asks, sounding thoroughly unbothered.

"*Away.*"

"Cool. I'll drive."

I veer harder left. "I'm not getting in your car."

"Cassidy—"

"No."

"Cricket—"

"Don't *Cricket* me."

He walks ahead of me now, cutting me off, standing between me and the street.

"I'm not letting you walk home."

"I'm not walking. I'm getting a ride-share."

He snorts. "Yeah? You want to explain to your brother why you were standing on the curb in stilettos at midnight waiting for an Uber after your coke-mule finance bro got dragged out in cuffs?"

I freeze.

He smiles like he's saying *Gotcha*.

"I hate you," I mutter.

His smile falters—just slightly. The cocky glint in his eyes dulls for the briefest moment, like someone hit the dimmer switch.

"I know," he says quietly this time.

Not smug. Not teasing. Just...knowing. Like he's remembering the last time I said those words too. The party. The two girls he was with and the wreck he left in his wake.

I blink hard and look away.

The air shifts between us—charged and suddenly too still.

He doesn't say anything else. Just steps back and holds the door open again.

I don't meet his eyes as I climb in.

But I feel the memory settle between us.

Unspoken and heavy.

The silence stretches for just a moment—long enough to settle like a weight between us—before Jaxon throws the car into gear like the devil himself is on our tail.

I shriek, slapping a hand against the door and the other straight out, grabbing for something—anything—to keep myself grounded. That "something" ends up being his forearm.

The McLaren roars, the engine snarling like a beast as we weave through traffic with speed that is 100% illegal and 1000% unnecessary. Meanwhile, Jaxon's driving like we're on a lazy Sunday cruise to the farmer's market. One hand on the wheel, completely relaxed. The other still under my death grip.

"You maniac!" I hiss, fingers digging into muscle that—unfortunately—doesn't budge in the slightest. "Do you have a death wish or are you just trying to scare the shit out of me?"

"I'm just driving," he says, smirking like it's the most reasonable thing in the world.

When I finally manage to peel my hand off his arm, I see the faint red marks I left behind.

"Sorry," I mutter, brushing my hair behind my ear.

His eyes dip to my legs first, slow and unhurried, before rising to meet mine. "I didn't mind."

A few minutes later, he swings into a parking lot with a dramatic turn that makes the tires squeal. I catch a glimpse of a small food truck gathering—three trucks angled like a triangle, with picnic tables and string lights strung between them.

"What are we doing here?"

He shrugs as he pulls into the center of attention, matte-black supercar gleaming beneath fluorescent parking lights. "I ruined your dinner."

My eyes roll so hard I practically see the back of my skull.

It wasn't ruined, not really. Brad was about three seconds away from asking me back to his apartment where he probably had a neon 'hustle' sign and a fridge full of protein shakes. Jaxon might've saved me from having to invent a fake emergency.

Not that I'll admit that.

He parks, engine purring as heads turn in all directions. People stare like Batman just showed up to fight crime.

I reach for my door, but it won't open.

I swear to God I'm pulling on the handle but before I can glare hard enough to melt the window, Jaxon rounds the car with casual confidence, rubbing the back of his neck like he doesn't know every woman in a ten-mile radius is watching him. One hand is shoved into the front pocket of his jeans, making the thick muscle of his arm flex beneath the sleeve of his black tee.

When he opens my door, he holds out a hand.

I hesitate.

Then I take it.

His palm is warm. His fingers wrap around mine like he's done it a hundred times before.

I ignore the way it makes my skin hum.

But he doesn't step back. He just stands there—so close I'm practically pressed between him and the car. His body heat wraps around me. His scent—clean, warm, woodsy—settles in my lungs. He's so tall I have to look up to meet his eyes, which are nearly black under the low lights. Intense. Endless.

It's not just his size or strength that makes him feel overwhelming.

It's him.

Jaxon has always been gravity.

And right now, I'm fighting like hell not to fall into it.

"I had a craving for tacos," he says, voice low.

I narrow my eyes.

Tacos are my weakness.

That wasn't a statement. That was a question without asking one. A test. A reminder.

Like he's saying he knows me.

"Well…" I say coolly, lifting my chin. "I suppose I could choke down a taco or two."

His grin hits full wattage. It's the kind of smile that

could make the devil give up his throne and retire. And the moment I see it, I instantly regret opening my damn mouth.

My cheeks burn but it does the trick, and he finally takes a step back, releasing me from the pull of his orbit.

"Shall we?" he says, tipping his head toward the trucks.

I sigh like this is a massive inconvenience.

But I follow.

Because apparently, humiliation comes with a side of carnitas tonight.

Chapter 8
Cassidy

The smell hits first—slow-roasted meats, warm tortillas, something cheesy and fried. It's a full-body assault. I could die happy right here in this parking lot.

But instead of heading to the trucks, Jaxon veers off toward one of the empty picnic tables near the string lights. He spreads a leather jacket I hadn't noticed on one of the benches and pats it.

"Sit."

I blink. "I can't sit on your jacket."

The look he gives me in response makes my stomach dip and my thighs clench.

"You could sit—" he cuts himself off, glancing away briefly, then back. "You can sit on it."

His jaw ticks and I sit, pretending not to notice. He doesn't push, which is somehow worse.

Before I can gather a retort, I hear footsteps behind me. An older woman—short, round, and radiating grandmother energy—approaches with two paper baskets filled to the brim with tacos. A young boy, maybe ten, follows with another set of baskets, steam rising from the contents.

The woman grabs Jaxon's cheeks like he's five years old and kisses both of them loudly, muttering something in Spanish too fast for me to follow.

Jaxon responds fluently. I had no idea he could speak Spanish.

I pretend to be extremely interested in whatever's hiding under all that chopped chicken.

The woman pulls two bottles of orange soda from her apron along with sets of plasticware, handing them off with a smile. Then she and the boy vanish like food-truck fairies into the night.

He cracks open one soda and hands it to me before opening his own.

I finally dig through the pile of food—and gasp.

"Are these... tell me these are cheese arepas."

He smirks over his bottle, leaning back against the table edge. "They're cheese arepas."

I nearly sob.

"They're just like those ones at that horse track you guys used to take *Warcry* to."

The name hits me like a whip crack—our prized black stallion growing up. Dominion's sire. Fierce, wild, untamable. Suddenly I'm nine years old again at the racetrack with my mom. Sitting with Jaxon and my dad eating cheese arepas. Warcry starting the legacy that Dominion would finish.

I tear into the food like it holds the answers to life's

mysteries. One bite in, and my eyes flutter closed as the creamy cheese, crispy edges, and spiced chicken melt across my tongue.

I moan. "Oh my God."

Eyes closed, head tilted back slightly, pure bliss in edible form.

When I open my eyes, Jaxon is staring at me. Not subtly, either.

He's got the end of the plastic fork between his teeth, not even pretending to eat. His expression is somewhere between curiosity and something darker. Something I'm afraid to name.

"I've been searching for arepas like these for *years*," I manage between bites. "And you've known about this place the *entire time?*"

I stab the top of his hand with my fork—lightly. Playfully.

He doesn't even flinch. Just grins and finally takes a bite.

We eat. We talk. And somehow, it's... easy.

Too easy.

That's what makes it dangerous because I have to keep Jaxon Kane on the other side of that closed door.

"You're richer than God and you're getting free tacos from food-truck Abuela? You're the worst."

He shrugs, all smooth nonchalance. "I pay their bills."

I pause, my eyes widening. "You pay their bills?"

"Maria threatened to cut off my fingers if I tried to pay for the tacos too."

That makes me laugh—unexpected and full. It slips out of me before I can stop it. "You're such an asshole."

"I'm pretty sure she's serious," he continues. "I keep the lights on. She feeds me."

"But... why?"

"Have you seen me in a kitchen? I'd blow up half of Manhattan."

"No, you idiot." Only I could get away with calling the one of the worlds smartest men an idiot. "Why do you pay their bills?"

He shrugs again, like it's no big deal. "Because I can. And they're good people."

He says it like it's nothing.

Like it didn't probably change their lives.

I study him for a second longer, chewing slower now. This boy who pulled a live cricket from my hair, forever coining my nickname, has turned into a man who hands over rent money like it's spare change and speaks Spanish like he was born into it.

But what gets me most... is the way he still knows exactly what I love.

Not just the tacos, but the arepas. The ones exactly like the racetrack where I have some of my happiest memories.

When my mom was full of life and healthy. I'd almost forgotten what she looked like back then.

But one bite, and it's like every memory surged forward in perfect detail.

"Thank you," I murmur before I even realize I've said anything.

Jaxon looks over, brows lifting slightly.

Then he flicks a piece of shredded chicken at my forehead.

"Hey!"

"You were getting too sentimental," he says with a smirk. "Had to keep you humble."

By the time we hit the quiet stretch of road that winds out of the city and into the hills, my stomach is full, my skin still warm from the soft glow of string lights—and my mood is surprisingly light.

Until his phone rings and the name on the screen flashes bright.

Eve.

And just like that, the air turns sour.

I glance at it, then look away quickly, annoyed with myself. It's not like I have any claim over him. I don't. We aren't anything.

He answers on speaker, casual. "Yeah?"

The woman doesn't wait. She launches in like she owns the line.

"Jax, this is an emergency."

Jax.

Huh. Only his friends call him that. So, at minimum, she's in deep enough to drop the nickname.

I bite my tongue, turning my face toward the window.

"I left my lucky hair clip in your car the other day."

Oh, perfect.

His girlfriend was just sitting in this very seat, apparently marking her territory with claw clips.

I glance down. Sure enough, nestled in the door's compartment is a brown clip.

I pick it up and hand it to him.

No words. No eye contact.

I feel his gaze flick over to me, linger longer than it should.

"Who the fuck has a *lucky* hair clip?" he mutters.

"I do," Eve snaps back. "And I need it for the auction tomorrow."

Auction?

A chill prickles across my arms.

Auction.

For a second, my chest tightens—because that word hits too close to home. But the auction for our estate is still a week out.

Still... the way she says it. Like it's important. Like she expects him to be there.

"I told you, I don't go to the auction," Jaxon says, completely unfazed.

Eve huffs. "Fine. I'll swing by and pick it up."

Wonderful.

She knows where he lives.

He's definitely fucked her. Or is fucking her.

I cross my arms tighter and turn away from him completely. The countryside whips by, dark and blurred, but I can still feel his eyes on me in the reflection.

"Sure," he says at last, and I can *hear* the smirk in his voice. "Stop by whenever."

They hang up and the silence stretches between us,

brittle and heavy. He doesn't say a word—but I can tell he's waiting. Bracing to see if I'll crack first and I do. I just can't help it.

"Your girlfriend sounds very pretty."

My voice betrays me. It cracks on *girlfriend*, and I hate myself for it.

"She's not my girlfriend," he says evenly. "Eve's just a good friend."

"Hm."

I don't believe him.

Men and women don't *just* stay friends without attraction being involved. Especially not when they're the kind of good friends who leave hair clips behind in luxury sports cars.

"So," I ask, trying to redirect the acid bubbling in my chest. "What's this auction?"

He's quiet for a beat too long.

"Ah… nothing. Just a charity auction The Black Ledger hosts it every year."

"And you don't go because you're morally opposed to donating to charity?"

When I turn to look at him again, his lips are twisted in a smug little smile. A secret tucked behind his teeth.

"Let's just say," he says slowly, "they're not auctioning off the typical charity gala items you're used to seeing from the uber-rich."

He turns up the long gravel road to our property. The white fencing catches the headlights like bone, glowing ghostly in the dark.

"What is that supposed to mean?" I press.

He glances at me, all shadows, and sharp edges.

"They're a bit more... *carnal* in nature."

I blink because that confuses me more.

And pisses me off.

He's talking in riddles, smug and mysterious and maddening. And now all I can think about is the woman who had this seat before me, maybe even got these same fucking tacos, breathed in this same cologne.

Suddenly nothing feels special.

Right back to where I started remembering why I keep him on the other side of a door that I can never open. Never again.

He barely rolls to a stop when I grab the handle and try to yank the door open.

"Thanks for the lift." It doesn't open and I swear under my breath. "Is there a way out of this death trap?"

He's holding back a grin, but his eyes are smoldering. Then, without warning, he leans across me. His entire body invades my space—his shoulder brushing mine, his breath warm against my neck. I suck in a sharp gasp and that was the wrong move.

It goes right past his ear.

He definitely heard it.

He probably also heard me *inhale* him like some deranged cologne-sniffing junkie.

Goddammit.

He pops the door open effortlessly, then looks at me. Voice low. Warm. Intimate.

"Good night, Cricket."

I say nothing. Just step out and slam the door harder than necessary.

Screw him.

I don't have time to play games with the dickwad from my past who needs to stay there. I've got to figure out how to save my house.

But as I walk up the steps, his words echo in my head.

They're a bit more carnal in nature...

What the hell does that mean?

Are people selling... *themselves?*

And he said "the uber-rich."

If that's true... this might be exactly what I need. Because I may not have money, power, or connections. But I *do* have one thing of value.

And I've been looking for the right person to give it to for weeks now.

Maybe this is my saving grace.

A soft whinny cuts through the dark, and I turn toward the stables.

Saving Grace. Our other champion. The one pregnant with Dominion's foal. The one I named when I was ten, believing in signs and fairy tales.

She kicks once, like punctuation.

My smile is faint, but real.

Maybe it *is* fate.

And Jaxon won't be there. He said so himself. And with my brother gone, this is sounding more perfect by the second.

As I step into the house and close the door behind me, Jaxon's taillights disappear down the road like the last flicker of a warning I'm going to ignore.

I don't know what this Black Ledger auction is but by morning, I will.

Chapter 9

Jaxon

Why I got dragged out to this thing is beyond me.

No, that's a lie.

I know exactly why I'm here.

Lucian Vale called me personally.

When *the* Lucian Vale—owner of The Black Ledger, Lord of Brooding Billionaires, Destroyer of Joy—puts your name on speed dial, you don't ignore his calls. Especially not when you're the one who promised his precious auction tech would run so smooth it could seduce a nun.

Which, to be fair, it does.

I didn't just upgrade his systems—I rebuilt the whole damn thing from the ground up. Security, encryption, tracking protocols for the Companions, client filters, hidden backdoor logs for safety. He wanted seamless. I gave him bulletproof. Hell, I even launched a custom app this year—sleek, anonymous, and sinful as hell—to showcase the *very* sultry items up for bidding tonight.

And when The Black Ledger auctions something, it's never simple.

It's experience, indulgence, fantasy.

And the ultra-wealthy eat it up. They pay, beg, donate to get on the guest list. Every year, the auction grows more exclusive, more excessive, more... debauched.

This year it's being held on one of The Black Ledger's skyscraper balconies. The kind of balcony that makes OSHA weep—half a football field long, lined with fire features and plush seating, the kind of lighting that makes everyone look like sex, and not a single expense spared.

The champagne flows like water, the DJ is working the crowd into a slow, rhythmic frenzy, and the air itself feels charged—like everyone's teetering on the edge of something wicked.

The Ledger Girls are out in force tonight—every last one of them wrapped in that signature shade of Ledger red. Some draped in silk, others in velvet or lace. They're mingling with the bidders, giving them a taste before the bidding even starts. A whisper of what could be theirs—for the right price.

And Eve is up on the block again.

She is every year.

God knows what wild, carnal package she's offering this time—something involving leather, poetry, and mild emotional trauma, if I had to guess. Whatever it is, it's worth millions. She always draws a crowd.

I flick her hair clip at her from across the bar. "Your weird-ass lucky charm, ma'lady."

She snatches it midair like it's a bar of pure gold and

presses a kiss to it, then tucks it beneath the bar top like she's invoking some ancient sex witch spell.

"May the best pervert win," she tells me with a wink.

I pull up my admin login on the auction app just as Lucian arrives.

He doesn't make an entrance—he *is* the entrance. He moves like he owns the air around him. Black slacks, sleeves rolled, top buttons open, no jacket. A storm disguised as a man. Everything about him screams power, control, menace. The kind of guy who doesn't just *run* empires—he devours them.

He strides toward me, scanning the crowd with that cold, calculating gaze like he's already reading every bid before it's made.

"The bids are about to start," he says. "We good?"

I lean back against the bar and grin, "Maybe. This is just the beta version so I guess we'll find out together."

His eyes narrow. "You test me on my auction night?"

Which is why I mouth off as much as possible.

Because whatever snark I throw tonight, he'll make me pay for it in the ring tomorrow.

And let's be real.

I'm always looking forward to it.

I toss him a mock salute. "Relax, boss. The app's perfect. Wire transfers are already syncing in real time. The charities are preloaded and ready to receive their cut as soon as the final bid's locked."

Lucian watches the room like he's hunting for problems, but I know he trusts me. He just doesn't *do* relaxed.

"I'll stick around for the first few rounds," I add, "but I

can monitor the rest from my phone. If anything glitches, I'll catch it before anyone notices."

He nods once, then steps over to the bar and orders his usual—whiskey, neat. The kind of drink that doesn't bother pretending to be soft.

"You bidding on anything tonight?" he cuts his eyes at me like a challenge. He already knows my answer and it feels like he's daring me to make him wrong.

I snort. "You already know the answer to that."

He arches a brow.

"I only use the Ledger girls for one thing, and this isn't it."

Lucian hums, unreadable as always. Then, casually, like it's not a command, he says, "Stay awhile. Eat something that didn't come out of a takeout container. Enjoy the spectacle."

He takes a sip of whiskey, eyes back on the crowd.

"Never know," Lucian adds, swirling his glass, "you might see something that catches your attention."

I'm about to turn back to the bar when I spot Elijah fucking Carter.

Of course he's here.

Tech money. Daddy's money, to be specific. And just enough facial symmetry to land on one of those *Top 40 Under 40* lists that make investors cream themselves.

He slinks up beside me, glass of something amber in hand, smug as ever. "You here as the hired help?"

I smile without showing teeth. "Still playing with code you stole from college kids and pretending it's innovation?"

He laughs, but there's a twitch in his eye. Good. I hate this fucking guy.

He took my first real software pitch and resold it under his name when I was thirteen. Called it a "mentorship." I called it what it was—intellectual theft. Two years out of college, I eclipsed his empire. Now I own half the companies he wishes would return his calls.

He blinks, clearly not expecting the hit. "Still got that mouth on you, huh?" I finally look at him. Really look. And I let the edge creep into my voice.

"You're still the guy who cashes in on the scraps," I say, slow and sharp. "I'm the one they build the fucking table for."

He stiffens.

"Now stop wasting my time."

And then, like the coward he's always been, he grins and slinks away—already retreating, but not without tossing one last jab over his shoulder.

"Looking forward to outbidding you tonight."

That's laughable.

If I ever cared to step in, he wouldn't last a round with how deep my pockets go.

Elijah Fuck-face joins the rest of the hoard and the first round of bidding starts not long after. Pretty tame stuff, compared to what I know is coming later. Romantic weekends. Private yacht excursions. One girl's offering some kind of sensory deprivation retreat, which—look, not judging, but that's a hard pass for me.

The auctioneer works the crowd like he's orchestrating a

slow, seductive waltz. He teases a *"last-minute addition to the catalog—one worth staying until the end."*

I snort into my drink. Yeah, right. It's always the same thing. A high-end flesh market dressed up in red silk and velvet lighting. The Companions design their experiences, sell them to the highest bidder, and hope the winning client is more charming than creepy.

Bidders go after the girls they want, or sometimes they just want to outbid their enemies. Ego over desire. It's all posturing with a boner.

Still, I'll give Lucian credit—he runs a clean empire. The Companions *set* the terms of their contracts. Every single one of them. The clients follow those rules, or they get a very personal visit from Lucian himself.

And trust me—that is not the kind of house call you want.

But he was right about dinner.

I park myself at the bar, claim a plate stacked with grilled steak skewers and lobster dumplings, and watch the chaos unfold from afar. The food's decadent. The entertainment, even better. Drunk billionaires throwing money around like it's Monopoly and all the girls want Boardwalk. I sip whiskey and fix a few backend settings when the admin panel pings with a slow transfer.

No big deal. I reroute the traffic and fix the bottleneck in under thirty seconds.

And then, because I'm apparently a glutton for chaos, I check on Cassidy.

She's been unusually quiet on social today. No breakfast

post or *Get Ready With Me.* No story with Dominion or her grooming Saving Grace.

Honestly, I figured she blocked me after my call with Eve.

She definitely got jealous.

And I definitely enjoyed it.

But then my thoughts shift to her mom.

What if today's a bad day? What if something's wrong?

Shit. I should've checked earlier.

Her Snap location is turned off—which is mildly irritating—and when I open our messages, I see that her notifications are silenced.

Now I'm getting that tight feeling in my chest. The one that doesn't mean lust or ego—it means something might actually be *wrong.*

I shoot her a quick text:

> JAXON: You alive, Cricket? Tell your mom I said hi.

The message sits there, unread.

Damn it.

If something's going on with Mrs. Hayes, Jonathan will never forgive me for not being there.

I toss a few bills on the bar—enough to cover the food, the drinks, and a solid bribe—and give the bartender a nod. I'm already moving toward the exit when the auctioneer's voice cuts through the air with new energy.

"Ladies and gentlemen, our final lot of the evening. A last-minute addition, submitted just this morning."

I slow just slightly, curiosity tugging at me.

"An exclusive offering—something never before sold at The Black Ledger's auction."

He's milking the moment.

"A once-in-a-lifetime experience from a Companion offering something... truly special."

I keep walking. Yeah, yeah. I've heard this kind of pitch before. Probably someone offering a public scene or a week of full submission—some kink-laced fantasy for seven figures.

But then the words hit:

"Her virginity."

I stop cold.

That's... bold. Even for this place. A virgin auctioned off in front of a sea of wealthy men with God complexes? That's a hell of a risk.

The auctioneer continues, voice all velvet and heat.

"She's twenty-three years old, smart, stunning. This is a limited, one-time-only experience. No repeat bookings. No extensions. A singular, unforgettable event."

I'm halfway to the door when he says her name.

"Please welcome to the block... Cassidy Hayes."

The blood drains from my face.

I turn, slow as death, and look toward the stage.

No.

No fucking way.

Chapter 10

Cassidy

To say I'm nervous doesn't quite cover it. My heart hasn't stopped racing all day, and I've run through this plan so many times it hardly feels real anymore.

I've almost backed out more times than I can count but still—I'm here—about to sell my virginity off to the highest bidder.

Last night, right after Jaxon dropped me off, I went straight to Jonathan's room. He's in the UK for the next month, and I didn't bother being careful. If Jaxon knew about The Black Ledger, there was a good chance Jonathan did too.

It didn't take long to find his tablet tucked in the night-stand and I've known his password for years so I went right in.

At first, I told myself I was looking for answers— about the mortgage, about everything. But I kept focus on the auction and finally, I found something. A booking confirmation from a few weeks ago.

I remembered the date—some fancy black-tie event following a golf tournament. Jonathan said it was for networking. It wasn't. It was an escort bought through The Black Ledger.

The realization hit slow and sharp. If Jonathan had used it... Jaxon probably had too. That thought stayed with me longer than I wanted to admit.

I clicked the link into the client portal and saw his full history—dates, payments, preferences. Things I didn't want to know.

But I also found what I needed.

The Black Ledger's downtown address. And an invite to the upcoming auction, disguised as a charity gala.

Jonathan had RSVP'd no and I actually felt relieved —briefly.

But the auction was real. And so was everything it represented.

By the time the sun rose, I knew what I was going to do.

I'd show up in person. I'd find whoever was in charge and I wouldn't take no for an answer.

Because like it or not, this was the only option I had left.

Now that I'm here—wrapped in a red sequin gown that clings like sin and catches the light with every breath—I can't stop retracing the steps that brought me to this moment, wondering if any of them were the right ones.

Then I remember Jonathan's text from this morning.

No *"How's Mom?"*

No *"Where are we staying once the house is gone?"*

Just a cold list of tasks like everything is normal, like our lives aren't crumbling.

That was the final push.

I'm not just doing this to save our home—I'm doing it to make a statement. A defiant, furious *fuck you* to the person who left me to clean up his mess.

Eve finds me backstage as the current lot winds down. She's dressed in a deep crimson gown, every detail immaculate, her presence quiet but commanding. The kind of beauty that turns heads and holds them. And she's nothing like I expected.

Kind. Grounded. Even gentle.

She and another Companion, Sienna—closer to my age—spoke with me this morning. It wasn't a sales pitch. It felt more like a soft checkpoint. They asked the right questions. Made sure I understood what I was walking into. And at every step, they reminded me I could walk away.

But I didn't.

I never mentioned Jaxon. I couldn't risk it.

He said this kind of thing wasn't for him—that he wouldn't be here. And I made sure it stayed that way. I shut off my location, silenced every notification, and put my phone on airplane mode before the Ledger team got to work.

And they didn't hold back.

A full-body wax I wasn't emotionally prepared for. A massage with oils I wanted to bottle and hoard. Then came the glam—hair, makeup, everything curated with precision. And finally, the red dress collection.

Gowns in every shade of scarlet, worn only by Companions beginning or ending contracts. Symbols, I'm told.

The one I chose—or maybe the one that chose me—fits like a secret. All shimmer and movement, as if I were dipped in heat and starlight.

It's no wonder this place commands what it does. It's not just luxury—it's power. The exclusivity alone gives me hope that someone might pay enough to keep the bank from taking everything.

Hope that this choice, reckless as it feels, might still mean something more than shame.

The moment comes and I'm led toward the stage, but the curtain shields me from view. I can hear the crowd—restless and humming with anticipation. Voices overlap, a low thrum of wealth and want. The lights beyond the velvet glow too bright to see past, but I catch a glimpse of tuxedos and tailored suits. Men with money. With appetites.

And they're all waiting for *me*.

The auctioneer's voice cuts through the noise, smooth and confident.

"She's twenty-three years old. Smart. Stunning. A first-time Companion offering something this stage has never seen before."

He lets the silence stretch, lets the tension tighten like a drawstring.

"This is a limited, one-time-only experience. No repeat bookings. No extensions. A singular, unforgettable event."

My breath catches. My knees threaten to give way.

Eve steps beside me, her hand warm on the small of my back.

"Good luck, honey," she says, soft and steady, and some-how, that helps.

The curtain rises and the lights blind.

I start my walk—each step carrying me deeper into the craziest thing I've ever done.

"Please welcome to the block..." A pause. "...Cassidy Hayes."

The curtain lifts, and as the lights flood over me, a hundred hungry eyes lock on—my breath catches, knees nearly buckling under the weight of being watched, wanted, and appraised.

And the bidding begins.

Ten thousand.

It hits like a slap.

Not because it's offensive—but because it's *real*. This is happening. I'm standing on a stage in a designer dress, auctioning off the one thing I swore I'd never give away this way...to someone that doesn't matter... and it starts at the cost of a used car.

A flick of a paddle and it jumps to twenty.

Then thirty.

I try to stay steady, rooted to the center mark just like Eve instructed. Don't pace. Don't fidget. Don't act like prey.

But all I can think is—*five million.*

That's what the farm is worth. The land. The stables. The house my mother sketched on a napkin the week after she married my father. Every inch of that property holds something sacred. And if I want to keep it—if I want to give my mother a home to come back to when her next round of treatment is over—I have to reach that number.

Five million dollars.

That's the prayer. The bargain I'm silently offering up to any god who might be listening.

Forty thousand.

Fifty.

The auctioneer's voice rolls steady, and the bids trickle in like water building to a boil. But they're still crawling. I've seen the numbers from the earlier lots. Most hovered in the tens of thousands. A few cracked six figures. Eve broke two million, but it was a weeks-long contract and she has a following. A reputation.

I have none of that.

I'm just the hype piece. The mystery virgin. The final lot, saved for the end in hopes the novelty alone might make someone curious—or stupid—enough to bid higher.

Seventy-five thousand.

A hundred.

I force myself to breathe through it. To keep my expression soft and blank, my eyes drifting over the room like I'm above it all. But my heart is pounding so hard I feel it in my teeth.

I scan the space the best I can past the lights, looking for something—*anything*—to ground me.

And that's when I see a silhouette, moving slowly up the center aisle. Hands in his pockets. Shoulders square. Casual. Purposeful.

At first, I think it's just another bidder making his way toward the front for a better view.

But the closer he gets, the more the shape starts to crystallize.

The swagger. The build. The sleeves pushed to the elbows.

My stomach drops.

No.

No no no no no—

Fuck.

He steps into the light, and my entire body goes still.

White button-down, open too far. Tattoos curling down his arms like smoke. The kind of fury in his eyes that turns blood cold.

Jaxon.

My worst-case scenario made flesh.

He's not supposed to be here. He *wasn't coming.* I shut off my location. I turned off my phone. I did everything to keep him from knowing.

And yet—here he is.

Looking at me like I've betrayed him.

Looking at me like I'm not a girl on a stage anymore... but a woman he *intends* to claim.

A man stands near the front and yells out, "Two hundred and fifty thousand!" like he's announcing a Super Bowl touchdown.

Jaxon turns his head, slowly, toward the voice.

The guy's grinning like he's just started something. And maybe he has. Because there's something loaded in the way he stares back at Jaxon—like they know each other. Like he *wants* to be seen. Like this isn't about me at all.

My chest tightens.

Jaxon says nothing. Doesn't flinch. Hands still in his pockets, jaw tight, gaze unreadable.

Then he turns back to me.

I can see that calm, careful rage simmering just beneath his skin. The kind that doesn't explode—it *erupts.*

"Five hundred thousand," he says flatly.

And just like that, I know the gloves have come off.

The other man throws back seven-fifty. Then a million.

Every number he throws out, Jaxon doubles.

Two million.

Four.

Eight.

I can't breathe. I can't move. I can't *look* anywhere but him.

Because Jaxon never takes his eyes off me. Not even when the auctioneer recites the totals with more and more disbelief. He's locked in, throwing out numbers like they don't matter. Like they're loose change.

The room has gone silent around us, except for the gasps and murmurs. No one expected this and Christ, neither did I.

"Fifty million," Elijah calls, his voice sharp and triumphant.

The entire audience loses it. People are whispering, stunned. Someone actually chokes on their drink and coughs.

I take a shaky step forward, lips parting. "Jaxon—"

But he doesn't move. He's planted like a monument of fury, every muscle coiled tight beneath that white shirt.

"One hundred million."

"*Two* hundred million." The competitor boasts and that does it.

Jaxon exhales through his nose—slow, measured—then, to my utter horror:

"One billion dollars and..."

He reaches into his back pocket, pulls out his wallet, cracking it open like it's nothing more than an inconvenience.

"Let's see," he says, pulling out cash fanning through the bills. "Two hundred and thirty-three dollars and..."

He pauses to dig in his pocket.

Yes. His actual pocket.

The man pulls out change.

"...Seventy-four cents."

And then—*he throws it.*

The bills flutter like confetti as they scatter to the ground at the man's feet, coins hitting the marble with a metallic clatter.

The room *erupts.*

Gasps. Laughter. Someone in the back actually yells, "Holy shit."

Jaxon turns his body fully toward his competitor, hands shoved casually back in his pockets.

"Say another fucking number," he growls, voice low and sharp as a knife. "And I'll double it again, Elijah. Fucking *try* me."

The guy opens his mouth—then closes it. Swallows hard.

Jaxon has him and he knows it.

Everyone does.

The auctioneer—who's been riding this chaos like it's the Kentucky Derby—steps in with perfectly timed drama.

"Going once…"

Silence.

"Going twice…"

The tension cracks like thunder.

"…Sold."

His voice rings out like a gavel.

"To Mr. Jaxon Kane."

Chapter 11

To say I'm pissed doesn't even scrape the surface.

I'm a fucking inferno in a white button-down, barely keeping it together as I storm through The Ledger's interior halls.

The Companions are taken backstage after their lots are over, tucked away in private rooms while their contracts are finalized.

Cassidy's back there too.

But she's not a Companion.

She's not some woman trained to stand on a stage and auction off pieces of herself to the highest bidder. She's not polished seduction or curated fantasy.

She's Cassidy.

My Cass—

I stop that thought cold.

Mine?

No.

Yes.

I don't know.

She's not mine, but she sure as hell isn't *theirs*.

And not like this.

Not offering up her virginity to a crowd of champagne-soaked billionaires like it's some kind of limited edition.

My stomach churns at the thought.

If I'd walked out earlier—if I'd not been curious to see what the big deal was on the last lot—some mother fucker, like Elijah, could've walked away with her. Fucking Elijah. That smug little bastard with too much money and no conscience. He would've bragged about it for the rest of his life. Turned her into some story he'd retell to dinner guests with a smirk and a brandy.

I nearly choke on the idea, shoving past a server and barely register his startled noise. The poor guy trying to guide me toward the private suites looks like he's debating pissing himself or running.

He fucking should.

I'm hanging on by threads.

The moment he points out the door, I don't wait. I don't knock. I push through like a storm, half expecting to find her crying. Ashamed. Scared.

But what I get instead—

She whirls around the moment I burst in.

Hair wild. Dress glittering. Her eyes—fucking hell, her eyes—blazing with fury.

No fear. No apology.

Just fire.

And it's aimed right at me.

Her shoulders are squared. That glittering red dress

hugging her curves like temptation incarnate. But there's nothing soft or seductive about her right now.

She's furious. And so the fuck am I.

"Are you out of your goddamn mind?" I bark, stalking toward her. "What the hell were you doing on that stage?"

Cassidy crosses her arms, chin high. "Whatever I damn well please."

"You were auctioning off your virginity, Cassidy!" My voice spikes, something wild and frantic clawing its way up my throat. "To a fucking room full of strangers."

"And?" Her voice is deadly calm. "My body, my rules. I don't have to explain myself to anyone—especially not you."

I reel like she slapped me. She doesn't back down. Doesn't flinch.

I don't know whether I want to shake her or lock her in a room and never let her out.

The door opens again, and Lucian walks in—with Eve right behind him.

Lucian barely steps into the room before I have him by the collar.

"You son of a bitch," I snarl, slamming him back against the wall. "How could you let her go up there? She's not one of your girls. She's not a Companion."

Lucian's body hits hard, but he doesn't even blink. His hand comes up fast and grabs my shirt in return, his eyes just as pissed as mine.

"She's a grown fucking woman, Kane," he grits out. "She walked in this morning. Signed the paperwork herself. This wasn't some conspiracy. We didn't even know you two were acquainted."

"Acquainted?" I spit. "She's—"

I choke off the word. Mine. Mine in ways I can't even explain.

Eve leans against the doorway with a drink in hand like she's watching pay-per-view. "This is so much better than last year's auction."

"Cancel the contract," I growl, still staring Lucian down.

"Don't you dare," Cassidy snaps.

I whip around to her, stunned.

She steps forward. "If he's not paying, then put me back up there. Or give it to the last bidder."

"The fuck you will," I bark, eyes wide. I bend at the knee to get closer to her eye level, trying to make her see me. "Cass, are you out of your damn mind? Do you even hear yourself right now?"

She stares me down like she's not scared of the monster I feel like. "Are you? You look like a goddamn maniac."

Eve nods. "He does look incredibly caffeinated."

I glare at her. "No. You're *my* friend. You take *my* side."

Eve shrugs with a smirk. "Chicks before dicks, my guy. If it's a man against a woman, I'm on her side every time."

"What the fuck." I blink at her.

"I appreciate female rage." She finished with a close-lipped smile that's not actually friendly.

"Lucian," Cassidy snaps. "Put me back up there. This is my choice, not his."

Something in me breaks.

"Fine," I grit out, pulling my phone from my pocket. "We're fucking doing this."

I open the payment portal and hammer the numbers in, punching the screen like it insulted my mother. A second later, the phone dings.

"Paid. A billion-dollar contract."

Cassidy plants her hands on her hips, unbothered and smug. "One billion, two hundred and thirty-three dollars and seventy-four cents... to be exact."

Eve chokes on a laugh.

Lucian doesn't smile. But his mouth twitches. Close enough that I want to fucking slap him.

I jab a finger at Cassidy. "Oh, you're so fucking funny, aren't you?"

"Sometimes," she says sweetly. "When a maniac isn't breathing down my back."

My fists clench. My jaw aches.

"Does your brother know about this?"

Her smile doesn't fade. If anything, it sharpens.

"What do you think?" she asks, voice silk and sin. "You wanna be the one to tell him?"

I stare at her, breath locked in my chest.

She takes a slow step closer, eyes burning into mine, daring me.

"Tell him you bought his little sister's virginity?"

Eve lets out a low whistle. "Oh, this is getting juicier."

"You're not helping," I mutter, dragging a hand through my hair.

Cassidy stands across from me, arms crossed, lips set in a hard line. She's not backing down. She never does.

Goddamn her for being so fucking stubborn.

"Is it money? Is that what this was all about?"

Because if she needed it—really needed it—she could've just come to me. I'd give her anything. All she had to do was ask. But instead, she walked into this world, put herself on that stage, and gave every man in that room a chance to bid on what never should've been up for sale.

And still... she won't tell me why.

She doesn't owe me that. I know she doesn't. But it doesn't stop the anger from curling around my ribs like barbed wire.

"It's my prerogative." She answers plainly.

It's always like this with us—two storm fronts waiting to see which one will break first.

So fine.

She wants to play by the rules? Then I'll give her rules.

I bought the contract. I'll honor it. Every single line. Every stipulation. Let's see if she's ready for what that actually means.

I take a step closer, lowering my voice. "You ready to give yourself to me, Cricket? Because that's what this is now. No more hiding behind bravado. You signed the paper. And now you belong to me."

Eve shifts her weight with a smirk. "Well, this turned awkward fast."

She punches something on the control panel mounted to the desk. The contract lights up on the TV screen above it, crisp and glaring.

"We need to set a duration," she says. "The contract requires a mutually agreed end date."

"Ninety days," I say without hesitation.

Cassidy lifts her chin. "A month."

My jaw tightens. "Why a month?"

"Stop with the fucking questions." she says flatly. "One month."

She's pushing me—again. Always testing, always drawing a new line in the sand, and daring me to cross it. It's infuriating how calm she is, how easy she makes it look to stand there and act like I didn't just spend the last half hour watching men try to buy her.

I hold her stare, jaw locked, breath tight. I didn't even know what I was going to say until the words flew out of my mouth.

"Move in with me."

Her head snaps toward me. "What? I can't move in with you."

"Then it's ninety days."

She hesitates, eyes darting like she's searching for an escape hatch. But there isn't one. Not anymore.

"Move in with me," I say again, low and firm. "And I'll agree to a month."

I can already see the battle happening behind her eyes. The calculation. The tension. But I also see the moment she realizes she doesn't have another move.

She exhales slowly. "Fine."

My grin is slow and sharp as I step into her. Taking up the space in front of her so she either has to step back or hold her ground.

She doesn't budge.

I lower my mouth close to her ear, smelling her perfume

and letting my exhale tickle her neck and whisper, "Good girl."

Cassidy stiffens, and I feel the pull in my gut that only she ever causes. This tension—this fire—it's not going anywhere. Not now.

I turn to Eve. "Update the contract. Thirty days. She moves in tomorrow."

Eve looks at Cassidy. She pauses a beat before sealing her fate and nodding in agreement.

The traitor, who used to be my friend, starts tapping the tablet again. Lucian watches in silence from the back wall, arms crossed like he's just here to make sure no one sets the room on fire.

Too fucking late for that.

I glance back at Cassidy. Her chin's still high. Her jaw tight.

But I can see that flicker in her eyes.

She thinks she's won. That she still has control.

Poor thing.

She doesn't realize yet—I already own her.

And I plan to make sure she feels it.

Every single day. Over every inch of her body.

I'm still standing way too close for this to be considered cordial, but I give her one more lingering look before I take a step back.

"See you in the morning, Cricket." I wink and see that fire light back up. "I'm looking forward to getting to know you–" I let my eyes run down the seductive curves of her body, "so much better."

It's move-in day with Jaxon Kane.

A sentence I never thought I'd think to myself.

Not even in some long-lost daydream or "what if" fantasy. Certainly not like this—after standing on a stage and selling my virginity to the highest bidder.

God.

I still can't believe it happened.

Can't believe I looked up, in the middle of that blinding spotlight, and saw him walking down the aisle—storm in his eyes, fury in his stride.

It felt like being caught red-handed in the middle of the most reckless decision I've ever made.

Now, less than twenty-four hours later, I'm supposed to live with him for a month.

What the fuck am I doing?

I pull out my phone and open the banking app, checking to see if half a billion dollars has hit my account yet.

Of course it hasn't.

Not that I expected it immediately, but still—I can't help the flutter of nerves in my chest. The contract said half now, half at the end. After... we've...

I can't even finish the thought without my stomach doing anxious cartwheels.

Jaxon Kane. One billion dollars. For my virginity.

It's absurd. Completely and utterly ridiculous.

And I'm the one who made it happen.

I try not to think about what comes next. About what it means once the second half is paid. About what I will have to do.

Instead, I focus on packing.

One large suitcase for clothes. A duffel bag for shoes. My cosmetics bag, and my backpack with all the essentials— laptop, sketchbook, headphones, and three half-read books I won't finish but bring anyway.

Once it's all packed in the trunk of my car, I make my way inside for breakfast with my mom.

Or rather, I eat while she sips at her tea.

She looks well this morning. Slept better than usual, but there's something off, something that makes her seem smaller. Paler. Could be the dark head wrap or the oversized black sweater swallowing her frame, but still... I notice.

The hair loss has been hard on her. The cold that never seems to leave her bones, even harder.

But her face lights up when she sees Saving Grace in the pasture, grazing with Dominion.

"Still think it was genius," she says softly, cupping her mug. "Breeding those two. You'll lock in the best bloodlines in the league."

I smile as I chew, then swallow. "That was the idea."

She nods, eyes distant for a moment.

"Cass... when I'm not here anymore..."

I stop breathing.

She doesn't look at me, just keeps her gaze fixed on the horses.

"When that time comes, I want you to keep them going. Even if you don't race them. Just... keep them. Take care of them. Make sure they're loved."

"Mom," I say, too fast, too defensive. "Don't talk like that."

"I'm just saying—"

"You're not going anywhere." My voice breaks, and I have to look down at my plate to pull it back together. "You're going to get better. And when you do, we'll race them together like we always have."

She finally looks at me. Her smile is soft. Sad. But she nods.

"I'd like that."

Not long after, she tells me she's tired and heads back to bed. I help her to her room, tuck the blanket around her shoulders, and kiss her temple before slipping out again.

But I can't leave yet.

I can't face him yet. Not with a fucking hurricane swirling in my stomach.

So, instead of driving to his building, I head for the stables.

I climb the worn stairs to the second story—the old hay loft Daddy converted into my art room six years ago. It smells like pine and dust and acrylic paint, and the second I step inside, I breathe a little easier.

The emotions are piling up, too many to hold at once, so I pick up a brush.

Because painting is the only thing that makes me feel like I still belong to myself.

The strokes are bold. Chaotic. The colors clash—deep reds slashing across pale yellows, streaks of dark green cutting through swaths of violet.

It doesn't look like it should make sense.

But it does to me.

I can see it, even if no one else ever will.

The gaping mouth. The fists tangled in long black hair. The motion in the blurs of paint, like wind or movement or panic caught mid-breath.

It's a woman screaming.

Not outwardly—but from the inside.

It's me, bleeding my inner turmoil onto canvas in broad, unrestrained brushstrokes.

I don't know how long I've been painting.

When I finally step back, my legs are tight from standing too long, my hands are speckled in dried paint, and the sun has shifted halfway across the sky.

Shit.

It's mid-afternoon.

I was supposed to leave hours ago.

If I don't get going soon, Jaxon will probably send a damn SWAT team to find me. I wouldn't put it past him.

I scrub my hands on a paint-stained towel and check on Mom before heading back to my car. I already staged the lie

—told her I got commissioned for a piece by some downtown gallery. My first one.

Said they were setting me up with a furnished apartment for the month so I could focus and hit the deadline.

Her face lit up when I told her and that made my guilt increase tenfold. She's the only one that supported my art. Told me I could do anything. How much talent I had. Made Daddy build the studio and buy me every color of paint available.

My brother always said it was a waste. Made me feel like the pictures in my mind were pointless. That going to college for my art was a hobby until I got married. Because that's all I could be good for.

Being married and becoming a mom. Like my life had nothing else to offer but that.

Mom always wanted me to see how far I could go.

She was genuinely upset when I moved back in to take care of her. She wanted me to live my life. Not be stuck in limbo while she fights cancer.

How on earth would she ever think I could leave her like this. Especially with Daddy gone barely two years.

Even now, I want to stay. To tell Jaxon to fuck off and that I'm not leaving her. That I need to spend as much time with her as I can in case I never get to again.

But this is the only shot I have to fix what's coming. To save the only home we've ever known.

That if she does close her eyes one day, if cancer wins, the last thing she'll see is this place she loved so much.

With one look back at the house, I blow a kiss hoping the soft breeze carries it to Mom.

And then I leave before I can change my mind.

The city rises up around me like a steel mirage. Towering glass and polished concrete, the buzz of wealth radiating from every corner.

I've never been inside Jaxon's penthouse before. Just heard stories. Seen the occasional background in a photo from an afterparty or one of Jonathan's rare humble-brag mentions.

But the building itself is massive. Intimidating. The kind of place that doesn't just whisper money—it screams it through Italian marble and staff that anticipate your every need.

I pull up to the valet and barely roll down my window before someone steps forward and says, "Good afternoon, Ms. Hayes. Mr. Kane let us know you'd be arriving. We'll take care of your bags."

Of course he did.

They already know my name. Know my car. Like this is some kind of luxury hostage situation.

A uniformed man grabs my suitcase and duffel while another opens the driver's side door. "We'll park it in Mr. Kane's private garage."

Private garage.

Of course.

I climb out, smooth my shirt, and take a long, calming breath before stepping through the sleek glass doors. The lobby is all shadow and shine—dark granite floors, cascading lighting, minimalistic furniture that costs more than my entire wardrobe.

An attendant leads me to a private elevator at the back. Not just exclusive. Personal.

Because why wouldn't Jaxon has his own elevator?

I roll my eyes as the doors glide shut behind us, sealing me in with the uncomfortable weight of my own reflection and the polite man seeing to my bags.

We begin the smooth, silent ascent to the top.

To him. To the man that is going to take my virginity.

My brother's best friend. The man I once loved.

The elevator doors glide open, and I instantly hate it.

Not the penthouse.

The penthouse is... breathtaking.

Floor-to-ceiling windows stretch across the entire far wall, flooding the space with sunlight and a panoramic view of the city skyline. The furniture is modern but somehow comfortable—sleek lines, deep colors, oversized pillows arranged in curated chaos.

It smells like him.

Like cedar and bergamot and sinful confidence. Like he bottles his cologne and pumps it through the air vents. Or lights candles made from his ego and masculine rage.

Everything is warm wood and polished steel. There's a living wall of greenery in one corner, an open kitchen that looks like it belongs on the cover of a magazine, and—of course—a breathtaking infinity pool on a private balcony.

Because what self-respecting man-child billionaire doesn't need a pool for an endless rotation of bikini-clad houseguests?

Then I hear footsteps. That lazy gait I know better than I should. He comes out from the hallway wearing absolutely nothing but black jeans and a motorcycle helmet.

Tattoos crawl over his chest and arms like inked temptation. His skin gleams with a light sheen of sweat, his abs tight.

I lift my eyes back up and find he's removed the helmet. His smug mouth halfway to a smirk.

I swear my ovaries try to claw their way out of my body.

"You shower in that thing?" I manage, proud I got the words out without openly drooling.

"Aww," he teases, pulling his wallet from his back pocket. "You trying to see me naked already, Crick?"

I narrow my eyes as he tips the valet a crisp hundred without breaking stride.

"Please. Don't make me vomit." We both know I'm a fucking liar. He's gorgeous.

His smirk widens. "You're just mad you liked the view."

"I've seen better," I lie.

Jaxon starts the tour like he's hosting a real estate show.

"This is the living room. The balcony doors open fully. Whole indoor-outdoor thing. This"—he points to the glass-walled room filled with gym equipment—"is where I pretend to work through my daddy issues instead of going to actual therapy."

"Impressive," I say, dry. "Do you have a spreadsheet for emotional suppression, or is that just muscle memory by now?"

He leads me to the kitchen with the reverence of a man showing off a Lamborghini.

"I'm a danger in the kitchen so a chef keeps this stocked a few times a week," he says, opening the fridge.

Glass jars line the shelves—layered salads with vibrant vegetables, little containers of dressing on the side. More glass containers with prepared meals, ready to heat and eat.

Every shelf is perfectly aligned, color-coordinated, and terrifyingly organized.

"You're actually a serial killer, aren't you?" I ask picking up a jar and inspecting it. "You even have OCD salads."

He grins. "And yet you're still here."

"Under duress."

Jaxon grabs my suitcase and duffel like they weigh nothing and heads toward a bedroom that's on the other side of the penthouse to his.

The moment the door swings open, my breath catches.

All my stuff is already here.

My framed photos. My books. My clothes hanging in the closet—perfectly organized by color. My brush on the vanity. My favorite plush blanket draped over the foot of the bed.

"What the hell?"

"You were taking forever," he says, shrugging. "Figured you needed help packing."

"You went and got my things?"

"Pshht. No, I sent someone." He shrugs like it's nothing. "And you're welcome."

"You realize this is only for thirty days, right?"

"Sure." He shrugs but doesn't look at me.

Just drops my duffel next to the bed and lingers in the doorway, arms crossed. Watching me.

"I want to know why," he says eventually.

"Why what?"

"Why you did it. Why you went up there."

I avoid his gaze, setting my cosmetics bag on the vanity. "I don't owe you an explanation."

"I could hack you," he says casually. "I could find out."

"No, you won't." I turn and hold his stare. "You won't invade my privacy like that. Idle threats don't suit you."

He grinds his jaw. "You're infuriating."

"You're not exactly easy-breezy yourself."

The air grows thicker. Every second that passes coils tighter between us.

I stare down at the bed, fidgeting with the zipper on my bag.

"So, um," My voice is smaller when I finally ask, "When do you want to, um... do this?"

Theres a long pause but I can feel the shift in him. Like he went from Captain Annoying to Rico Suave in a blink.

"I'm not sure what you're talking about," he says, voice like silk-wrapped gasoline. "Can you be specific?"

"Seriously?" I snap, glaring at him. "You know exactly what I mean."

"Do I?" he tilts his head, pure menace and mischief.

"You're infuriating." I huff and I know I sound like a pouty brat. "You probably just plan on holding me hostage until the month is over, don't you?"

He steps closer. Close enough that the heat from his body ghosts over my skin.

"Oh, I intend to get what I paid for, Cricket." He steps behind me, his hands go to my arms and slide up them. I feel his nose in my hair as he takes a deep inhale, then lowers his mouth next to my ear.

His voice drops, dark and deliberate. "And you'll beg me to do it."

I lift my chin, refusing to back down as I turn and face him. "I won't beg you for a single thing."

His smirk is slow. Dangerous.

"Keep telling yourself that, baby."

Chapter 13
Cassidy

Something's wrong.

I know it before I even open my eyes.

A high pitch warning going off in an endless shriek that pulls me from sleep.

There's a weight in the air—thick and bitter—that scratches at the back of my throat and makes my nose wrinkle. Not the soft, warm scent of detergent and cologne that lulled me to sleep last night. This is something darker. Smokier.

Something is on fire.

My eyes snap open.

I jolt upright in bed, coughing once, then twice. The scent hits harder now. Smoke—undeniable and aggressive. Not the faint kind from a blown-out candle. The *oh shit, the house is on fire* kind.

I throw the blanket off, stumble to my feet, and rush for the door, nearly tripping over my duffel bag on the way out.

My heart is hammering now, fully awake and fueled by panic. I don't even think to grab a robe.

The hallway is hazy—soft gray streaks wafting through the morning light. Somewhere up ahead, there's the unmistakable *whoosh* of a fire extinguisher being triggered and a string of muttered curses.

I follow the sounds, barefoot and wide-eyed, and round the corner into the kitchen and promptly stop dead in my tracks.

Jaxon Kane. Shirtless. Barefoot. Holding a bright red fire extinguisher like it's an extension of him.

The stove is a *literal inferno*. Orange flames dance up the backsplash, licking toward the ceiling as smoke billows upward. He sprays the extinguisher at the base of the flames, eyes narrowed in concentration, face flushed with effort. Muscles tense, jaw tight, hair a mess.

He looks like a firefighter calendar shot gone very, very wrong.

He finally gets the fire under control—foam now coating half the kitchen—and lowers the extinguisher with a groan, panting, covered in a sheen of sweat and disaster.

He looks up, breathing hard. His hair is a mess. His tattoos glisten. His eyes meet mine—and even through the haze, I swear I see amusement crack the surface of his exasperation.

Then he nods toward the smoldering mess behind him and mutters, "Well... breakfast is ready."

I blink at the scorched scene in front of me.

There's nothing salvageable. Not a single pan or piece of food that doesn't look like it crawled out of hell.

A laugh bubbles out of me before I can stop it—half amusement, half disbelief. "What was this supposed to be?"

Jaxon steps back and gestures vaguely at the wreckage, like he's unveiling a masterpiece. "Eggs?" he says, hopeful.

I giggle again, covering my nose as he moves to the far wall and pushes open what I thought were just floor-to-ceiling windows. But they glide outward on hidden hinges, turning into massive glass doors that disappear into the wall. Suddenly, the smoke has somewhere to go—and the balcony becomes part of the living room, flooding the space with fresh air and sunlight.

"I've never in my life seen anyone catch eggs on fire," I say, still staring at the battlefield of his stove.

He shrugs, not even a little embarrassed. "I'm a man of many talents."

His eyes drop, trailing down the length of me. I suddenly remember I'm standing in nothing but an oversized t-shirt—no bra, no pants, and definitely no defense against the heat in his gaze. The air between us tightens, charged with something I know better than to touch but can't help breathing in.

His brow arches. "Turn around."

"No."

This isn't just any shirt and we both know it. I suddenly want to kick myself in the ass for wearing it but I didn't even think of it. Because I sleep in this shirt more than anything else.

He steps forward slowly, a predatory glint in his eye. "Turn around, or I swear to God I'll force-feed you the charcoal eggs."

I back up a step, eyes narrowing. "You wouldn't."

"Try me."

Reluctantly I turn because it would look ridiculous if I tried to walk backward all the way to my room. I nearly feel his gaze on me just as hot as the fire a moment ago.

"Is that..." he pauses, voice a little hoarse. "You sleep in *my* shirt, Cricket?"

God I'm so fucking stupid.

I glance over my shoulder. "It's just an old shirt."

We know it's not. It's his. His old baseball shirt with his name on the back. "KANE" and the number "18". My birthday.

I've always wanted to ask if he picked the number or if they gave it to him. But I'd die first.

Jaxon had bought a house for himself and his mom, Sandy. I was barely thirteen and he was celebrating with a pool party. Jonathan pushed me in at night when the swimming was over. My clothes were soaked, and he gave me this shirt. A pair of boxers too.

Our parents came to pick us up and he told me to keep them. And I did.

He takes another step closer. "Just an old shirt huh?"

"Yup." I swallow hard, crossing my arms over my chest to hide my nipples that are hardening with each second. "I didn't even pay attention when I put it on."

Another step. "Sure you didn't."

His eyes drop again, and for a second, I think he might kiss me—right here in the smoke-scented kitchen, with the fire extinguisher still on the counter and a burned pan still hissing behind us.

But instead, he backs off, and leans against the kitchen island. Stomach muscles flexing as he's still calming his breathing.

"Get dressed," he nods toward my bedroom door. "I'll take you to breakfast."

***

Back at Jaxon's apartment, he disappears behind his office door, mumbling about a few meetings and that he won't be long.

I head to the guest room—the one that's mine for the next thirty days—but I barely make it past the bed before my phone buzzes with an alert.

I freeze when I see the bank notice of a deposit.

$500,000,000.

I blink, then blink again, thinking maybe my eyes are playing tricks. Maybe there's a glitch. Maybe the comma's in the wrong place. But no—it's real. All of it.

Half a billion dollars.

And change.

In my name.

It doesn't even register at first. I sit down, phone still in hand, and try to catch my breath.

And this is only half.

Half of what my virginity was apparently worth.

That thought alone is enough to send me spiraling. But I don't let myself go there. I can't. Not right now.

Because this money—this unimaginable, world-altering amount—could fix everything.

Not just the house but... everything.

I pull myself together, change into jeans and a t-shirt, and send Jaxon a quick message letting him know I'll be out for a bit.

By the time I pull up to the house, my nerves are a wreck. It looks the same as it always has—but at the same time it doesn't. It looks different.

Maybe it's the adrenaline still humming in my veins. Or maybe it's the task I'll have to carry out soon that enabled me to have this money.

I make a beeline straight to the art studio, where I hid the mortgage papers.

After I threw them on Jonathan's floor, and he left for the UK, I went back in there for them. That was careless to just leave them around for someone to find. To take to mom and give her stress she doesn't need.

He had taken the letter with my doctor's exam with him and I clinch my jaw remembering it was gone.

My heart clenches as I call the mortgage company and start the transfer. The process is mechanical—routing numbers, security codes, verification steps—but my hands shake the entire time. Every second feels like a countdown. Like someone's going to call and say it's too late.

But then...the transfer is complete.

And just like that, the mortgage is gone. Paid. Cleared. No more foreclosure notices. No more threats. No more shame.

I press my palms to my face and let out a shuddering breath. Tears burn at the edges of my eyes—grief and relief tangled up in one overwhelming release.

This house was never just a structure. It's memories. It's safety. It's my mother's final years.

And for a terrifying moment, I thought I'd failed her. And my dad.

I allow myself to cry—just for a moment. For what we almost lost.

But I hear Ben downstairs with Grace and I suddenly feel so selfish. Since finding those papers, I'd only been worried about this house. About us. I hadn't even thought of Ben.

He lives here too. For decades, he's lives on the property and taken care of the horses.

If Jonathan stopped paying the bills, he probably hasn't pain Ben either.

Ben is brushing Grace when I find him, her pale-blonde coat glinting under the late sun. He glances up with a crooked smile as I approach.

"I didn't know you were here, Cass."

"Didn't mean to interrupt," I say, running a hand down Grace's neck. She nuzzles me, always so sweet and aware.

There's a knot forming in my gut but I have to ask.

"Has Jonathan been behind on your pay?"

Ben hesitates, eyes drifting to the horizon. "Well... yeah," he admits, voice quiet. "Last few months have been a little light. I figured, with everything going on with your mama, maybe it just slipped through the cracks."

It didn't slip.

It was ignored.

I swallow the rage and the guilt, pull out my phone, and open the banking app again. "I'm paying you today. The full amount. Plus a bonus."

He protests, of course. Says it's not necessary, says I don't have to do that.

But I do.

I do because it's the right thing. Because he's earned it a hundred times over. Because he stayed when everything else was falling apart.

He grips my shoulder after the transfer goes through and says something about my father being proud. I can't look at him when he does. I think if I do, I'll cry again.

Inside the house, I find Shanae in the kitchen.

Her expression shifts the second I ask the same question. She doesn't try to lie. Just smiles that knowing, tired smile and tells me not to worry.

I pay her too. Quietly. No fanfare. And I make her promise not to tell my mother.

"She doesn't need the stress," she agrees, squeezing my hand. "And I already knew. Don't worry—I've been keeping it from her."

We go over the care schedule for next week since I won't be around much.

She asks about my *art* commission and I change the subject to ask her to arrange another overnight nurse to help fill the gaps. She's already on it.

It shouldn't surprise me, how on top of things Shanae is. It never does. But it still makes me grateful every damn time.

My mother is sitting by the window when I check on her, a book in her lap and her eyes on the pasture beyond. The horses move slowly in the golden light, grazing near the fence.

"Hey, sweetheart," she says softly, looking up.

"Hi, Mama." I lean down, kiss her forehead, and settle the blanket around her legs. "You good here for a bit?"

She nods. "I've got everything I need."

I stay there a little longer, just to breathe in the comfort of her presence. Of her voice. Of this moment that could've so easily slipped through my fingers.

When I finally pull away, I head back to the studio—my space, my sanctuary.

That feeling of drowning is threatening to pull me away. And there is only one place I can let it all go.

The Italian takeout is going cold on the counter, untouched, the smell turning my stomach the longer it sits. Her favorite place. The one she used to beg for when we were younger—extra garlic knots, creamy pasta, the kind of food that sticks to your ribs and tastes like home.

But the box is still closed. The food untouched.

And the girl it was meant for is still not fucking here.

I call her again.

Straight to voicemail.

Again.

I pace the length of the kitchen, jaw clenched so tight I can feel the tension pulsing behind my teeth. Every step is a fight not to let this get under my skin.

It was hours ago when she texted she was going out.

I didn't see it and then when I replied and asked about dinner, she didn't answer. No big deal. I can make a decision without her.

I ordered food while maintenance erased the rest of the evidence that I nearly burned the entire building down this morning. Only a few cabinet doors needed to be replaced so no big deal.

It was fine until my mind started working against me. Where she was. If she had another date. What is going on that's she's hiding. Refusing to tell me why she did all this to begin with.

When the door finally opens, I don't think—I just *react*.

She strolls in like nothing's wrong and hums some quiet tune under her breath as she kicks off her shoes.

Like I haven't been pacing this fucking apartment for hours wondering where she was.

"Where the hell have you been?"

She blinks at me, eyebrows lifting like I just accused her of murder. "Excuse me?"

"I've been calling you."

Her arms fold across her chest, slow and deliberate. "And?"

"And you didn't answer."

"I didn't realize I needed to report for parole, officer."

I stare at her, stunned at the calmness in her tone. At the sheer audacity of it. "That's not what I said."

"It's what you meant," she shoots back, stepping further into the kitchen for a bottle of water.

"You were gone for hours, Cassidy."

She takes a drink of water, clearly set on ignoring me now.

I shake my head, jaw tight. "You don't get to ghost me like I'm no one."

Cassidy whirls on me, eyes narrowed like she can already see the fight coming. "I didn't ghost you. I went out."

"Without telling me."

"I didn't know I needed your permission."

"You don't," I snap. "You just needed to say something."

She throws her hands up. "Why? Why do *you* care so much?"

I don't answer.

Because I can't say what I'm actually thinking. That I was worried. That every minute she was gone felt like a punch to the gut not knowing who she was with. That I hate how easily she can still make me feel like I'm helpless and pissed off and obsessed.

But I don't say any of that.

Instead, I fall back on the one thing I know she can't argue with.

"Look—if this isn't working for you, Cricket..." I pause, letting the silence stretch. "Feel free to cancel the contract. Give the money back."

Her expression shifts.

Sharp. Wounded. Defensive.

She crosses her arms, hugging herself like it's the only thing keeping her from throwing something. "Are you serious right now?"

"You don't want to be here? You have a way out."

"I'm not giving the money back," she says, every word coated in fury.

"Then I own you, Crick." I step into her space making

her look up at me. "I own this body." I run the back of my finger down her cheek.

She parts her mouth and I zero in on it. My finger continuing the light trail I'm blazing down her. Touching her in a way I never have before.

"I own your time."

My finger slides over her full lip and I want to take it between my teeth. I keep going down her neck, over her collarbone before I flatten my hand on her chest. Dragging back up her neck, I reach around and grab and fistful of hair at the base of her skull and pull.

"And soon,"

I step into her fully, my body flush against hers and I can see her pulse racing at her neck. I drag my nose up the column of her throat and when she gasps, my cock twitches.

"Soon, I'll own this pussy." I step back and look her dead in her green eyes, full of fire and now... also arousal.

"So you can answer a fucking text message."

Her jaw clenches so tight I can see the muscle ticking.

"Got it, Cricket?" I let go of her hair but I don't step away.

She holds my stare, letting me feel the full extend of her anger before she finally answers—through gritted teeth—"Fine. I've got it."

I nod once, cold and sharp. "Good."

She turns, storming toward the bedroom, but tosses the last word over her shoulder like a live grenade.

"Good."

The door slams shut behind her.

I smell bacon before I even round the corner.

For a split second, I think maybe she's trying to make peace but when I step into the kitchen, that hope dies a quick, brutal death.

She's at the stove, moving with slow, deliberate ease—like she has all the time in the world and not a single thought about me. Her back is to me. No greeting. No glance. Just that same infuriating silence that's hung between us since last night.

And on the island is one plate.

One fork.

One cup of orange juice.

One cup of coffee already poured and waiting.

Everything about it screams *intentional.*

She finishes plating her food and moves past me without even brushing my shoulder. Takes her spot at the counter, slides onto the stool, and eats like I'm not standing five feet away watching her pull a power play with scrambled eggs.

Wow. You can make eggs without turning them into a nuclear bomb.

Whoop-de-fuckin'-doo.

I grab a bowl from the cabinet, fill it with the first cereal I see, splash some milk in the bowl and lean against the fridge like I couldn't care less.

And I don't. I don't even *want* bacon.

We exist like that for a while—her slowly slicing into her

toast with unnecessary precision, me making sure the fridge doesn't escape while I crunch through my breakfast like I'm chewing nails.

When she finally stands, I think maybe she's done with this little game—maybe she's ready to apologize before retreating back to her room.

But instead of walking away, she turns to the coffee pot.

She pours the last cup—I didn't get any coffee yet, but whatever—and wraps both hands around the mug like she's savoring a private victory. Her movements are slow, precise, like she knows I'm watching and wants me to feel every second of it.

Then she glances at the fridge.

The creamer's behind the door. She knows it. I know it.

Still, I stay exactly where I am, shoulder propped lazily against the stainless steel, bowl of cereal in hand, doing my best impression of someone utterly unbothered.

She doesn't say a word.

Neither do I.

I lift another spoonful to my mouth, focusing on the sugary swirl of colors and the dull scrape of metal against ceramic—anything but the fact that I can feel her next to me. She's standing close enough to reach the handle, but not quite close enough to push me out of the way.

For a moment, I think maybe she'll give up. Maybe she'll wait.

But no.

She opens the other fridge door.

It swings wide—faster than it needs to—and clips my elbow right as I bring the spoon to my mouth.

The impact jolts my arm and launches a full arc of cereal into my face. Cold milk splashes across my chest, dripping in lazy trails down my abs before hitting the floor in a slow, humiliating patter.

A fluorescent-colored ring sticks to my cheek. A purple one lands in the waistband of my sweats.

There's a bright green one perched on my knuckle like a silent witness to me being slapped in the face by some fucking cereal.

She remains completely silent.

Doesn't look at me. Doesn't blink. Doesn't even pause as she reaches into the opposite door, takes the creamer from its place, and pours it into her coffee like nothing happened.

And I just stand there, staring over the top of her head as she moves. My face still wet. Milk sliding down my side. Cereal clinging to my skin like a goddamn garnish.

She returns the bottle to its spot in the door, gently closes it, and walks away without so much as a glance in my direction.

Her steps are unhurried. Her mug is full. Her expression remains unreadable.

And I don't say a thing.

Not because I'm not pissed—I am. I'm fucking furious, and sticky, and dangerously close to launching this entire bowl into the sink.

But I'm not going to break.

She's the one who started this. She's the one who walked away yesterday. And I'm not giving her the satisfaction of thinking I'll be the one to cave.

Not a fucking chance.

I'll choke on this fucking cereal if I have to but she's going to be the one that cracks first.

Chapter 15

Jaxon

Captains log, Day 2 of the silent standoff.

Morale is low. Discipline is lower.

Yesterday was hell.

At some point between her cereal assault and my vow to keep my damn mouth shut until she gives in, we seemed to reach a mutual, unspoken agreement: if we're going to be petty, we're going to be *extra* about it.

She started the escalation.

Somewhere around noon, she changed into shorts that were—at best—three inches of fabric and attitude. Black, skin-tight, unapologetically short. Paired with a sports bra that was definitely more bra than sport.

Then she hit my gym.

My gym.

Just strutted in, put on her headphones, and climbed onto the treadmill like it was hers.

I watched from the security feed in my office for a full minute before I caved.

Went to my room. Dropped to the floor, doing as many push-ups and sit-ups as I could squeeze into five minutes.

Just enough to justify the sweat.

Then I splashed water on my chest, let it drip down my abs, and threw on a pair of hoochie-daddy shorts.

It wasn't subtle.

I entered the gym like I was walking into a battlefield and chose my weapons carefully—specifically, the weights directly in front of her.

Started with squats. Deep, heavy, slow. Made a show of adjusting my stance. Of rolling my neck. Flexing just a little harder than necessary when I stood.

She held her ground until I transitioned to hip thrusts.

I adjusted my slutty little shorts a bit to get more of my V on display. Definitely saw that quick side-eye she tried to hide.

The bar and heavy weights across my pelvis. A deep dip down and thrust up. Flexing my stomach. The grunts. Mm, the grunts. Some of my best work.

I have to be honest; it was even giving me a semi.

And, that's when she left.

No eye contact. No *fuck you Jaxon.*

Just powered down the treadmill, grabbed her water, and walked out like the room had caught fire.

In my opinion, that was a win.

But today... today she's out for fucking blood.

I step out onto the back patio with a protein shake in hand, fully prepared to act like she's invisible.

What I'm *not* prepared for is the bikini.

Correction: The whisper of fabric tied together with

string and very questionable engineering. The kind of suit that doesn't really say *"I'm here to relax,"* so much as *"I dare you not to look."*

And damn it, I'm looking.

How could I not?

She's stretched out on one of the loungers by the pool, sunglasses on, legs just barely spread like she doesn't know exactly what she's doing to me.

Like she doesn't know that every inch of her is driving me absolutely fucking insane.

I take a slow sip of my shake and sit down at the patio table like her tits aren't beaconing to me through that little white scrap of nothing she dares to call swimwear.

I didn't come out here to engage.

I came out here to enjoy the new *Sports Illustrated* spread —front and center in their tech and finance feature.

"The Sex Tech King of Silicon Valley."

Their words. Not mine.

But I didn't exactly fight them on the phrasing.

The cover is glossy and indecent. Shirtless. Oiled up. One hand gripping the back of my neck, abs flexed, every tattoo on display.

And I make sure she sees it.

I position the magazine just right, pages open on the table, angled perfectly in her line of sight. I lean back in the chair, slowly flipping through the spread like I'm admiring the lighting. Like I'm not watching her watching *me* watch *myself*.

That's when she starts to move.

It's subtle at first. Just a shift of her shoulders, a tiny

adjustment in her lounge chair that makes her breasts bounce behind the thin stretch of white bikini top. My eyes drop before I can stop them, catching the way the fabric doesn't fully cover her, showing a bit of skin under her breast.

She bends her knees slightly, lets her legs sway.

Just a little but enough to catch the angle of her thighs and the barely-there triangle of white covering what I already know is untouched.

And fuck me—she *knows* exactly what she's doing.

My dick throbs, already thick and hard beneath my swim trunks, straining against the thin material with every teasing shift of her hips.

I glance back down at the magazine, pretending to be interested in the words I haven't read once.

I will *not* break.

Then she fucking flips over.

Hands and knees.

Ass in the air.

Back arched in a curve so perfect I could sketch it from memory.

She pretends she's adjusting her towel—tugging at the corners, smoothing it down—but the performance is for *me*, and we both know it.

My spine locks.

She reaches for her phone and the motion makes her ass jiggle.

A soft, rhythmic bounce that nearly ends me.

I nearly choke on my own breath as she widens her knees just slightly, enough to shift the angle, enough to show me exactly what that little bikini bottom is hiding.

My cock jumps, painfully hard now, twitching in my trunks like it wants to punch through the fabric.

Holy Christ, she's wet.

I can *see* it.

A faint, damp patch clings to the stretch of fabric between her thighs.

She's turned on.

This is *turning her on*.

And fuck, I love it.

I want to bury my face between those legs, slide that little bikini to the side and taste how hot this little game has made her. Run my tongue over that soaked fabric, then tear it off with my teeth and lick her until she forgets her own name and sobbing mine.

My hand drops beneath the table. I squeeze the head of my cock through my trunks, trying to ease the pressure before I lose all sense of reason.

Pointless.

It only makes it worse.

Every nerve in my body is begging me to flip her over, drag that flimsy scrap of a bikini down, and tongue-fuck her until she's trembling under me.

But then reality slaps me across the face like a goddamn brick.

Jonathan's little sister.

I close my eyes for half a second and exhale through my nose, jaw tensing until it aches.

The memory punches back fast and brutal—Jonathan at

the party six years ago, shoving me against the wall when he caught us coming in from the garden. His voice, low and threatening:

"She's seventeen. You touch her, and I'll end you."

I swallow the bitterness. The frustration. The throbbing need.

And I make a choice.

I stand up, toss the magazine onto the table, and dive headfirst into the pool like I'm escaping a fire.

The cold water hits my overheated skin with a jolt, but it's not enough to cool me off. I push hard through the water, lap after lap, trying to outrun the image of her bent over and soaking wet.

When I finally climb out at the deep end, I grip the edge of the concrete and pull myself up in one smooth motion, letting the water roll off my body, every muscle flexed from restraint.

She's still on her lounger, pretending not to watch.

So I take *her* towel—the one folded neatly on the table beside her—and shake the water from my hair like a dog, making sure it sprays just enough to mist across her thighs and stomach.

She flinches, just barely, but I catch it.

And as I walk past her, dripping and silent, I don't look back.

Because this war is far from over but right now, I have to jack my dick off before I pull her bikini fabric to the side and run my finger up her wet cunt.

Her bedroom door is open.

I tell myself that's not a signal.

She's on her bed, propped up on one elbow, tablet resting on her thighs while some show plays—low volume, no subtitles. Her attention stay on me, but she fights to keep it hidden.

I pace the corridor just outside her room, phone pressed to my ear, pretending this is just a casual late-night call.

But I make sure she hears *who* I'm talking to.

"Hey, man. How's London?"

It's her brother on the other end of the line.

The one who doesn't know I'm doing so much more than keeping an eye on his little sister. The one who would lose his goddamn mind if he saw the way I looked at her. Wanted her. Fought the urge to smell her sweet cunt her every damn minute of the day.

I lean against the opposite wall, letting my voice stay steady while stick my hand just under the waistband of my sweatpants.

My grey ones. My thin—grey—sweats.

There are two things I know for sure:

One—these pants are like kryptonite for women.

Two—I wear the ever-loving fuck out of them.

And right now they're doing *exactly* what they were made for.

They're clinging in all the right places—just thin enough that you can make out the shape of my dick. Even the head of my cock, which is slightly hard.

Just enough to tease.

To tempt.

To let her *wonder.*

I see her shift on the bed, glancing over her tablet, her eyes narrowed right on my dick. She runs her tongue across her bottom lip, and I feel a drop of cum leak out.

Fuck. I want to pull my cock out right now. Slide my hand up and down my shaft while she watches me. Come hard and see if she'd crawl over here to me and lick up my mess.

"What's that man?" I blink, having to get myself back to the conversation. "Yeah, Cass is being a good girl."

I keep my eyes on her when I say those last two words.

Her eyes narrow and she slams her tablet shut, standing up.

Apparently she only owns the smallest goddamn clothes in existence.

She walks past me without a word, wearing silk pajama shorts that are barely shorts at all. Her ass is round and smooth, the fabric clinging like it's one wrong breath from giving up entirely. Her top is paper-thin, camisole straps slipping just enough to reveal the curve of her shoulder.

No bra.

And her nipples are hard as fuck.

Visible. Distracting. Dangerous.

She's never been this undressed around me.

Never looked so effortlessly, infuriatingly sexy.

I try not to look. I *try.*

Who the fuck am I kidding. I don't try. I fucking look.

I watch the bounce of her hips, the delicate sway of her

breasts. But there's a mirror at the end of the hallway, and it betrays me.

Her eyes catch mine and she smirks. Just the corner of her mouth curving like she knows she's killing me and enjoys every second of it.

And fuck, she's beautiful.

I shift my stance, forcing myself to keep talking—to stay cool while I boil alive. "Three more weeks?"

"Sure, I can keep her in my sights for three more weeks. No problem, man."

Do you mind if I fuck her senseless the entire time? I keep that question to myself.

She returns a moment later with a bowl of ice cream, stolen from my freezer like this is *her* apartment. *Her* kitchen. But it could be hers. I'd give her anything she wanted.

I step closer to her doorway, stretching my arm to grip the top trim as I lean, blocking the path back to her room just enough to make her hesitate.

She slips by, slow and casual, and her breasts brush right against my bare torso. That cami so fucking thin it feels like skin to skin. Soft warmth and the unmistakable friction of hard nipples dragging across my ribs.

I stop breathing.

My grip tightens on the doorframe, knuckles white.

She turns once she's inside her room, still facing me. Her eyes hold mine like she's waiting for something.

Like maybe she's going to say what we're both thinking.

Hang up the fucking phone and kiss me.

And if she did God help me, I'd do it so fucking fast.

And hard. With everything I've been holding back for years.

My gaze drops—*just for a second*—to her chest. Pebbled nipples pressing through that scrap of a cami like they're waving goodnight.

Then right when I look back into those green eyes, she slams the fucking door.

Right in my goddamn face.

I jerk my head back just in time to avoid taking it to the nose.

And all I can do is stand there, hard as a fucking rock, wondering how long we can keep this game going before I kick this fucking door down and take what I paid for.

Chapter 16
Cassidy

Once again I'm about to make myself right at home in my closet—well, *Jaxon's* guest room closet.

The bedroom door is locked. Music's playing low from my tablet, something upbeat enough to sound like I'm just getting ready for the day.

I slip into the closet and close that door too.

And then I strip out of the cami and shorts. My panties are soaked, and they join the pile on the floor in an instant.

The vibrator is already in my hand and turned on before I'm on my knees.

I don't waste a second pressing it straight to my clit.

Relief crashes through me instantly, sharp and almost painful, tangled with the sweet, unbearable tension of knowing I'm seconds away from falling apart.

My hips start rocking against it without permission, like they've been waiting for this.

And of course—just like last night—my thoughts go straight to Jaxon.

The same man I've hated and wanted in equal measure for more years than I'm ready to admit.

The same man who's dominated every fantasy I've had for two straight days.

In my head, he's everywhere—his mouth between my legs, looking up at me with that smug, infuriating smirk before diving back down. His chest against my back, lips at my neck, hands everywhere.

My free hand drifts up my stomach, cupping my breast through nothing but bare skin. I pinch my nipple and my hips jerk against the vibrator, my pelvis finding a steady rhythm that has heat coiling low and tight inside me.

It's too easy to imagine his mouth there instead. His tongue circling. His teeth catching.

The pinch makes the pleasure spike so sharp I almost cry out.

Almost.

But I bite it back.

I can't make a sound. I can't let him know how close I've been to breaking. How wet I've been for him. How many times I've come in this closet, imagining him.

The thought should embarrass me—the slick, wet sounds of my own fingers brushing against myself while the vibrator hums against my clit—but it doesn't.

It turns me on even more.

Because I can imagine exactly how much it would turn *him* on.

Last night's grey sweatpants flash into my mind. The outline of him thick and heavy beneath the thin cotton. In this fantasy, I hook my fingers into the waistband, drag him down in the hallway, and sink onto him right there—mounting him, bouncing on his cock until I can't breathe.

I know he's big.

Really fucking big.

I got a glimpse of his dick once. Something I try to forget but never can.

Feeling him inside me would be the kind of stretch that would hurt at first, then ruin me for anyone else.

I imagine his hands gripping my hips, his mouth open in pleasure as I take every inch. That mouth... always that mouth. Smirking. Teasing. Pushing me to the edge just to watch me fall.

And I want it on me. Sucking my nipple—

I pinch harder, and the orgasm slams into me so fast I almost lose my grip on the toy.

Keeping quiet is a war. Every muscle trembles with the effort not to moan too loud, my head tipping back as I bounce in place, working the vibrator over my clit in tight circles, pinching at my nipple in time with each pulse.

My moan is barely a whisper, my breaths ragged and broken as the climax rolls through me in hot, relentless waves.

I keep going until my thighs tremble and my clit's too sensitive to touch.

The toy slows, my hips settle, and I finally switch it off.

The aftershocks are enough to make my legs twitch, my

pelvis still pulsing as I breathe deep and try to come back down.

The satisfaction will probably hold me over until lunch.

Probably.

And if it doesn't?

Well... I know exactly where I'll be.

I feel lighter now. Relaxed. Or at least... enough to fake it for the next few hours.

I clean myself up, slip into fresh clothes, and start planning my next move.

The pool's on the agenda again, so I pull out a new bikini—black, with a tan lining under the mesh that makes it *look* sheer but really isn't. It's a trick of the light, like one of those magic-eye puzzles. You'll stare because you think you're seeing something you're not.

I tie a black mesh wrap low around my hips, knotting it to the side so it slants just enough to give the illusion I'm constantly about to lose it.

I know my body's good. Hourglass curves, a waist narrow enough that I've been accused of Photoshopping in pictures, hips that have their own opinions about denim sizing. I've always had more up top than my friends—full breasts that barely fit into anything made "for my size."

And Jax? Yesterday, he had a hell of a time not staring.

Today's top is smaller. Triangle cut. A little more skin. Definitely more under-breast—just enough that I can imagine his thumbs slipping underneath, right where no one's ever touched me before.

The thought alone makes me grin.

Since pancakes are his favorite, I decide they're going to

be *my* breakfast. Just enough for me. I find a "pancakes for one" recipe on Pinterest, swipe my phone off the charger, and head into the kitchen.

The first cabinet I open? Empty.

Weird.

I check the next one. Also empty.

I know this kitchen was fully stocked yesterday—*I cooked in here.* So unless the pots and pans decided to grow legs overnight, I'm being messed with.

I check the dishwasher, just in case. Bone dry. Not a single plate or pan.

Fine. Cereal it is.

Except when I open the dish cabinet, there's nothing. Not a single bowl. Not even a chipped mug.

Fine.

I grab the cereal box from the pantry, a gallon of milk from the fridge, and march to the table. No bowl, no spoon—just me, dry cereal straight from the box, chased with a swig of milk from the jug.

It's absurd. It's petty.

And I'm committed.

That's when Jax walks in.

His eyes flick to me as I tip a handful of cereal into my mouth, then lift the gallon and drink.

I know exactly how ridiculous it looks, and I make no move to hide it. If anything, I double down.

The sight must catch him off guard because for a split second, I swear he's about to laugh. His lips twitch, the corners lifting in something dangerously close to a smile before he shuts it down.

All I get is a faint smirk as he grabs a bottle of water from the fridge and walks out.

It's not a win.

But it's not a loss either.

I head toward the linen cabinet by the pool door, humming to myself, determined to keep my mind on the mission—bikini, towel, pool, win the day.

Except when I open the cabinet, I freeze.

The towels—*all* of them—are stacked neatly on the very top shelf. Too high for me to grab without a chair or a step stool. Which I'm sure is *exactly* why they're there now.

I stretch anyway, fingers grazing the edge of the lowest one, but it's no use.

And of course, this is the moment Jaxon chooses to walk in.

He doesn't say a word—just steps up behind me. Close. Too close. The heat of his body slides in against my back like a shadow, his chest just shy of brushing my shoulder blades.

I tell myself I should move, but instead I keep reaching.

Because I can feel him there.

And because I know damn well what kind of picture I'm making in this bikini—the bottoms sitting low on my hips, the wrap tied to the side barely keeping anything modest, the top cut just small enough to keep him wondering.

He leans forward, arm lifting to the cabinet above mine. Of course he's not actually helping me.

No towel is being passed down. No space is being made.

Instead, he's taking his time, rifling through whatever's up there like he's searching for buried treasure, all while his hips stay perfectly aligned with mine.

Every time I push up onto my toes, my ass grazes his crotch.

And every time, he doesn't move away.

If anything, I think—no, I *know*—he presses in that tiniest fraction more. Enough that I can feel him starting to harden. Enough that my own thighs clench and my pulse trips over itself.

I should turn around. I should end this right here—grab the back of his neck, pull his mouth to mine, and finally know what he tastes like.

But the idea of making him snap?

Of seeing him lose every ounce of control he's been holding onto these last two days?

That's a far better reward.

So I keep stretching. Keep reaching. Keep brushing up against him like it's all part of the effort.

When I finally "give up," I huff a little laugh and head toward his room instead.

His bathroom has towels. And no witnesses.

I step inside, grab one from the neatly folded stack, and turn to leave—just in time for him to walk right past me.

He doesn't stop. Doesn't even glance at me.

He just hooks his thumbs into the waistband of those grey sweatpants and strips them off in one smooth motion.

And there's... nothing underneath.

Nothing.

My face goes instantly hot, like I've stepped into a sauna.

I make a noise—something between a choke and a cough—that I try to disguise as clearing my throat, but it's useless.

I keep my eyes glued to the floor, willing my legs to move, but my traitorous gaze flicks up at the exact wrong time.

He steps into the shower. Completely bare-assed.

It's firm. Perfect. And I hate myself for looking.

Except I don't stop there.

Because when he turns slightly, I catch a flash of the front.

Hard. Really hard.

And yes—really big.

I spin out of the doorway before I make a bigger fool of myself, clutching the towel to my chest like it's some kind of shield, but my face is still burning as I head for the pool.

It's too cloudy for tanning.

Not that it matters—he's not even out here.

So instead of lying in the sun, I've spent almost an hour on the pool deck doing yoga poses in my tiniest bikini. Deep stretches, slow bends, every pose I can think of that shows off the way my body moves.

I know he has cameras out here.

I know he's watching me.

And yes... I like it.

It's the same way he found me in the gym yesterday—already a little winded, his skin damp with sweat. He'd joined me like it was a coincidence, but I know better.

I hope he's in his office right now, eyes locked on the monitor, one hand under the desk, making himself come to the sight of me.

By the time I'm done, I'm starving for lunch.

I pad into the kitchen, still in my bikini, hair messy

from the humidity. I go straight for the fridge, already prepared to eat a jarred salad with my fingers... or chopsticks... or hell, maybe a fork if I can find one, though I doubt it.

The fridge is just as annoyingly neat as it's always been—labels facing forward, jars in perfect rows like soldiers. I grab one and twist the lid.

Nothing.

I try again. No luck.

The sound of footsteps pulls my head up just in time to see him walk in.

Black leather pants.

Helmet in hand.

I tense my jaw. *Of course.* More thirst trap videos for his motorcycle crowd, no doubt. Not that it bothers me. Not that I care where he goes or who he tries to impress.

I grab another jar and try again. Still nothing.

He reaches past me, opens the fridge, and pulls out a jar of fruit. He pops the lid without a hint of effort—no struggle, no grunt, just that easy twist of his wrist.

Then he starts making a smoothie.

And watching me.

I try a potholder for better grip. Then another jar. Nothing.

It's not until I attempt a jar of fruit that I realize what's happened—every lid in this fridge is sealed like it's been locked by the gods themselves. The pickles? Same.

He's tightened them. Every single one.

I glance at him from the corner of my eye. He's leaning against the counter now, drinking his smoothie straight from the blender container because, of course, there are no cups. His eyes never leave me.

Daring me.

Daring me to ask for help.

To be the one to break the silence.

I don't.

I slam the last jar down a little harder than necessary, straighten, and pull open the drawer where he keeps the takeout menus. Inside are a few leftover fortune cookies and random chopstick packets. I grab three cookies, hold them tight in my hand like they're a prize, and walk toward my room.

Right back to that fucking closet.

But it didn't fucking help.

If anything, it only made me more strung out.

I kept going until my thighs shook, until my hips couldn't stop moving. Twice in a row—my knuckles shoved between my teeth to muffle the sounds, the vibrator never once leaving my clit until I couldn't tell if I was still coming or just trembling from the effort.

When it's over, I'm flushed, sweaty, and somehow even *more* wound up.

I need air.

I change into actual clothes and head for the elevator, already imagining the quiet of the ride down to the lobby, maybe a walk outside—anything to put distance between me and him.

But just as I'm about to press the button, he's suddenly there.

Jaxon steps into my space like he owns it, reaching right across me to hit the panel before I can.

He's close. Too close. His body brushes mine, forcing me to turn slightly to the side.

God, he smells good. Clean and warm, with something darker under it. The heat of him seeps through the thin fabric of my shirt. His shirt strains across his shoulders, every line of him designed to make me swallow hard.

I turn my head—just to look away. Just to breathe.

But it only gives him better access.

He moves in, close enough that his chest presses into mine, his breath warm against the side of my neck. I feel him inhale, slow and deliberate, and it's like being pinned in place by something I can't see.

The heat in my chest spikes, running lower, heavier.

His lips hover near my skin. I feel him part them, and for one reckless second, I think—*he's going to kiss me.*

The thought hits me so hard it makes my sensitive clip pulse and I flex my thighs. A sharp, high-pitched moan escapes me before I can stop it. My hand flies to my mouth, my eyes wide.

He pauses.

The entire penthouse feels like it goes silent with him.

And then I feel the curve of his mouth against my skin. The smug, quiet smirk.

He leans back just enough to press the elevator button.

But before the doors slide open, he dips in again, close enough for his lips to brush the shell of my ear. His voice is low, steady, and annoyingly happy with himself.

"I won."

The doors part, and he steps inside. I stay right where I am, arms crossed over my chest, scowl on my face aimed at him.

"I'll bring back takeout," he says, glancing back at me while he leans casually against the elevator wall.

I flip him off as the doors close, catching the sound of his laugh just before they seal shut.

This is going great.

Better than great, actually.

I've had a hard-on for what feels like forty-eight hours straight, but I can't remember the last time I had this much fun. She's stubborn, petty, and absolutely incapable of backing down—and I'm enjoying every second of watching her try to beat me at my own game.

The Thai bags swing from my hand as I walk back toward the penthouse, the smell filling the elevator. I ordered enough for six people, all because I couldn't decide between the curries or the noodles... and maybe because the idea of her rolling her eyes at the excess makes me want to smile.

Hell, I *am* smiling.

I hadn't even planned on leaving today. But when I saw her dressed and heading for the elevator earlier, I knew I couldn't let her get away without pushing things up another notch. And I did. The look on her face when those doors closed—priceless.

When I step inside, she's in the kitchen, pretending not to watch me set the bags down.

"I didn't know what you like," I say casually, tearing open a container, "so I got a little of everything."

"Thanks."

One word. Bitter enough to curl at the edges.

I bite back a grin but knowing she's a little salty, I turn on a cold case crime show. They've always been her favorites.

We eat in relative silence except when we chime in on the crime and who could have done it.

My mind keeps going back to her on that auction block.

The question she won't answer.

Why?

I could push her. Ask why she's going through with this like she's got something to prove. But I already know I'm not going to get the truth—not yet.

Still, the thought nags at me.

Last night I remembered something—her brother's set to get back in three weeks. Right at the end of our thirty-day agreement. I'd suggested ninety days at the start. *She's* the one who blurted out a month.

I wonder if the two things are connected. Probably just wanted this over before he got home.

The show is over, and we put away the leftover food for later.

"Going to take a bath," she says after putting the last of our dishes in the dishwasher. "Then turn in early."

My pulse ticks up a notch, at the little treat I have in store, but I keep my expression neutral. "Sure. Enjoy."

The infinity tub in her bathroom could fit three people comfortably, water pouring from a waterfall faucet. You let it run the entire time—it's part of the design.

After she disappears into her room, I finish clearing the containers from the counter, stack the leftovers neatly in the fridge.

Every few minutes, my eyes drift back to her closed bedroom door.

I walk over once or twice, putting my ear to it and listening. Waiting.

To kill some time, and keep from going insane, I fix the jars in the fridge.

Yes, I tightened every single one, so she'd have to ask for help. Hid all the kitchen ware too. Everything. Right down to the last teaspoon.

Something was going to make her talk to me dammit.

It's been about thirty minutes when it happens.

A sharp scream cuts through the penthouse, followed by her voice calling my name.

My pulse kicks and I go into acting mode.

I charge down the hall, throw open her door for water to come rushing past my shoes, flooding into the penthouse.

The bathroom floor glistens under the light, and I bite back a grin—this is already better than I expected.

"I don't know what happened," she says, panicked. "I thought the water was draining. Jax, I'm so sorry."

I'm barely listening.

Because she's standing in the tub, a thin robe clinging to

every curve of her naked body. The fabric's soaked through, nearly transparent. Her black hair is twisted into a messy bun, a few strands sticking to her damp neck.

She looks perfect.

I could pick her up and set her on the bathroom counter right now and sink into her until she's screaming my name for a very different reason.

Her voice cuts through my thoughts. "Stop staring like a pervert."

I force myself to blink, to breathe, to remember that this isn't the moment to lose control.

She starts to step out of the tub, and instinct takes over. "Don't." I close the distance and slide my arms under her before she can argue.

Water sloshing with each step.

The tile is slick, and the last thing I need is her cracking her head open.

I lift her easily, bridal style, wading into the water without caring that my shoes are getting drenched, and carry her into my room.

Now she's pressed against my chest, wet and warm, and every step makes it harder to think about anything except peeling that robe off and seeing if she's as soft as she looks.

But instead, I set her down in my bathroom, grab one of my towels, and hand it to her.

"I'll call maintenance," I say, my voice lower than it should be.

And then I leave before I do something that'll end this night in a way I can't take back.

Maintenance gets here fast. Two guys with a shop vac

have the water gone in no time, but the damage is already done—drywall's saturated, cabinets warped. The head guy explains the drywall will take a couple days to replace, but the custom vanity? That'll take weeks to get a new one in.

She's sitting on the edge of my bed while they talk, looking smaller than she normally does, hands twisting in the towel like she's bracing for me to be furious.

When I walk the crew out and close the door, she's still sitting there, staring at the floor.

I lean against the frame. "Well… seems your room's out of commission for a while."

Her head snaps up.

"So you're going to have to bunk in here with me."

She blinks. Then narrows her eyes like she's just solved a crime. "Jaxon Kane. Did you do this on purpose?"

I give her my best confused look, brow furrowing just enough to make it believable. "Why the hell would I flood my own penthouse?"

She doesn't buy it for a second.

"I'll take one of the other guest rooms," she says, standing and marching for the hall.

"That's the only one."

"Bullshit." She starts opening doors. Surely convinced a penthouse this size has more than two bedrooms.

It does.

But the second she opens the first extra room, she freezes.

"Is this… a server room?"

"Pretty much."

She frowns at the wall-to-wall racks of hardware and blinking lights.

"Fine, I'll sleep on an air mattress in another room," she mutters, heading for the next door.

The second room? Same thing. Full of racks and cabling. And cold enough to see her breath.

"What the hell, do you have your own fucking data center in here?"

"Pretty much," I repeat, leaning in the doorway.

She slams it closed and checks the last one.

Same setup. Same sub-zero temperature.

"And why is it so cold?" she asks, pulling her wrap tighter.

"Servers run hot. They need to be kept cool."

She crosses her arms. "You're single-handedly contributing to global warming."

I press a hand to my chest in mock offense. "I'll have you know I use only clean thermal energy, thank you very much."

She rolls her eyes, but I catch the faintest twitch of a smile before she turns away.

I circle us back to the only thing that matters.

"Your room's out of commission. You're sleeping in my room."

"No," she says flatly.

"Yes," I counter.

"I'll take the couch."

I shake my head. "Not happening."

She plants her hands on her hips. "Why? Afraid I'll get crumbs on your precious throw pillows?"

I step closer, lowering my voice. "Because if you sleep on the couch, I'll just throw you over my shoulder and tie you to my bed."

Her lip's part like she's not sure whether to be offended or flustered.

I lean in. "And between you and me, I'd fucking love to see what you look like tied to my bed."

She fights it—puts up one of those stubborn little walls of hers—but it's a losing battle. Eventually, she exhales through her nose like she's conceding to a war crime.

"Fine," she mutters. "But don't try anything funny."

She disappears into her damp room for clothes. When she comes back... well, I'll be damned... I have to actually bite my lip to keep from whistling at her.

She's wearing my old shirt again.

And... son of a bitch... my boxers.

She doesn't look at me when she walks in, which is probably for the best, because I'm not hiding the way my eyes track her every step.

I'm already in bed, laying down with my hands behind my head, and watch as she starts building a wall of pillows between us. It's a process—stacking, adjusting, testing the distance like she's drafting architectural plans for a fortress. Then she crawls under the covers and makes a point to stretch as far to her side as humanly possible.

I cock a brow. "What is this... a purity fortress?"

"You can't be trusted." She barks back as she rolls onto her side so her back's to me.

I hit the switch on the wall, killing the lights, and exhale a long, slow breath. The sound comes out part sigh, part moan. I feel her tense at it.

There's a beat of silence that stretches out. Her tension basically radiating around the room.

After a moment, she says quietly, "I was at my studio."

My brows pull together in the dark. "Huh?"

"Where I was when you asked."

It takes me a second to process that. She's finally giving up a piece of her stubborn resolve, and it makes me smile.

"I checked on Mom and the horses," she continues, "and went to my art studio for a few hours."

"I've never seen a studio at your house."

"It's in the barn."

I think about that for a moment, then nod in the dark.

"Good night, Cricket," I say, turning onto my side.

And I try—really try—not to think about tearing down that pillow wall and pulling her into my arms to see what her lips feel like on mine.

Chapter 18

Cassidy

Jaxon has been holed up in the largest of his extra bedrooms for days. I'm still not sure what he's doing in there, but it's loud. Things keep getting carried in and out. There's drilling. Cursing. The occasional *thunk* that sounds like he's dropped something heavy enough to dent the floor.

The guest room I flooded—*or he* flooded, depending on who you ask—is still being demoed, so whatever project he's working on has taken over this space instead. His tech rooms.

Right now, I'm at the table with my iPad, sketching while he takes apart something that looks...expensive. Cables and shiny metal guts are spread across the table like he's dissecting a robot. Music plays low from his playlist— one of my favorite songs comes on—and before I even realize it, I'm smiling.

He's singing. Quiet, almost under his breath. But he's good. Not in a trained, perfect way, but in a deep, easy way that slides under your skin. His dark hair falls slightly in his eyes as he works, brows drawn together in concentration, tongue caught at the corner of his mouth.

God, he looks cute when he's focused.

I must be staring, because he glances up and hits me with one of those panty-soaking smirks that should be illegal.

"What?" His voice is low, teasing.

"Nothing," I say quickly, forcing my eyes back to my screen even though my cheeks feel warm. I keep the smile, though. I can't help it.

He watches me a moment longer, like he's debating whether to call me out, then goes back to work. A minute later, he's humming again. Then singing. Softer this time, almost mumbling like he doesn't even realize he's doing it. I never knew he liked to sing. I wonder if he actually does... but I don't press.

The room he's working in is making me jealous. The windows are massive, flooding the space with the kind of light that would make painting here a dream. I keep imagining a giant easel in the corner, canvases leaning against the walls, the smell of turpentine instead of soldering metal.

He walks past carrying another armful of tech, disappearing into the next room when my phone chimes and kills my mood in a second.

JONATHAN: Someone's coming by the house to grab something this afternoon.

CASSIDY: Who? And what are they "grabbing"?

A few minutes with no reply I send another.

> CASSIDY: Hello?

> Who is coming by the house and what are they supposed to be getting? Some details would be nice.

Still no reply back. Like I'm not worthy of one. Like the specifics don't matter.

I debate inviting Jaxon along but there's just some family secrets that need to stay in the family. This is one of them.

I push my chair back. "I'm going to check on Mom. I'll be gone for a while."

His head pops out of the doorway. "You'll be back for dinner?"

"Yeah," I promise, grabbing my bag.

His mouth quirks like he's about to say something, but instead he just nods and disappears back into his mystery project.

***

Mom's feeling good today—one of those rare, bright afternoons where her energy holds steady—so we decide to walk down to the stables together. The sun's warm, the breeze carries that mix of hay and sweet grass, and for a little while, it almost feels normal.

We're giving Grace some extra oats when my phone buzzes in my back pocket. I wipe my hands on my jeans and pull it out.

JONATHAN: They'll be there in 5.

I frown, reading it twice like maybe I missed something. *They?* My stomach knots. I fire back immediately.

CASSIDY: Who is "they"?

Three dots never appear. I'm already typing again before I can think.

CASSIDY: Jonathan. What's going on?

No reply. The longer I stare at the screen, the worse the bad feeling gets—like the air itself is thickening around me.

I'm still glaring at my phone when the crunch of gravel pulls my attention up. A truck and a horse trailer ease into view, kicking up dust behind them.

Everything in me goes cold.

"I wonder who this is." Mom asks, both of us watching the truck back up to the barn.

"I'll found out." I try to sound reassuring but my heart is pounding in my throat.

Two men climb out, both in work boots and dusty ball caps. One pulls a folded paper from his pocket before he's even close.

"This Emerald Ridge Farm?" the first one asks.

I hesitate. "Who's asking?"

The second one tips his chin toward the trailer. "We're here for the horses. Dominion and Saving Grace."

It's like the words don't register for a second, and then they slam into me so hard my knees nearly give. *What?*

"No," I say immediately. "No, you're not."

"Cass?" Mom's voice cracks and sounds so small just behind me. "What is this?"

The first man holds the paper out. "Got the receipt right here, ma'am."

"This has to be some mistake." I shake my head, already pulling my phone back out. "I'm calling my brother."

Jonathan still doesn't answer. I call again. And again. Straight to voicemail.

Panic is building fast in my chest, making it hard to breathe. My fingers fly over the screen and I send off a quick text to Jax—*Are you busy?*—but nothing else. Not yet.

"Ma'am," one of the men says, voice firm, "we don't want trouble. Just here to pick up the stock."

"They're not stock," I snap. "They're family. And you're not taking them."

Things turn sharp fast.

Mom's color drains in seconds, her hand trembling as it grips the stall door for balance. "Cass..." Her voice is faint, thin, and it cuts through me like glass.

The men exchange a look, and I get a sinking feeling this is about to get really bad. Because their patience is gone before we've even started.

One steps in closer, but I move to block his way to the stall. "Ma'am, we were told you'd resist. But our job is to get these horses loaded. This is nothing personal."

"The hell it isn't," I snap, my finger pushing the call

button again as I keep my eyes hard on him. The other is opening their trailer.

When I take a second to spare a look at Mom, the second man moves quickly around me, heading straight for Dominion. My pulse spikes as I catch sight of the big gelding side-stepping nervously, ears flicking back.

"Stop!" My voice cracks, sharp and desperate as I end the call my brother keeps ignoring.

"Cassidy, I—" Mom sways where she's standing, her breathing shallow. I move toward her instinctively, ready to catch her if she goes down, but every step I take toward her is another step away from the stable. My heart is tearing itself in two—do I help her or stop them?

"Shanae!" I whip my head toward the house. "Shanae!" I shout again, my voice carrying across the open acreage. From here, I can see her small figure emerge from the house.

"Help!" I yell, waving an arm. "We need help!"

By the time I look back, the man's got the stall door open and Dominion's trying to back into the far corner, muscles tense.

My feet are moving toward him but the second man's hand closes around my arm, firm enough to keep me in place but not quite bruising—yet.

"Don't make this harder than it has to be," he says, low and final.

"Get your hands off me!" I bite back, yanking my arm out of his grip. Hot tears spill out of my eyes and my throat feels like it's tightening.

My phone rings in my hand and I answer without looking, spitting the words out through a sob. "How could you do this?"

"It's me," Jax's voice cuts through, low and steady but he's caught on to the panic in my tone.

I gasp, the words tumbling out before I can stop them. "He sold them, Jax. The horses. Jonathan sold them." My voice breaks completely, ugly sobs shaking me.

There's a pause on Jaxon's end of the line. The unmistakable roar of his bike in the background. "Get Big Ben," he orders, voice like steel. "Don't let them leave. I'm on my way."

Shanae comes running up just as Mom's knees buckle.

"Mom!" The word tears out of me, sharp and panicked. I try to rush into the barn, but the man in front of me grabs me with both hands, yanking me back. My phone slips from my grip, hitting the dirt and hay with a dull *thud*.

"Let go of me!" I growl, twisting against him.

Shanae reaches Mom first, slipping an arm around her shoulders and guiding her toward the nearest chair. "I've got you, I've got you," she murmurs, but her own voice is shaky.

"Ben!" I shout, scanning the property. His truck isn't here. My heart lurches. Please, God, let him be in the pastures. Please don't let him have gone into town.

"Call Ben!" I scream at Shanae while I keep struggling against the man's grip.

The first guy is already inside the stall with Dominion, and the big gelding's eyes are wide, whites showing as he tosses his head. The other horses are starting to react— snorting, stamping, restless in their stalls.

"Stop!" I yell, the sound raw in my throat. I slam my heel down on the man's foot and drive my boot into his shin. He cusses, jerking me forward before regaining his hold.

Over his shoulder, I catch sight of Shanae pulling her phone out, her lips moving fast. I can't make out the words over the roaring in my ears. My heartbeat is pounding so loud it drowns everything else out.

Then I see Dominion being led out with a lead rope, muscles bunched, fighting the pull with every step.

Something inside me snaps. I thrash harder, my nails digging into the man's wrists, my boots scrambling for leverage. He swears again, shoving me forward until my front smacks into the barn wall.

"Enough!" he snarls, pressing his weight into me, using his body to pin me there. His breath is hot on my neck, his voice low and threatening. "We're taking these horses, sweetheart. One way or another."

Dominion rears back, whinnying in panic, but the man at his lead keeps yanking him forward, bit by bit toward the trailer. My chest aches watching him fight, his hooves skidding in the dirt, but it's not enough. He gets him inside. The sound of the gate clanging shut is like a death knell in my ears.

Helplessness crawls up my spine, but I can't stop fighting. My arms are burning, my muscles screaming from straining against the man holding me, but I won't give up. I can't let them leave. I shove and twist, trying to push him off me, but it's useless.

Then I hear a truck engine and a shout.

I whip my head toward the sound and see Ben's pickup

skid in sideways at the front of their truck, big and loud and perfectly blocking their way out.

Thank God.

Ben jumps out before it's even fully stopped. "Get away from the horses!" he shouts, his voice booming across the yard. He's a big man and in his younger days he would probably give both these men a run for their money.

"He has Dominion!" I call out, my voice raw.

The man holding me shoves his forearm against my throat so hard it cuts my words off mid-breath. "I'm tired of hearing your mouth," he growls, leaning in so close I can feel the spit when he says it. He's choking me. Rage twists his features, and for the first time, I think he might really hurt me.

Ben's already stepping into the trailer, and I hear muffled shouting. Then a grunt—and Ben goes flying backward, landing hard on the ground outside, clutching his jaw.

"Don't hurt him!" I scream like my voice has any power here.

"Ben," Mom calls out from her chair, her voice weak and trembling.

"Stay with Lilly!" Ben barks toward Shanae as he pushes up to his feet, blood bright at the corner of his mouth.

But Ben's not done—he's storming into the barn now, just as the second man steps down from the trailer, Dominion secured inside.

"Please," I sob, my voice breaking. "Stop."

Ben's got a metal shovel in his hands now, swinging it once like a warning. "Don't you come near this horse."

The man squares off with him, voice low and threatening. But before he can take a step, a sound cuts through the air—sharp, distinct, getting closer.

A motorcycle.

My heart jumps. I know that sound. I've heard it for years.

Jaxon's here.

The scream of his bike echoing like a warning across the atmosphere tells me he's riding like he's bringing hell with him.

His bike is getting louder—closer—and the fight surges back into me. I push off the barn wall with my feet, catching the man holding me off guard. He stumbles back, swearing, but keeps his grip.

Ben swings the shovel again. "Get back!"

The man wraps both arms around my stomach, trapping my arms to my sides, squeezing so hard my feet leave the ground. I can't breathe. Can't scream.

I kick wildly, thrashing my head back. My skull connects with his face, and the sickening crunch of his nose breaking rings in my ears.

He cusses loud, grip loosening just enough for me to suck in a breath.

"You fucking bitch," he spits, his arms clamping down again before he hauls me up and throws me to the ground.

The impact rattles my bones. Dirt grits into my eyes and mouth. The air is knocked from my lungs, and for a moment, the world tilts sideways and spins the wrong way.

"Cassidy!" Mom's scream rips through the chaos.

"Sit down, Lilly!" Shanae's voice, closer, panicked.

Then—movement. A streak of black in my peripheral.

The man is yanked away from me so fast he stumbles. Jaxon's still wearing his helmet as he drags the man back and, in the same motion, slams a fist into his face. He yanks the man forward by the shirt, driving his knee up hard, then pulling his head down to meet it. Bone meets bone with a sick crack.

The man drops, and Jaxon's on him like a predator. "You fucked up touching her." The words are low, deep—and nothing like the Jaxon I know. This voice is darker. Deadlier.

I feel the crack of a bone as much as I hear it and wince.

The man screams. Jaxon rips his helmet off and is at my side in the next heartbeat, hauling me upright and sitting me against the wall.

The man is screaming, holding is arm and rolling on his back like it's the only thing he can do amid the pain he's in.

"Are you hurt?" His eyes are wild, pupils blown wide so the deep brown is almost gone. "Are you okay?"

"Grace," I choke out, my voice breaking.

He presses a quick kiss to my forehead, his breath still hard. "Get to your mom, baby."

He hauls me to my feet just long enough to steady me, then he's gone—storming into the barn, his shoulders rigid with fury.

Chapter 19

Anger isn't enough to describe what's in me right now.

This isn't anger.

It's the kind of fury that could burn a man's soul to ash.

I step into the barn, flexing my fingers before curling them into fists. My body is coiled tight, ready to break something.

Ben's holding one of the assholes back with a shovel. His pissant of a friend is on the ground, crying like a bitch with a broken arm.

I round on the one still standing, getting right in his face, chest to chest, and shove him back hard. "Get the fuck out of this barn."

He stumbles, surges back out of control, but stays on his feet. Then the idiot charges me—grabbing me around the waist and ramming me back into the wall.

Cassidy yells my name. God help me, she better stay put.

These assholes don't realize what they've just asked for. I fight for fun. This is nothing more than a fucking warm-up.

The guy's still pushing at my midsection, trying to land punches to my ribs, but I block every one. I drive my elbow into his shoulder, putting my weight behind it. I feel the joint shift under the blow. *Yeah, I know that fucking hurt, you cunt.*

I bend, wrap my arms around his waist, and lift. Using every ounce of strength and momentum, I slam him to the ground with a grunt.

"My God, Jax." I hear Cassidy's mother. I can nearly feel the worry in her voice. I wish she wouldn't waste it on me. I don't need it. But these mother fuckers do.

I'm on him before he can think, busting his nose with the one punch. Blood sprays. My forearm locks on his throat, pinning him there and he knows I've got him.

"Why are you here?" I growl pushing harder, enjoying hearing him choke.

He struggles, trying to breathe. I wait a few seconds before I ease up just enough to tease him.

"We—bought the horses outright," he rasps against my hold.

"What'd you pay?" I press down again to emphasize that I'm not fucking playing around.

"They're worth more than money." He's trying to pull against my arm to give himself some space to breathe. His face turning from red to purple. "They're legends."

"I didn't ask for your fucking opinion. How much?"

I press down more and he can't fucking breathe at all now. His body squirms and he finally taps on my forearm in a frantic plea of surrender. I stand, grip his shirt, and haul him up—tearing the fabric—before shoving him toward the open barn door.

"How much?" I repeat, walking him backward past the three women—Cassidy kneeling beside her mother, Shanae standing like a shield in front of them. My eyes cut to Cassidy. Dirt smears her cheek. Her hair's tangled. My hands start to shake. My eyes water with how fucking angry I am.

"No. We want the horses."

I see a paper on the ground and snatch it up. $75 million.

"I'll give you $150 million to forget the horses and get the fuck out of here."

"Jaxon..." Lilly's voice is disbelieving, but I throw a hand back, keeping her where she is. I know what I'm doing.

The man laughs. "You crazy?"

"You want me to answer, or do you want me to show you—again." I take a step forward. "$200 million."

He hesitates a moment thinking it over. He side-eyes his buddy and then his focus is back on me. "...Three hundred."

"Deal. Ben—get the horse."

The tension shifts in an instant. Like a band as snapped and is rewinding everything backward. The man glances at his friend. "You good?"

The one with the broken arm glares at me, spitting a curse that I don't appreciate him saying in front of Mrs. Hayes.

I kneel, force the tremble out of my voice—it's not fear, it's fury—and make it almost a whisper. "If her mother wasn't here watching, I would've fucking killed you for touching her. So shut the fuck up."

I pull my phone, hit the contract for my finance manager. "I need an immediate wire for three hundred million to this fuckwad I'm about to hand the phone to." I say, never taking my eyes off the man I fought inside this barn.

"Fuck you," he spits, but he takes the phone and steps aside, answering the questions coming at him to start the transfer.

I pace between them and the women, hands on my hips, keeping myself between the threat and what's mine.

It takes Ben a few minutes to get Dominion calmed enough to lead him off the trailer and back into his stall. "I'll move my truck," Ben says. I give him a short nod but keep my eyes on the assholes. My blood's still hot and I don't trust them for a second.

The man tosses my phone back and hauls his buddy up by his good arm. Ben joins me, both of us locked on them, not ready to breathe easy until they're fully out.

Since Ben is here too I turn back to Cassidy—and before I can say a word, she's on me. Practically jumping in my arms, holding on like she'll drown if she lets go.

"Jax," she sobs into my shoulder, squeezing me tight.

A million emotions slam into me all at once, so strong my body shakes with them. I keep replaying seeing her hit the ground, the pain on her face. The way she curled in on herself when she couldn't breathe.

"Shhh," I wrap her up, my arms locking around her just as fiercely. "It's okay now," I murmur into her hair, squeezing my eyes closed and pressing my face into her neck.

She's trembling. So am I.

"Don't let me go, Cass," I tell her low, just for her. "Don't let me go or I'll go kill them."

Her arms tighten, her face tucking against my neck like mine is to hers. I shift us just enough to keep them in sight.

"Okay," she whispers back. "Don't leave me."

I exhale hard and hold her tighter. *I don't fucking plan on it, Cricket.*

Their doors slam. The truck roars to life and pulls away. Ben trails after them, making sure they're gone.

The tension starts to bleed out of me, but I'm nowhere near calm.

I palm the back of her head, threading my fingers into her dark hair and breathing her in like it's the first clean air I've had all day.

Two thoughts stick in my mind and won't leave.

I'm never leaving her alone again.

And I need to have a talk with my friend.

Cass checks on the horses, running her hands over their necks like she needs to feel for herself that they're still here. Dominion's still edgy, ears flicking back, but he's breathing easier now. Saving Grace noses at her pocket, searching for treats, and Cass rubs her velvety muzzle, whispering something I can't hear.

I scoop her mom up without a second thought. She's

light—too light—and I can feel the way she leans into me like the last hour drained her completely. There's no way she could walk all the way back to the house.

As we're crossing the yard, she pats my cheek weakly. "Thank you, Jackie. You've always been brave."

I glance down at her. "Not sure brave is the right word for what I just did."

She smiles faintly. "It is. You were always like that— even when you were a boy. Remember that awful goose you saved me from at the county fair?"

A short laugh escapes me. "I've never met a goose that could best me."

That earns me the smallest chuckle, which is good—her color's still pale. Cass trails beside us, watching her mom like she's afraid she might shatter if she blinks too long.

By the time we get back to the house, her eyes are half-closed. I lower her onto the her bed gently. "Should we make her something to eat?" I whisper, glancing over my shoulder at Cassidy.

She smirks, and it's the first real sign of her usual self since all hell broke loose. "Might be safer if we don't. You almost burning your penthouse down trying to make eggs."

I huff out a laugh. "That was a one-time thing."

"Mm-hm," she says, clearly not buying it. "She'll want to sleep. We can just go."

Shanae gives her a hug and reassurance her mom will be okay with a little rest, but I can see how guilty she feels leaving.

Outside, she hesitates at her car, looking toward the

barn where my bike is still laying on its side. "I'll meet you at your penthouse or should I follow you?"

"Neither," I say, holding my hand out. "I'll drive your car. I'll send for my bike later."

Her eyes narrow playfully as she drops the keys into my palm. "Okay, but this is *not* your McLaren. You can't drive it like a demon."

"Aww, come on," I grin, heading for the door. "Let me open her up just a little."

Cass rolls her eyes, but I can see the corner of her mouth twitching, even if it is still a little sad over tonight's events.

Big Ben hollers that he'll stash my bike in the stables and Cassidy glares at me when I rev her cars quiet little engine.

<hr>

The ride is quiet. I can feel her staring out the window, lost in whatever's running through her head. I can't stop replaying it all—the way she answered the phone. How that prick threw her to the ground, the sound she made when she hit.

My hands tighten on the wheel.

And under all of it is the question I can't shake: *Why the hell would her brother sell those horses?*

Even I know what they're worth. Dominion and Saving Grace aren't just valuable—they're legendary. A Triple Crown Winner. Champions. Mated. A bloodline people would kill to get. They're priceless.

In the penthouse, she disappears down the hall,

mumbling something about a shower and clean clothes. I can't sit still, so I order dinner while she's gone.

When she comes back, damp hair curling at the ends, I lean against the counter. "You up for a surprise?"

Her brows pull together. "That depends."

"Trust me," I say, taking her hand.

I lead her to the largest of my extra rooms—the one I've been working in all week. The door's still shut and I stop her there. "Open it."

She pushes it open and freezes.

It's an artist's dream in here—everything she's ever had in her own studio, and more. Giant canvases leaning against the wall. Sketchbooks—her favorite kind—stacked high. Jars of brushes. Paints lined in neat rows.

She turns to me, eyes glassy. "Jax... I—"

She looks around again, swallowing hard. I know what she's thinking. That this is temporary.

Why do all this if she'll only be here a few more weeks.

Yeah. About that...

"You can take it all with you when you leave," I lie to her before she can say she fight me on it. "At least now you don't have to go home every time you want to paint."

She steps into me, hugging me around the waist with a whispered *thank you*. Then again, tighter this time. "And thank you for earlier. For the horses. I'll—"

I cut her off and tilt her face up to mine with a finger under her chin. "If you say you'll pay me back, I'm wiring those assholes another three hundred million."

Her lips press together, swallowing something I can't read before she nods.

I pull back just a bit and hold her stare, willing her to answer my question. "Why would your brother sell them?"

She exhales hard, looking away. "You don't know the same Jonathan that I do." And that's it. No more. She walks away before I can press her.

The service bell rings with our dinner, so I drop it—for now.

But I'm going to find out what the fuck that means.

I'm having the most amazing dream.

Of course it's about Jax.

That mouth of his—God, it's sinful. Wicked. Devious in every possible way. In my dream, he's between my legs, his tongue sliding over me like he knows exactly what I need before I even know it myself. His hands are holding me still, but I can't stop moving, can't stop chasing the heat building in me.

My face is buried in the pillow, muffling the broken sounds slipping out of me as he works me over. He takes his time—slow enough to make me beg in my head—until I'm riding the waves he gives me, hips rolling helplessly, falling apart just for him.

And then—

I wake up.

The pleasure still clings to me, my thighs tight around the pillow I'm hugging between my legs. My chest is rising fast, breaths uneven, skin warm all over.

I blink, and my stomach drops.

Jax is right there on his side. Head propped up on his hand.

Staring straight at me.

That smirk on his face says *everything*.

"That," he drawls, eyes glittering, "sounded like an amazing dream."

I groan, dragging the pillow over my face. "I wasn't dreaming."

His smirk deepens. "And you tore down the great wall of chastity."

"You're annoying."

"And you're horny, Miss *'ugh, right there.'*" He mimics my high, breathy, moaning voice with such obnoxious accuracy I want to throw something at him.

So I do. The pillow smacks him in the chest, and I sit up. "Grow up."

I stomp to the bathroom and slam the door, because I'm pretty sure if I stay out there another second, he'll find a way to make me combust just from that smug look.

When I come back out, he's not in his room. Thank God.

But my victory is short lived because he's sitting on the kitchen counter, shirtless, coffee in hand. Another mug—already made the way I like it—sits waiting for me.

He's got pancake ingredients spread across the counter like he actually knows what to do with them.

I eye him. "Presumptuous of you."

He shrugs, taking another sip. "I'm happy to make you pancakes... if you want to go ahead and get the fire marshal on the phone."

I roll my eyes but push past him to start measuring. I've got my mom's pancake recipe memorized—though really, it's Jaxon's mom's recipe. She'd taught it to my mom years ago, back when she came to the house on weekends to cook, always bringing Jaxon with her.

I can still see it clear as day—Saturday mornings, the three of us at the table, the air warm with the smell of syrup and butter. One of my earliest memories.

"Why do you like pancakes so much, anyhow?" I ask, cracking eggs into the bowl.

He leans back on his hands watching me. "You know we were poor. Had to make food stretch sometimes. But pancakes..." He shrugs. "I could have as many as I wanted."

Something twists in my chest, hot and sharp. I knew his childhood was rough until his mom, Sandy, came to work for us, but I never knew the details. I want to ask, but before I can, he changes the subject.

"But I have more important questions."

I narrow my eyes. "I know where this is going."

"Were you dreaming about me?"

"No."

"Liar. Was I good?"

"Wouldn't know."

"I'm happy to do a reenactment if you like."

I smack him on the arm with the spatula, trying not to smile. "Get out of my kitchen."

He grins like he's already won, and I get back to flipping pancakes, pretending my face isn't hot.

He slides off the counter and comes up behind me.

My pulse kicks instantly. I've imagined this exact scenario—*him* behind me—more times than I'll ever admit.

"What are you doing?" I ask without turning, spatula still in my hand.

"Just keep cooking."

He moves my hair over one shoulder, and when he leans in to breathe me in, my knees almost give. "You've never had sex before."

I smirk to cover the fact that my stomach is in free fall. "A quick one, ladies and gentlemen."

He chuckles low against my skin, and it sends a shiver all the way down my spine. Both of his hands glide slowly down my arms, unhurried, like he's learning every inch.

"Have you fooled around any?" His lips brush the side of my neck.

God, if he only knew how many nights I've thought about his mouth there. "A little," I admit, the words coming out breathier than I'd like.

His grip tightens, like the answer matters more than it should. Another kiss, lower. "Tell me what you've done, Cricket." His palms skim my hips, moving forward and down toward my pelvis—closing the last bit of space between us until I feel the unmistakable hardness pressed into my lower back.

"I've kissed," I say, barely above a whisper.

He hums against my skin, lips finding the bend of my neck and shoulder. "What else?"

One hand slides under my shirt, stopping just beneath my breast. My breath catches when his thumb trails lightly across the soft skin under my breast. The other drifts down my thigh, his fingers slow, purposeful, and I swear my heart might burst through my ribs.

"I've been fingered before."

"Mmm," he murmurs, mouth warm on my skin again. "Who, Cricket?"

"Who?"

"Who did you let touch you?"

I swallow hard and hope he remembers. "I'm sure you remember Matt, from that party?"

His hands tense on my body.

"We dated for a while."

"I see."

Do you Jaxon? Do you see you rejected me and pushed me into his arms?

"And did you come?"

I swallow, embarrassed at the truth. "No."

"What a shame." His palm covers my breast now, thumb rolling my nipple. I moan, leaning my head back against his chest without thinking. I want more. God help me, I've *always* wanted more from him.

"I can show you how good it can feel, baby." His lips graze my ear, making every hair on my body stand on end. His other hand moves between my legs, slipping inside one of the legs of the boxers I slept in. His fingers rubbing over my pussy like he already owns it. "Fuck, Cricket. You're soaking your panties."

He rubs his fingers over my panties and my mouth drops open. His mouth is on my neck, kissing. Licking.

"And you're burning our breakfast,"

"Shit." I snap forward, sliding the pancake onto a plate

before I forget entirely. My hands aren't steady, and the pan feels heavier than it should.

"Keep cooking, beautiful," he says, voice low and thick, like a promise. "Let me make you come."

It doesn't sound like a question—but it is.

I nod, pouring more batter onto the pan with shaking hands, my mind spinning with the reality that this isn't a dream anymore. He's actually touching me. Talking to me like this. And I know we're crossing a barrier that we'll never return from.

His hand slides under the waistband of my panties, and he groans the second his fingers meet me.

"Christ, Cricket... you're soaked."

I grip the edge of the counter like it's the only thing holding me up. I've dreamed about this man—about this exact touch—for years. But nothing in my imagination comes close to the heat in his voice right now.

He doesn't rush. His fingers slide between my pussy lips, stroking slow, deliberate lines over my clit. My hips jerk forward involuntarily, the spatula clattering onto the counter.

"Uh, Jaxon." I grit out, closing my eyes and biting my lip.

"That's it," he murmurs, his mouth near my ear, his tone a mix of praise and command. "Just feel me."

My breath comes faster, shallow and uneven. Every stroke is maddeningly controlled, like he's reading my body and holding me right on the edge of something I've never felt before.

"You're already trembling for me," he says, his lips

brushing my neck. "That's good, baby. I want you just like this for me, every time."

I don't even have the sense to answer. I just nod, sucking in a breath as his touch circles and glides, pressure alternating until I'm gasping.

He keeps talking, voice low and steady, anchoring me in the intensity. "Let me take care of you. You just stay right here and come for me."

My legs are weak, thighs pressing together, but his free hand grips my hip firmly, holding me exactly where he wants me. I can feel the restraint in his movements—how easy it would be for him to push harder, faster—but instead he controls it, keeps it steady, winding me tighter.

"Breathe, Cricket," he reminds me when my chest locks. "That's it. Just like that. You're beautiful with my fingers in this sweet cunt." He licks up the column of my neck, sucking the sensitive skin just under my ear.

"Oh, my God."

I moan and groan, losing it. I've been touched before, a little. But never like this—never with someone completely focused on *me*, coaxing every reaction out of me like it's the only thing that matters.

"Jaxon." I breathe out, my hand clamping around his wrist as he works my pussy.

"That's it baby." His other hand slides under my shirt again, squeezing my breast, pinching and twisting my nipple in time with the movements of his fingers on my clit. "Give it to me."

"Yes." I sound like I'm both begging him and worshiping him. "God, please, just like that."

"Keep—"

The tension builds sharp and hot until it bursts stealing the rest of my plea. My knees almost buckle, my body rocking against his hand as I come, breathless and completely undone.

He slows but doesn't pull away right away, easing me through it, stroking me softly until the aftershocks fade and I'm leaning all my weight into him.

"Good girl," he says against my ear, and the praise makes my stomach flip all over again.

I'm not even pretending to finish the pancakes. My arms feel heavy, my chest still rising and falling too fast.

He finally pulls his hand free, turning me around and I watch in dazed disbelief as he slips his fingers into his mouth, eyes locked on mine. He moans like I'm the best thing he's ever tasted. "So sweet," he murmurs. "Just like I knew you'd be."

He leans down like he's about to kiss me. My pulse jumps so hard I swear he can hear it.

I tilt my head without thinking, eyes heavy-lidded from the orgasm still humming through me. My mouth parts, my breath catches. God, I want him to.

But he pauses there—close enough that I can feel the heat of him, smell the faint mix of coffee and soap and *him*. His eyes flick down to my mouth, linger there, and then... he pulls back. Slowly. Smirking like the devil.

"Thanks for breakfast," he teases, reaching past me to grab a plate. He piles on pancakes, drizzling syrup like I wasn't just moaning out his name seconds ago.

I grab a hand towel and snap it against his arm. "Wash your hands first."

"Not a fucking chance," he says, eyes glinting with wicked amusement. "I'm going to smell your sweet pussy on my fingers all day, Cricket. Because you were delicious."

My jaw drops, my whole body lighting up all over again.

He just winks and strolls toward his office, leaving me standing there—burning just like the forgotten pancake still smoking on the stove.

Chapter 21

S he's been buried in that studio I put together for her since the day she opened the door. I'd like to say I'm annoyed she spends so much time in there, but the truth is—I love that she loves it.

Whatever's on that massive canvas, it's got her whole attention. She won't let me see it, won't even give me a hint. Says she never shows anyone her paintings which makes me want to walk in there even more.

A knock comes to the door, and my building concierge carries in a package. "For Miss Hayes," he says.

Shanae told her about it earlier this morning and she said she's pick it up in a few days. I sent someone from the building to get it for her.

When I carry it into the living room, she looks at it, then at me. "That seems like a waste," she says, taking the box.

"Do you know how much I pay to live here?" I arch a brow. "They would literally help me commit murder if I asked with a *Will there be anything else, Mr. Kane?* when we were done.

She shakes her head, smiling faintly, but when she looks down and sees some fancy crest on the side of the box, her expression changes. Tightens.

It's from her brother.

Her stomach visibly sinks, and that puts me on alert immediately. I watch as she opens it, pulling out neatly folded shirts, a necklace, all marked with the same crest.

"Is this Jon's new business partner or something?" I ask, already feeling the itch of curiosity.

Her answer is short. "Or something."

I study her. "Why do you two got beef all of a sudden?"

Her gaze flicks up to mine, and there's a hardness there that wasn't before. "This isn't new. He's always been an asshole to me."

"Do you want to talk about it?" I ask the question carefully knowing I'm pushing into territory she'd like to keep me out of.

Without answering, she dumps everything back into the box, carries it to the kitchen, and drops it straight into the trash.

"I'm going into the studio," she says, already walking away.

I let her go for now. But I'm not done.

I send off a text to Jon to see if he can talk, then I drive fifteen minutes to the gym where Lucian is already on a bag like it owes him money.

Lucian is owner of The Black Ledger, king of his own

empire, and one of the only people I'll get in the ring with for fun.

Eve's here too, sitting in a chair and rubbing both breasts.

"Ew?" I hold one hand out in confusion. The other clutches my gym bag.

"What? My nipples hurt," she announces the second she sees me. "Just got them pierced."

"Oh, well hello to you too, *Judas*," I say dryly. "We'll file that under: Things I didn't need to know."

"Hello, you salty bitch," she fires back. "Still pouting from the auction?"

"From being stabbed in the back by my *friend*? Yes."

"You'll get over it. I'm sure your billion-dollar lot will kiss it and make it better for you." She winks.

Lucian chuckles from the ring, tossing me a pair of gloves. I climb in, and we start warming up—easy jabs, controlled footwork. We both like taking our frustrations out in here on each other. We're evenly matched, which means no one's ego gets too bruised, and we both know it's never personal.

I've known Eve a few years now. Lucian just as long.

The Ledger girls are practically part of my payroll, but I've never had a sexual contract with one of them. Just to accompany me to events to keep hordes of social-ladder-climbing women from approaching me.

I know what the press says about me having a new girl on my arm every week, but I don't give a shit as long as I can keep my peace and privacy.

Lucian gives me a look between swings. "You're in a good mood. Has something to do with your auction lot?"

I shrug, though there's no point in denying it. "Maybe. Cassidy's... different. Been *different* a long time now but it's bothering me—why she did this in the first place."

Eve cracks two first aid cooling packs and sticks them in her shirt, holding them to her breasts. "Oh, that's so much better already."

"This is horrendous by the way." I throw a jab at Lucian, and he moves out of the way with a chuckle. "Just in case you wanted to know if you were traumatizing your friends."

"Just hack her." She doesn't even acknowledge me, leaning her head back and closing her eyes.

Lucian winds up a spinning kick and I move out of the way quickly. "Come on old man. I saw that coming from last week."

"Keep it up." He dishes back to me. We both know Lucian could break my neck and I'd be dead before I hit the ground.

"I don't want to invade her privacy." I get back to Eve's suggestion.

"That's rich, coming from you," Lucian mutters.

"I want her to come to me and tell me because she *wants* to," I say, throwing a quick combo at Lucian, which he blocks mostly. I land one hit. "Not because I snooped around and forced it out of her."

Lucian grins like he knows something I don't. "You ready to do this, lover boy?"

I narrow my eyes and he smirks knowing it's time to stop holding back and try to beat the shit out of each other.

An hour with Lucian did the trick like usual. He mentioned a fight in a few days and I'm usually game to throw my name in the ring but I'm not sure if that is Cassidy's scene.

Back and the penthouse and showered, I push the fact Jonathan left me on read to the back of my mind. I've got better things to do.

Like take Cassidy out.

I didn't like how that package from Jonathan dimmed her mood, so I tell her she's coming shopping with me.

She tries to block me at the studio door before I can get a look at the canvas she's been working on. "Full u-turn. Out of here."

I try to look around her, but she moves with me, using her hands to block my line of sight. I saw a little but not enough to figure out what it is.

"You do know this *is* my house."

"And this is my... imagination."

"And I want to see it."

"Never. It's not for seeing."

"Is it of me? A nude portrait, probably," I wiggle my eyebrows up and down. She laughs and pushes me against my own hallway.

"Not in your life."

"I'd be happy to pose for you. You could draw me like one of your French girls." I play with my chest in mock seduction, but she can't stop smiling and that's all I want. "Just make sure you get my giant coc—,"

"You're the worst person I know." She claps her hand over my mouth to stop me from finishing a sentence that would be sure to make her cheeks turn cherry red. More than they already are.

I laugh against her hand and have to physically stop myself from pulling her against me. She rolls her eyes and comes with me without another fight.

We end up at one of my favorite motorcycle shops. The woman behind the counter—tattoos, piercings, perfect red lipstick—grins when she sees me. Cassidy's shoulders go just a little stiff.

"This her?" the woman asks, eyes flicking to Cassidy.

"Yeah," I say easily. "This is my girl."

Her heart might not say it out loud, but I *see* how those words land.

Kady already has a few things pulled for her. She's nice, but Cassidy's watching her too closely, like she's trying to figure out if we've ever fucked. I don't bother explaining yet because I love watching her squirm.

We get Cassidy fitted for riding gear—her own boots, jacket, gloves, helmet. She's nervous, but I can see the excitement in her eyes. She's been on horses her whole life, but never a motorcycle.

And God, she looks fucking amazing in gear.

By the time we check out, she's practically bouncing. The total hits the thousands, and I don't even blink. Not when I threw down three hundred million to save her horses. Not when I paid enough to buy a small country for her at the auction.

"You'll let me take you riding?" I ask leaning against the counter.

"Yes!" she says, bright-eyed, smiling—and I match it without even thinking.

Then she asks how I know Kady, and there's a little tension in her voice that I can't miss. *Is my little Cricket jealous?* God, I hope so. That would make my day.

"She's the owner," I tell her. "Been shopping here for years. Met her wife by coincidence a few months ago—did a job for some architect friends."

"Wife?" That eases her instantly.

"That's her—Frankie." I point to a framed photo on the wall of Kady with her arm around another gorgeous pinup glam type. "Didn't even put two and two together until I came back here for a new helmet."

She tilts her head. "Why did you need a new helmet?"

I grin. "Would you still come riding with me if I told you I crashed?"

"Jaxon!" she scolds, smacking my arm.

I laugh, pulling her into a hug that feels... easy. Natural. Flirty in a way that makes it hard to let go. "I'm just playing. I just wanted a new one."

Her laugh lingers in my head long after we leave, and I know one thing for sure—this girl belongs on the back of my bike, and right next to me.

Forever.

Chapter 22

Cassidy

It's been raining for days, the kind of steady, dreary gray that makes everything feel heavier.

I've been back to check on Mom once since those assholes tried to take the horses. She's been doing well—Shanae keeps me updated almost daily—but I still can't shake the image of her pale and shaking that day.

Yesterday, I got a text from Jonathan.

JONATHAN: We'll talk about the horses when I get back.

I didn't answer. Didn't even tell Jaxon. I just walked into the art studio he made for me and poured everything onto the canvas until my arms ached.

But today... today's different. Today I'm packing a bag because Jaxon's taking me out on his bike.

I've always wanted to ride on one. Never drive—God, no—but sitting on the back, holding on tight? That's always sounded fun.

The bike's already loaded on a trailer hitched to his truck when I come down. He's leaning against the hood, arms crossed, helmet sitting beside him like it's waiting for me.

"You ready, Cricket?" he asks, one brow lifting.

"As I'll ever be," I say, sliding my bag over my shoulder. "You're sure you're not going to kill me, right?"

He smirks. "I like you too much for that. Plus, you still owe me pancakes."

I roll my eyes, but my cheeks heat anyway.

We hit the road, and for the first hour, it's easy—just back roads and stretches of highway, the sky breaking into patches of pale blue. I pepper him with questions about riding—how long he's been doing it, the fastest he's ever gone, whether or not he's ever crashed.

He puts on music at some point, scrolling through his phone until something bouncy fills the cab. I recognize it in the first few notes and laugh. "Is this... the *Glee* soundtrack?"

He shoots me a quick sideways grin. "Of course it's Glee."

"Never would've pegged *you* for a man who enjoys musicals," I counter.

He starts singing along anyway—badly, on purpose—and I can't help joining in after a song or two. We're both laughing by the time the next season's soundtrack hits.

But somewhere in the last hour, my voice quiets. The closer we get, the more my nerves creep in.

He notices. Without a word, his hand finds mine on the center console. He threads our fingers together, warm and steady, and brings my knuckles to his lips for a quick kiss.

"Hey," he says, his tone softer now. "You're gonna love this. I promise."

I nod, but my stomach flutters when he doesn't let my hand go. He keeps holding it. Setting our joined hands on my thigh.

"Tell me about Dominion and Grace," he adds. "What made you think to breed them?"

It's easy to talk about them. About Grace's stubborn streak, about how Dominion won't let anyone else near her stall, about the way they run the pastures like they own them. Jaxon listens, asking small questions here and there, and by the time we pull into the nearly empty lot in the Catskills, I've almost forgotten to be nervous at all.

When we finally pull into a nearly empty lot, the clouds are breaking, and the air smells like wet leaves.

We get geared up. I'm dressed. Nervous, but excited. And Jaxon... he looks *happy*. Not just his usual smug contentment —there's an energy about him, like he's genuinely excited to do this with me.

I hope so, because *damn* he looks good. All black gear, all black bike, and the two of us match like we planned it.

He helps me with my gloves, then my helmet, giving me a quick lesson on how to be a good "backpack"—how to lean with him, where to put my feet, when to hold tighter.

Then he swings a leg over the bike and starts it up, the low rumble sending a thrill straight through me. He reaches back, steadying me as I climb on behind him, and for a second, my heart's pounding louder than the engine.

"Here, give me your hands," his voice comes through the

helmet's Bluetooth, deep and warm in my ear. I have to work not to shudder at the sound—like it's just for me.

I place my hands where I think they should go, but he reaches back, catching my wrists and pulling me flush against him. "Like this," he says, fixing my grip tight around him so I know how hard to hold on. He explains where to put them when he's not going fast.

Now I understand why they call it being a backpack. My legs are spread around his, his ass is in my crotch, and my chest is plastered to his back. Every inch of me is on him. The heat building inside me has nothing to do with the gear.

He eases us forward, taking slow loops around the lot so I can get used to the feel of the bike moving beneath us. Once I'm steady, he heads out onto the road.

We pass a storefront with wide windows, and I catch our reflection—him, all black leather and strength, me clinging to him like I belong there. He glances toward it, too, and I wonder if he likes what he sees. Because I do. I could make a habit of this... but I know it's temporary.

My brother will be home in two weeks, and this little game of ours will have to end.

We stop at a red light, and he plants one boot on the pavement to steady us. Sitting taller, he tells me where we're headed, one hand rubbing absently over my thigh as he does it—like it's second nature. And I'm thankful he can't see me smiling inside the helmet.

Because I am. He's doing a great job of making me feel... well, a lot of things but...like I'm really his.

The light changes, his hands return to the handlebars, and I hold on tight.

Chapter 23

Jaxon

I don't think I've stopped grinning since the moment she came downstairs. Three hours in the truck, music up, her singing along—sometimes badly, sometimes better than she'd probably admit—and she still looked fresh, eyes bright.

I'd forgotten how easy it could be to just... have fun with someone.

The poor woes of a rich boy, I know. But most people around me are there because they work for me. Or because they want something—money, a spotlight, a leg up toward something—and then they're gone.

My close circle is small. Really fucking small.

But I don't have to worry about any of that with Cass. She's known me forever. Seen me in rags that were too small and falling apart, and later in Jonathan's hand-me-downs. Better fitting, sure. Certainly the nicest things I ever had back then—but still, never mine.

She's seen every part of me... mostly. Not how things

were before my mom took a job with the Hayes'. And not lately, since we went our separate ways. That was my fault. I had my reasons.

I hated those reasons, but back then I believed them. I used to think Jonathan was right—that it was for her good.

But now... I'm starting to see a side of my friend I've never seen before, not until I started seeing him through Cassidy's eyes. And it's got me rethinking everything I thought I knew about him—what he's capable of, what else I don't know.

I shake it off. That's not for today.

Today is her. On the back of my bike, exactly where I want her.

I love having her there—the weight of her against me, her arms wrapped tight around my waist. Too tight at first, but it doesn't last. She loosens, finds her rhythm with mine.

We start slow, but I open it up a little more each time, feeling her excitement build through the way she leans into me. She's having the time of her life, and it shows—she's getting more comfortable by the second.

The turns are where I really test her. I start conservative, then push faster, dropping us lower into each lean. She listens well, matches my movement, and it feels good—how we fit together like this.

"Want to try something?" I ask when we hit a long bend.
"What?"
"Touch the pavement on the turns. Just your fingertips."
Her laugh is nervous. "You're insane."
"Maybe. But you'll love it."
The first few times she tries, she pulls back before she's

anywhere close. I don't push her—just take us into the turns smoother, lower, letting her feel how much control I've got.

Finally, on the third try, her hand skims the pavement. She squeals so loud it nearly bursts my eardrum.

I laugh through the comms. "Damn, Crick. You're gonna make me deaf."

"Worth it!" she shouts, still laughing.

And fuck, she's right. Everything would be worth it with her.

I'm fucking starving. And if I'm hungry, I know she has to be too.

"All right," I say over the comms, "you wanna go fast now?"

Her voice is incredulous. "That wasn't fast before?"

I feel her grip tighten, her body scooting even closer against me. I can't stop the grin that spreads under my helmet. Should've done this earlier.

"You trust me?" I ask.

I feel her nod, but then she says it out loud too. "Yes."

"Okay, baby. Hold on tight. Here we go."

The road ahead clears, and I lock in—eyes forward, weight balanced, her pressed warm and solid at my back. I lean us into the first curve and she comes with me, and then we're flying.

I push it as far as I think I can safely take her. Not as much as I'd do riding solo, but still a hell of a lot faster than anything we've done today.

And she loves it. I can feel it in the way she moves with me, the way her laughter cuts through the comms like pure adrenaline.

We eventually roll into a little hole-in-the-wall spot I know—best burritos on the planet. The guy behind the counter recognizes me instantly, greeting me like we're old friends.

Cass tilts her head. "Everyone seems to love you everywhere you go."

I smirk. "Yeah, well... I'm incredibly lovable."

She glances at me over her menu. "Do they not know you're a giant turd?"

I laugh. "A turd. You're so mature, Cricket."

I've been watching the clock all afternoon, but not because I'm in a rush to get back.

There's a spot I want to take her to—one I've been saving. If I time it right, we'll hit it just before sunset.

The road winds upward until we pull off to a small dirt lot. From there, it's a short hike to a wide rock ledge that overlooks the valley. We sit side by side, legs stretched out, the warm stone beneath us radiating the last of the day's heat. The view is all soft oranges and pinks bleeding into each other, with streaks of purple at the edges. Lightning flickers way off in the distance, far enough to be beautiful, not dangerous.

She's looking at the horizon, but I'm looking at her.

"Pretty, huh?" she says without glancing my way.

"Yeah," I answer, but I'm not talking about the sunset.

The light catches in her eyes when she finally looks at me, and for a second, neither of us says anything. I can feel the shift, that quiet stretch of time where everything slows. My heart kicks up, which is ridiculous—I've kissed plenty of women. But she's not plenty of women. She's *her*. My Cricket.

She must see something in my face because her lips part, and she stops fidgeting with the zipper on her jacket. There's this stillness in her, like she's holding her breath without realizing it.

"You've got that look," she says softly, almost like she's teasing but too curious to commit to it.

"What look?"

"The one you get before you do something you're not supposed to."

I smirk, leaning in just slightly, close enough to watch her pupils expand. "Maybe I'm about to."

Her lashes lower for a second, then lift again, meeting my eyes head-on. She knows. I can feel it in the way she tilts her chin up a fraction, not pulling away.

The space between us disappears slowly, my hand finding the side of her jaw. She's warm, her pulse thrumming under my fingertips.

When our lips finally meet, it's soft at first—testing, savoring—but it builds fast. Her mouth fits mine perfectly, and the world around us fades until there's nothing but her, the taste of her, the way she exhales like she's been holding that moment in for years.

It's the best kiss I've ever had.

Thunder rolls closer, low and heavy, and then the first drops fall. We pull back, glance at each other, and the shared grin says everything.

We make a run for the bike, the rain turning from playful

to a downpour in seconds. She's laughing by the time we reach it, hair plastered to her cheeks, jacket dripping.

Before she can grab her helmet, I catch her wrist and pull her in again. This kiss is different—harder, wetter, full of the rush from running through the storm.

"Every girl needs to be kissed in the rain at least once in her life," I murmur against her lips.

She smiles like she's storing the moment somewhere permanent and kisses me back, rain and all.

The rain's not letting up. It's not just a shower—it's the kind that soaks you straight through in seconds.

"We'll need to wait it out a little," I tell her, swinging a leg over the bike and looking around for some kind of shelter. There's nothing but wet trees, a narrow strip of road, and the view behind us swallowed by gray.

But she doesn't move toward cover. "I don't want to," she says. "Feels nice."

She's standing there with her face turned up to the sky, rain dripping down her hair, her jacket molding to her body in all the right ways, and I swear she's going to kill me.

Then she looks at me sideways. "How many other girls have you brought out on your bike?"

"None." My voice leaves no room for doubt.

Her brows lift. "None?"

"You're the only one I've put on the back of it."

Her lips twitch. "Have you ever had sex on it before?"

Only in every wet dream I've had about her for a long time. But I shake my head. "No."

She tilts her head. "Then how would that fantasy go?"

I grin, get back on the bike, and pat the space in front of me. "Come here and I'll show you."

She climbs up, straddling the tank, her ass in my lap. The contact is immediate and addictive. I rock my hips into her, slow at first, my hands sliding over her rain-slick thighs. She's warm under the gear, every shift of her body pressing against me just right.

One arm wraps around her, pulling her tighter as my other hand slips between her legs. My fingers find her through the damp fabric, adding steady pressure to her clit while I rock her forward and back. The rain's pounding on us but neither of us cares.

I lean in to her ear, my voice low. "If we weren't in the middle of a storm, I'd take my time. Strip you bare. Have you riding me right here until you couldn't remember your own name."

Her breathing's heavier now, her hips moving with mine, and I know I've got her.

I shift, lifting her like she weighs nothing, turning her around to face me. She's perched on the gas tank, her knees bracketing my hips, and I'm already imagining her there without all this gear.

"I could eat you like this," I tell her, sliding my hands under her thighs.

I hook one leg over my shoulder, making her lean back against the handlebars to keep balance. The way she looks at me right now—lips parted, eyes dark—I know she's drenched under those pants, and not from the rain.

I kiss the inside of her thigh, slow, before biting just hard enough to make her yelp.

"Thought so," I murmur.

I pull her back down to straddle me, my hands gripping her ass, moving her hips against me. Her arms loop around my neck, and when I kiss her again, she grinds on me like she's been waiting for this all day.

She leans back, bracing herself on the handlebars, working her hips in slow circles over my cock. The friction's brutal in the best way. I keep my hands on her, guiding her pace, murmuring in her ear,

The wet leather squeaks against my gloves, and every drag of her body over my cock has me fighting for control.

"Does this feel good?" I murmur against her ear.

She nods, breathless.

"Say it, Cricket."

"It feels... really good," she admits, the words almost a gasp as her forehead presses to mine.

"Yeah? Tell me what you like about it."

Her hips stutter, but I keep her moving, pushing her to stay with me. "I like... how close you are. The way you're holding me. The way it—" She breaks off on a shiver when I press harder against her clit.

"The way it makes you what?"

"—makes me feel like I can't breathe... but I don't want to stop."

"Fuck," I groan, because she doesn't even know what she's doing to me. "Feels good for me too, baby. So fucking good. You're about to make me come and I haven't even slipped inside you yet."

Her nails dig into my shoulders, her thighs tightening around my hips. I can feel the tremors starting in her, the way her breath catches every time I grind her down and pull her back up. She's close—too close—and I want to watch her fall apart for me.

"Jaxon," Her mouth drops open and I nip at her full bottom lip.

"Fuck, Cricket... don't you dare stop."

Her head tilts back as the orgasm hits, a raw, unguarded cry tearing from her throat. It's not pretty or practiced—it's real. It's her. And it's so goddamn perfect it wrecks me.

I lose it with her, my hips jerking up into hers as the tension snaps hard and fast. The heat floods through me, and I let out a rough, guttural sound I couldn't hide if I wanted to.

I press my forehead to hers. Both of us panting. My hands rubbing up her soaked clothes. "You see what you're doing to me?"

Her eyes go wide like she's just caught on to what happened. "Wait... did you come too?" she asks it like there's a crowd listening, even though it's just us and the rain.

I don't bother hiding the truth. "Fuck yes I did. You drive me crazy, baby. Always have."

And I mean it.

Not even five minutes later, the rain eases up. We make it back to the truck dripping, and flushed. She's smiling in that way that makes my chest ache.

I load the bike while she ducks inside to change, peeling herself out of the soaked riding gear.

When she comes back out, I'm already unbuckling my pants.

Her eyes go wide. "What are you doing?"

I give her a look like it should be obvious. "What, you expect me to ride home for three hours with cum in my pants?"

Her mouth opens, shuts, opens again—no comeback. Just a little sputtered noise and a blush that shoots straight down her neck. I smirk as I strip out of the ruined jeans and toss them in the back with the rest of the wet gear.

She climbs into the truck, buckling in and facing forward like that's going to hide the fact that she's flustered as hell. I can't help it—I'm grinning the whole time.

We're barely thirty minutes into the drive before her head tips toward the window. It doesn't take long until she's out completely, breathing soft and even.

I steal glances at her when I can, watching the way her damp hair sticks in soft curls to her cheek, the way she's curled into herself like she's been doing that in my passenger seat her whole life.

I make sure to keep her seat warmer on so she doesn't get cold and think about putting a blanket in here for next time.

By the time we pull into the penthouse's private garage, it's full dark. She stirs when I kill the engine but doesn't wake all the way. I get out, circle to her side, and scoop her up without a second thought. She makes a sleepy noise but doesn't protest, her head resting on my shoulder, burying her face in my neck and exhaling deeply.

Upstairs, I lay her down in my bed, carefully removing her shoes and dry clothes. I slip my old baseball shirt on her before I reach under and remove her bra.

I press a kiss to her temple—a quiet, unguarded thing

I'm not even sure she feels. Her lashes flutter but she doesn't open her eyes.

Since the Great Wall of Chastity has officially been breached, I strip down to my boxers and slide in behind her, fitting my body to hers. She's warm and soft against me, and for once, I don't feel the need to think about anything else—no plans, no schedules, no Jonathan, no contract.

Just her.

I pull her closer, my arm banding around her waist, and let the rhythm of her breathing pull me under.

Chapter 24
Cassidy

The phone's on speaker beside me while I lean over my drafting table, but my brother's voice feels like it's right in my ear.

"What the fuck were you thinking, getting Jaxon involved with the horses?" Jonathan's tone is sharp enough to cut skin.

My stomach's already tight, my jaw locked. "What the hell was I supposed to do? They—"

"You should've stayed out of it. Christ, Cassidy, you make everything worse."

I hate that I can feel the burn behind my eyes already. I hate trying to talk to him while I'm crying. My voice comes out strained, like I'm choking on glass. "Well, maybe *you* shouldn't have told him to keep an eye on things."

There's a pause on his end, heavy and cold. "Don't fucking push me, Cassidy. I'll be coming back soon, and you won't be so fucking brave then. Will you? You piece of shit."

I flinch like he slapped me.

"And stay away from Jaxon. The last thing I need is to come home and find out my little sister's been throwing herself at him like some desperate schoolgirl. *Again*." His voice sharpens to a sneer. "You think he'll fuck you like it means something? He's fucked half the pussy in Manhattan. You think you'd be special?"

His chuckle is nothing less than a cold shiver down my spine.

"You'd just be another faceless whore he slid his cock into so keep your goddamn legs closed."

My throat closes because that stings more than anything he's ever said to me.

He hangs up. Just like that. No chance for me to say anything back. No chance to defend myself or tell him I hate him or that I'm going to let his best friend fuck me until I can't walk anymore.

The silence in the studio roars.

I stare down at my drafting table. I've already made a mess—pencils scattered, eraser crumbs everywhere—but isn't that what artists are supposed to do? Make a mess?

But maybe I can do something to clean this mess up. I have so much money left from Jaxon and the second half isn't even in my account yet. Won't be until the contract is over.

I could have enough now to set up a different future for us. Mom and me. Find better medicine, better treatments to help her. Find a way to cut the bindings Jonathan has placed around me.

I grab a fresh sheet of paper from the oversized pad and

pick up my graphite pencils, but the lines come out too soft. Too... polite. It doesn't match what's boiling in my chest.

I drop the pencil and reach for a thick stick of charcoal instead. It's heavy, unforgiving. The black smudges bite into the paper with every stroke—harsh, ugly lines, just like Jonathan's words. My hand moves fast, almost frantic, sketching shadows and walls, blending with my fingers until my skin's stained gray.

The picture takes shape before I've even thought it through. A little girl, crouched in the corner of a dark room, knees tucked to her chest, her hands clamped over her ears.

When I stop, my breathing's hard, my tears dry and tight on my cheeks.

I set the charcoal down and pick up my graphite again. Slowly, carefully, I draw one last detail—a single tear sliding down the little girl's face.

My mind won't stop replaying Jonathan's voice, over and over, spitting words meant to stick like burrs under my skin. *Stay away from Jaxon. Desperate schoolgirl. Whore.*

Except the reality doesn't match the picture he's painting. Jaxon's been nothing but careful with me—almost *too* careful. He's made sure my firsts were on my terms, that I wasn't just... swept along. My first time being *properly* fingered, my first time grinding in someone's lap until I came—he could've taken more, but he didn't.

And yet... I've seen the photos. The women on his arm at every event. A different face each time. Glossy hair, expensive dresses, perfect smiles. Like they're accessories to the suit and the watch.

Jonathan's wrong about a lot, but he's not wrong about this—Jaxon isn't mine, and I can't forget it.

I can't forget what I'm hiding from him. I have to keep my distance. I have to walk away at the end of this month with my heart intact, and he needs to let me.

Except... it's hard to keep your distance when someone keeps pulling you closer.

I push away from the drafting table and wander down the hall, more to get out of my own head than anything else.

I peek in Jaxon's office and he's on a call. I hear words that tell me shit is hitting the binary code fan.

Outage.

Failover.

He's got a black sharpie marker and he's busy writing things that could as well be ancient Greek for all I know. It looks stressful but he looks like he's in his element, so I don't bother him.

The fridge is a sad graveyard of takeout boxes.

I don't know how he lives like this, especially when his mom is such a great cook. Not "fancy restaurant" great— just food that's made with love. Steam that curls around you when you lean in to smell it and makes all your problems go away.

Yup. That's what I need. Something hot. Delicious. Something made with love.

One memory slips in. *"I'll tell you the secret ingredient."*

Sandy whispered while I rolled another meatball in my hand. I could barely see over the counter, so I was standing on a step stool next to her.

It makes me smile and I know exactly what will cheer me up.

I also know Jaxon will enjoy something not in a takeout container for a change.

I check the fridge and pantry, half-expecting to be disappointed, but you'd think this bitch is in this kitchen whipping up three meals a day with how much food is in here.

All the labels tell me someone stocks this for him. Probably cooks with it too so I suppose it's okay.

Inspiration hits and I start grabbing ingredients.

I roll up my sleeves, turn on the recessed speakers, and scroll until I land on something upbeat. Before long, a tiramisu trifle is in the fridge setting for dessert later. The kitchen smells like browning meat and simmering sauce. I set a big pot of pasta water on to boil, toss a salad together, and slice bread for garlic toast.

From down the hall, Jaxon's voice carries—low, clipped, and all business. "No, I don't care what the vendor says. If the load balancer's not up in the next five minutes, you tell them I'll be on the next flight and it won't be a friendly visit."

He strides in a moment later, phone still pressed to his ear, sleeves pushed to his forearms. He's the picture of controlled fury, rattling off instructions about data centers and backup servers, barely even looking my way—until the smell hits him.

Mid-sentence, he stops walking. His eyes lock on the stove. His brow furrows. And then, without a word, he ends the call with a sharp, "Handle it."

The phone hits the counter. "What is that?"

"Dinner," I say, like it's the most obvious thing in the world. "You're leaving?" I try to hide the disappointment.

"No. I already fixed the problem I just like making him sweat. My script will run in…" He looks at his watch. "Four minutes and thirty seconds and the data center will be back online." He comes closer, gaze fixed on the simmering pot. "*You* cooked?"

"Yes, Jaxon. I'm capable of boiling water."

"This smells like my mom's sauce. Which I know to be impossible because—"

He picks up the spoon, dips it into the sauce, and takes a taste. The second it hits his tongue, something in his expression changes. His eyes narrow, slow and calculating, like he's just caught me committing some kind of culinary crime.

"*She* gave *you* the secret ingredient."

I pretend not to know what he's talking about. "What ingredient?"

He points the spoon at me like it's evidence. "Don't play dumb, Cricket. My mother swore she'd take that to her grave."

I shrug. "Maybe I figured it out on my own."

"Bullshit." He sets the spoon down, stalking toward me. "Tell me."

"Not a chance."

Before I can retreat, he's closing the distance, herding me backward until my lower back hits the counter. He braces one palm beside my hip, leaning in just enough that I have to tip my chin up to keep his gaze.

"Garlic?" he guesses.

I smirk. "Obviously. Try harder."

"Wine?"

"Warmer."

"Red pepper flakes."

I shake my head. "You're terrible at this."

His eyes narrow, but there's a spark there now—playful, dangerous. He presses in until my hips are flush with the counter, his chest brushing mine. Then he leans in, close enough that I feel the warmth of his breath against my neck.

"Last chance," he murmurs before kissing the sensitive skin just beneath my ear.

I suck in a breath, but keep my voice steady. "Still not telling you."

He moves to the other side, lips grazing my jaw this time. "What if I wear you down?"

"You'd have to try harder than that," I whisper, though my hands have already found the edge of his shirt. Trailing under to touch his skin.

He pulls back just enough to meet my eyes, our mouths so close they could touch if one of us so much as blinked wrong. His voice drops. "Can I kiss you again?"

The question catches me off guard—not just the words, but the way he says them. Careful. Like he's asking for something fragile.

I nod, and he starts to close the distance—then pauses, lips hovering. "Can we make that an open authorization? Saves me having to ask every time—"

"Just kiss me, Jaxon."

His grin turns wicked. "Yes, ma'am."

The kiss is instant heat, deep and hungry. His hands find

my ribs, mine slide under his shirt, and then we're not just kissing—we're devouring. Tongues, moans, the press of his body into mine like he's been starving for this.

Something hisses behind me, sharp and angry, and I jerk back.

"Shit—!"

I push him away, spinning to the stove where the pot is boiling over. I grab the box of pasta and dump the noodles in, steam rushing up into my face.

Behind me, Jaxon's voice is pure amusement. "So the secret ingredient is... neglect? Just let everything boil over until it develops 'flavor'?"

"Says the man who flambés eggs." I shoot him a look over my shoulder. "And for the record, you're never getting the secret ingredient out of me."

He starts pulling plates and silverware from the cabinets, still smirking. "You know, I can figure out the world's most difficult schematics in seconds... but this? This is apparently beyond me."

"Maybe she just loves me more than you," I say, tossing the pasta once for emphasis.

He comes up behind me, arms sliding around my waist, his lips brushing my neck. "That wouldn't be hard."

I bite down that jolt that runs through my stomach. *He's not mine.*

Dinner ends up being exactly what I needed—the perfect antidote to the mood Jonathan left me in earlier. Between the simmering sauce, the warmth of the bread, and Jaxon's easy grin across the table, I almost forget about my brother entirely.

Almost.

"Tell the truth," I say, narrowing my eyes over my fork, taking my last bite. "You tightened all the jars in the fridge on purpose. Didn't you?"

He doesn't even try to look innocent. "Or maybe I just don't know my own strength." His mouth tilts into a smug grin. "And you should talk—assaulting people with refrigerator doors."

I can't help laughing at the memory from a few days ago. The cereal that went flying. The milk dripping off the tip of his nose while he stood there like a statue.

"Oh, it's funny, huh?"

Before I can answer, a warm splatter of tomato sauce hits my shirt.

I gasp. "Did you just—"

"Not so funny now, huh?" Jaxon says, grinning like the devil licking sauce off his fingers.

I grab a piece of lettuce with just enough dressing to be dangerous and toss it at him. "You deserved it."

"Well, I think you deserve this."

The butter knife is already in his hand, loaded with a generous glob. Before I can dodge, he flicks it. The butter hits me dead in the face with a wet slap.

I freeze. He freezes. Then he bursts out laughing so hard he doubles over, gripping his stomach.

I wipe the butter off slowly, stand, and round the table. He's still laughing when I slide my fingers into a handful of sauced spaghetti noodles and stop right in front of him.

"You want to know something, Mr. Kane?"

His grin falters just slightly. "Do tell me."

"I went back to my room," I say sweetly, using my free hand to undo a button on his shirt, "and laughed my ass off at that stupid blue Fruit Loop that stuck to your cheek."

I stretch his shirt open at the collar, and shove the noodles down his chest. Flattening my hands over his shirt, I smear my hands, pressing the cold pasta into his skin through the fabric.

"Oh, come on!" He leans back in his chair with a strangled sound, eyes wide, sauce dripping down his shirt.

I return to my seat, victorious.

"Oh, you think you're walking away from this?" He grabs the salad bowl, takes a handful, and flings it at me. Lettuce, dressing, and tomato chunks hit my arm and shoulder. "Consider that a counter-offer."

I lob a slice of bread back at him, hitting him square in the chest. "Stop being a child."

He scoops up a meatball and nails me in the neck. "Haha! Bullseye."

"That's it."

We're both laughing now, working around the table, pulling plates and serving dishes to our sides like we're defending territory. I get my hands on the serving platter of meatballs, the sauce gleaming under the lights.

"Take cover!" He calls out like he's commanding troops to retreat.

He dives for the kitchen, shielding himself behind the open fridge door as I fire one at him. "Are you seriously lobbing beef grenades at me?"

Another meatball sails and splats inside against a shelf.

He stares at it... then looks at me with a dangerous glint and a sneaky smile.

"Jaxon. Don't you dare."

"Oh, Cricket." He shakes his head in mock disappointment. "My sweet Cricket."

He reaches in and pulls out the tiramisu trifle, setting the beautiful glass bowl on the table. Layers of cream and espresso-soaked cake stare me down like they know what's coming.

"I worked hard on that," I warn.

He digs in with one massive hand, scooping up a pile.

"And I work hard at making sure I win every fight I'm in."

Chapter 25

"Jaxon Thomas Kane," I point at him like that'll stop him.

He grins. "Oh, using my full government name. That gets me hard."

I'm trapped between him and a chair. He rubs his hands together slowly, deliberately, the dessert squishing between his fingers.

"Jaxon?"

"Cassidy?"

And then slow, almost sensual, he smears the tiramisu down both sides of my face, slathering me in espresso cream. I squeeze my eyes shut at the chill, the squish as he trails it down my neck, over my collarbone, and wipes the rest across my chest.

His hands slide down past my hips, over my ass, and grip the backs of my thighs. It's the only warning I get before he lifts me like I weigh nothing.

I yelp, scrambling to hook my arms around his neck, but

he doesn't take me far—just pivots and sits me on the table beside us, plates and cutlery rattling under the sudden shift.

Then his hand fists gently at the base of my hair, tilting my head to the side. His tongue is hot against my skin, dragging a slow, deliberate path up my neck, tasting the tiramisu he just smeared all over me.

"Now for the fun part," he mutters against my skin.

The next kiss isn't sweet at all—it's greedy, messy, open-mouthed. He leans me back so he can grind into me, and I feel just how turned on he is. My pulse is hammering, my body already responding, arching into him.

He sits me up again but doesn't break the kiss. His fingers skim the hem of my shirt, and I know exactly what he's asking. I lift my arms without hesitation.

The shirt hits the floor a second later.

His thumbs brush over the thin cups of my bra, and my nipples pebble instantly under the touch.

"Beautiful," he whispers, pressing his mouth to my cleavage, right where my breasts spill just enough from the cups.

A quick flick of his fingers behind me, and the clasp comes undone like it's nothing to him. He slides the straps off my shoulders slowly, almost reverently, until the bra is gone and I'm bare in front of him.

Heat floods my cheeks under the intensity of his stare. He doesn't look at my face—he's entirely focused on my breasts like he's committing them to memory.

"We're going to be such good friends," he says, leaning in to press kisses to the soft skin before fixing his mouth over one nipple, sucking it into his heat and making me arch with a gasp.

I'm not sure this is normal. To feel so aroused by his mouth on my nipples because I swear I could come from this alone.

"Were you just… talking to my breast?" I ask, breathless.

He moves to the other one without missing a beat. "Shhh. We're getting very well acquainted."

The second nipple is worse—so much worse—and I swear I feel the ache deep between my legs. My clit throbs, and before I even realize I'm doing it, I start moving my hips against him, desperate for friction.

He pulls back just enough to look at me. "Do you want me to stop?"

"Don't you dare." The words snap out of me before I can think, sharp and needy. I fist the front of his shirt and drag him closer until his mouth is on me again. He smiles against my skin like he knows exactly how undone I am, his tongue circling my nipple while his fingers tease the other, pinching and rolling until I'm shivering.

Then his free hand drifts lower, to the button of my jean shorts. A deft flick, and it's open. The slow rasp of the zipper follows, and my whole body goes tight.

"Can I taste you?" he whispers, his lips trailing kisses along the side of my breast, lower to the soft skin beneath, then down to my ribs.

I nod, my breath catching.

I lift my hips, and his hands—big, warm, sure—hook into the waistband of my shorts. He eases them down, slow and deliberate, until they're off and forgotten on the floor.

I'm perched on the table, legs parted on either side of him, wearing nothing but my panties.

Thin, damp panties.

He freezes for a moment, his eyes on me, and something primal darkens his expression. "Fuck, Cricket... look at you."

The back of his finger drags over my center, and I feel the wetness cling to him even through the thin fabric. Then he pushes the edge aside and slides lower, slow and unhurried, until his knuckle grazes my clit.

A flush creeps up my neck. No one has ever seen me like this—no one has ever touched me like this—and I'm suddenly, stupidly aware of the fact that I've been in these all day. That I'm soaked for him.

I try to press my legs together, but his hands are there, firm on my thighs, holding me open. "I haven't showered—"

His grip tightens, thumbs stroking slow circles into my skin like he's soothing me, but his voice is anything but soft.

"I don't care if you've been rolling in the damn dirt, Cassidy. I want you exactly like this—hot, messy, and fucking dripping for me."

He hooks his thumbs into my panties and works them down my legs with unhurried focus, like unwrapping a present he's been dying to open. When they're gone, he grabs a chair from the table and sits, pulling me closer until I'm right at the edge.

"You're mine, baby."

He takes my left foot, placing a tender kiss on my ankle and props my foot on the armrest. He does the same to the other, spreading me wide until I realize—I've just become the meal.

"I bought you." He looks up at me, dark eyes locked on mine.

"I own you."

He rubs his big hands up my calves, giving my knees a gentle push. "So open those legs and let me see what a billion dollars tastes like."

The first brush of his breath over me makes my stomach clench. I've never... no one's ever done this to me before. My mind is a storm of *what if it's weird, what if I don't like it, what if—*

Then his mouth is on me, and every thought is obliterated.

He starts with slow, deliberate licks up my center, parting me with his tongue like he's savoring the taste of something forbidden. "Sweet," he murmurs against me, the vibration sending a shiver up my spine. "Knew you'd taste like this."

My hands grip the edge of the table, knuckles white. I can't stop my hips from rocking forward, from chasing more of that warmth, that pressure. He flattens his tongue and drags it up again, ending with a soft flick over a spot that makes me gasp and jerk.

His dark eyes look up at me. "There it is. That's where you like it, isn't it?" He doesn't wait for my answer—just goes right back, teasing me with the tip of his tongue, circling, pressing, retreating.

It's overwhelming. Too much and not enough. My thighs tremble, and he notices, his hands sliding up to grip them tight, holding me open, keeping me exactly where he wants me.

"Relax, Cricket. Let me take you there." His voice is low, coaxing, but there's a command in it too. He licks and kisses my pussy like he's making out with it.

Then he closes his mouth over me and sucks—slow and deep—and my entire body bows off the table. My hand flies to his hair, fisting it, and he groans like I've just given him something he's been starving for.

"That's it. You like this?" he says, tongue flicking faster now, relentless, like he's set on wringing every drop of pleasure out of me.

"Yes."

The heat in my belly coils tighter, tighter. My breaths turn ragged, and I'm pushing back on the armrests but he holds me firm. Like it frustrates him I'm scooting away.

He fixes himself over my clit and sucks with a growl. I explode inside.

My orgasm rips through me hard and fast, my thighs clamping around his head as my hips buck. It's not graceful, not pretty—I cry out, raw and unguarded, every nerve alight. And he doesn't let up. He keeps working me through it, licking, sucking, swallowing every reaction I give him like it's the only thing he's ever wanted.

By the time he eases back, I'm boneless, shaking, my chest heaving. He presses a kiss to the inside of my thigh and looks up at me with that smug, wicked grin.

"Worth every fucking penny."

She's still catching her breath when I pull back, lips wet, chin slick from her. She looks wrecked—flushed cheeks, glassy eyes, chest heaving—and I should stop.

I don't.

She thinks I'm done. Sweet, innocent little Cricket. She has no idea. I've dreamt about this for years—what she'd taste like, the sounds she'd make when I finally had her the way I want her. And now that I know, I'm not fucking done until I get my fill.

I bend and drag my tongue over her again, slow and deliberate. She jolts, a startled gasp breaking from her lips, and tries to push at my shoulders. "Jax—too much—"

A low growl rumbles from my chest. I stand, grab her wrists in one hand, and grab her soaked panties off the table. I use them to bind her hands together. Her eyes go wide, breath hitching when I grab her chin and make her look at me.

"Lay back," I tell her, voice low and rough. "And don't disturb my meal again."

She swallows hard but obeys, lying back across the table, arms above her head. Her breasts rise and fall fast, and fuck if that view doesn't go straight to my cock.

I lean forward and take one nipple into my mouth, sucking slow and deep just to feel her gasp and arch for me. My hand cups the other breast, thumb brushing over the hardened peak until she's trembling. She's so damn responsive—every flick of my tongue or roll of my thumb makes her breathe harder. I wonder if I could make her come just from this alone. I'm absolutely going to try one day.

But not now. Right now, I need more of her.

I drop to my knees and spread her open again, hooking her thighs over my shoulders.

She sits her head up to look at me and I swear I see her pupils dilate more. Like she's seeing a fantasy play out for real. And fuck, I hope so.

"Holy shit." She breathes as she lays her head back down.

Then I go in—tongue sliding through her pussy, circling that perfect little bundle of nerves, sucking until her back arches.

"God, you taste even better the second time," I murmur against her, my lips brushing her sensitive skin. Her hips twitch up, her bound hands pulling against the panties, and I press her thigh harder into my shoulder, holding her still.

She's sensitive, every flick of my tongue making her moan louder. I work her slow at first—long licks, gentle sucks—until her breathing starts to stutter. Then I pick up the pace, tongue stroking fast, my hand sliding down and rubbing the lips of her pussy.

"Fuck—Jax—" Her voice is broken now, desperate, and it's all I can do not to come in my jeans from the sound of it.

My mouth seals over her clit, and she shatters—hips bucking, thighs clamping around my head, a raw, unfiltered cry tearing from her throat. Her fingers thread through my hair and she pulls.

I don't stop until every last tremor leaves her body. When I finally pull back, she's spread out on my table like a feast, arms still bound, chest heaving, hair wild.

And all I can think is… she's mine now, and I'm never letting her go.

I wipe my mouth with the back of my hand, then kiss a slow, wet path up her stomach, over her ribs, until I find her mouth. Her wrists are still bound in her panties, and I pull them over my head so her arms loop around me, holding me there while I kiss her deep—stealing every last trace of her from my tongue.

"You taste so fucking good," I murmur against her lips, hands sliding over her sides, her hips, committing every curve to memory. She's completely naked, warm and soft in my arms, while I'm still fully dressed.

I could strip and take her now. God knows I want to.

But not until she asks me to. Not until she *wants* it as much as I do.

"You look way too smug right now," she says, a teasing glint in her eyes.

My brow arches. "Oh yeah?"

She smirks. "Yeah."

I don't bother with a comeback. I just scoop her up bridal-style and start walking toward the patio doors.

Her eyes widen. "What are you—Jaxon—"

"Well, gotta clean the smug off me, don't you think?" I say simply, stepping outside into the warm night air, the faint chlorine scent of the pool mixing with the dried marinara still stuck to both of us from earlier.

We're halfway there when she blurts, "Your phone!"

I skid to a stop, fish it out of my pocket, and toss it onto a lounge chair without looking. "Good looking out, Crick."

Then I grin down at her. "Now plug your nose."

Before she can protest, I take off running and leap straight into the deep end with her in my arms.

We break the surface with a rush of air, my arms shifting her so her legs wrap tight around my waist, her breasts pressing flush to my chest. Water slides between us, but it's not enough to cool the heat curling low in my gut.

I hold her like I never want to let her go, my mouth finding hers in a kiss that's all teeth and tongue, slow grinds turning to deeper ones as her moans mix with mine.

"You're going to make me addicted to you," I breathe against her lips, backing her up until her back hits the smooth tile of the pool wall.

Then I let a grin cut through the heat as I unbind her wrists. "And I know with one hundred percent certainty you're already addicted to my mouth now."

I make a point to smell them, giving them a slow lick with the flat of my tongue, before I toss them to the edge of the pool.

She tilts her head, challenging. "Oh, is that right?"

"My poor tongue will probably never get another day of rest again."

"You're too cocky for your own good."

"You damn right I'm cocky," I murmur, sliding one hand down between us, finding her clit with my thumb and circling slow.

Her breath hitches.

"I could hand you a black card with no limit," I murmur, keeping the rhythm steady, "and dare you to try and bankrupt me."

She lets out a choked moan, her head tipping back, eyes fluttering shut.

"You can wear whatever the fuck you want when we go out—because I can fight."

Her body tenses around me, the telltale sign she's close, and I lean in, letting my words rasp against her ear.

"And when you ride me with this sweet pussy," I growl, nipping her bottom lip and tugging, "you can lean forward and kiss me without my big dick slipping out."

She shudders, teetering on the edge, and I press harder, faster. "So I'll talk all the shit I want."

Her release hits, body clenching, a low cry spilling from her lips.

"And you'll moan my name while I do it." I say, feeling her pulse under my hand.

"Oh, Jaxon..." she gasps, exactly how I like it.

"You're so fucking beautiful," I tell her, running my hands up her slick body, cupping her ass and giving it a hard squeeze. She grinds against my cock, and fuck, I want to be inside her so badly I can barely think.

"Jaxon... can I ask you a question?" she says, voice soft but with that glint in her eyes.

"Of course."

She backs away, bracing like she's about to lift herself out of the pool. I help her, my hands at her hips, guiding her until she's perched on the edge. Goosebumps race over her skin, her body glistening under the lights.

Then she leans back, props her feet on the ledge, and spreads her legs wide—giving me a perfect, unashamed view of her pretty little cunt.

"Will you eat me out again?" she asks with a smirk that nearly kills me.

"Fucking shit."

I flop backward in the water like I've passed out, coming up with a hand over my face. She's laughing, but she's not moving—just sitting there like the goddamn temptation she is.

"I wasn't prepared for that, Cricket," I admit, getting between her thighs and giving her pussy a slow, deliberate kiss.

"If you go get that little white bikini on..." I trail off, pulling myself partly out of the water to give her a chaste kiss on the lips.

She smiles, legs drawing in a bit. "I knew you liked it."

I take her back into the water with me, my arms locked low around her hips and ass, keeping most of her out of the pool so I'm looking up at her—and at my new best friends, her gorgeous breasts.

I suck one nipple into my mouth, walking her toward the steps.

"You almost killed me with that thing," I murmur against her.

She giggles, and I swear I'd do anything to hear that sound for the rest of my life.

"It took every ounce of power I had not to slide that little bikini to the side and taste you right there." I set her down at the steps, grip tightening. "Now you get your tight little ass back out here with that thing on—so you can sit on my face."

When she turns, I bite one cheek, making her squeal.

I peel my wet shirt off, toss it aside, and drop onto a lounge chair to wait.

When she comes back out, I let out a low whistle. "Fucking gorgeous." *And all mine.*

I stretch out. "Get my pussy up here."

She crawls onto the chair, hesitation in her movements, and I can tell she's nervous.

I help her along, guiding her exactly where I want her. "Sit. Fully. No hovering."

"You won't be able to breathe," she protests.

"If I die, then I die. The doors of Valhalla would open and welcome me—it'd be the most honorable death I could hope for."

Then I pull her down, take one long, slow swipe of her wet cunt with my tongue and groan deep.

And as her taste floods my mouth, the thought hits me hard and unshakable. *God, I hope she falls in love with me... because I'm already fucking gone for her.*

Chapter 27

Shanae's name flashes across my phone.

It almost went to voicemail before I could answer at the last second.

"Cassidy." Her voice is too fast, too sharp. "It's your mom. She's... something's wrong. I'm taking her to the ER."

The bottom drops out of my stomach. "What? What happened?"

"She's been dizzy and her breathing's shallow. She tried to brush it off, but—"

"Okay. I'll meet you there." I cut in, already moving. I shove my feet into the first shoes I see and grab my bag with shaking hands.

Jaxon's in his office, headset on, speaking in a low, commanding tone that says something's going wrong with one of his companies. From the sound of it, whatever's happening is big—voices on the other end are frantic, his jaw tight.

I hesitate in the doorway, knocking twice softly. "Jax—"

His gaze snaps to mine, reading me in an instant. He doesn't say *hold on* or *one minute*—he just pulls the headset off and ends the call. "What's wrong?"

"My mom... Shanae is taking her to the ER." My voice wavers, and I hate it. "I need to—"

"I'll drive you," he says, already standing.

"You're working—"

He crosses the space between us in two long strides, tilts my chin up with two fingers, and kisses me—slow, steady, grounding. "I'm driving."

There's no arguing with him when he uses that voice. The one that leaves no room for debate but still somehow makes me feel safe.

I nod, my throat too tight for words, and he's already grabbing his keys.

I've never been so grateful for Jaxon's reckless driving. Today, it feels like salvation instead of a death wish. We're there in record time—no stoplights, no hesitation—just the city blurring past.

Shanae is standing by the check-in desk when we walk in, clutching her phone, relief washing over her face. "Well you two got here fast," she says, waving us through the waiting room.

Mom looks up from the wheelchair, and her whole face brightens at the sight of us—like the pain and fear disappear just for a second. My chest tightens so hard it's almost painful.

But when I see her, the breath nearly leaves my lungs. She's thinner than the last time I was here—only a few days ago, but she can't afford to lose *any* weight.

Her clothes hang looser, her cheeks are a little more hollow.

I bite down on the shock, force a smile like nothing's wrong. She doesn't need my fear on top of whatever she's dealing with. The way Jaxon's fingers tighten around mine tells me he notices too. He doesn't say anything—he just stays solid and steady beside me.

T he ER feels quieter now. Mom's sitting on the edge of the bed, looking more like herself, a faint blush back in her cheeks.

The doctor explains she had a drop in blood pressure when standing up too quickly—likely made worse because of dehydration from the chemo and radiation. Not uncommon, nothing life-threatening today, but it caused the dizzy spell that scared Shanae.

They gave her fluids, adjusted a few medications, and want her to follow up with her oncologist in three days.

Jaxon's been keeping Mom laughing for the last hour—ridiculous one-liners, exaggerated stories, even trying to convince her that hospital pudding is *Michelin star* quality. I appreciate it more than he'll ever know. Every smile he gets out of her feels like a victory.

When he excuses himself to the bathroom, the nurse comes in with a clipboard and a stack of papers. Shanae steps forward instantly.

"I'll take care of those," she says, then glances at me. "Go sit with your mama for a bit."

I drag my chair closer to the bed, slipping my hand into Mom's and resting my head on it. She strokes my hair like she's done since I was little, slow, and soothing, like she can calm every ache with just her touch.

"So, you and Jackie?" she asks softly.

I lift my head a little. "Hm?"

"Jaxon." Her mouth curves. "I saw him holding your hand. Is something going on there?"

I open my mouth, close it again. "Oh, I... don't know."

She leans back against the pillows, studying me with that all-seeing mom gaze. "I'm not surprised. Honestly, I'm more surprised it's taken this long. That boy has always looked at you like you hung the moon."

"No he hasn't." My throat tightens, and I let out a watery laugh.

"A mother know's these things." She keeps rubbing my head and I let the words settle a moment.

"So, if he were my boyfriend... would you approve?"

She smiles, warm and sure. "I couldn't hand-pick someone better for you. He may not show it outright, but I know what a man in love looks like. And Jaxon Kane has got it bad. Your father looked at me like that for decades."

That makes my stomach twist—not entirely in a good way. Mom notices instantly, her hand stilling on mine.

"When Sandy applied to work for us," she says quietly, "she and Jaxon were in a real bad way. I didn't care if Sandy could do the work or not. I wasn't going to turn them away. Paid her double the listing and gave her an advance."

She pauses, her thumb brushing over my knuckles. "I

never knew the details of their life before, but I saw how hollow Jaxon's eyes were. He was such a sad little boy."

She squeezes my hand. "But his mama saved him. Showed him what love's supposed to look like. And I hope he saw that in our home too. I know he's got a lot of love to give."

My chest aches, the weight of her words pressing into me.

"I know it might seem strange because you've known each other so long," she says gently, "but if you feel it in your heart, baby... follow it."

The door swings open, and there's Jaxon, rolling Mom's wheelchair in like he's just come up with the cure for boredom. Shanae's right behind him, clearly in on whatever scheme he's cooking up.

"I've got a great idea, Lilly," he says, all mock-seriousness as he parks the chair beside the bed. "We steal another wheelchair and you and me race to the car."

Shanae snorts. "Lord, you're ridiculous."

I can't help it—I chuckle, and Mom throws her covers off with a sparkle in her eye. "Please, boy."

I step forward to help her stand while Jaxon steadies the chair. Shanae moves in to support her other side, and together we ease her down into the seat.

"You couldn't beat me if you got started yesterday," Mom says, patting his hand with a smirk.

Jaxon grins and glances over at me. "Well... at least I know where you get your sass from."

"Cassidy..."

The voice is faint, barely there, but I know it instantly. My mom.

I whip my head toward the sound, but the hallway is endless, swallowed in shadow. Machines buzz somewhere ahead, a dull, urgent hum. I run—at least I think I do—but my legs feel heavy, like I'm wading through water.

"Cass, where are you?"

It takes forever to reach her.

She's in the hospital bed, skin pale against the thin sheets.

"I'm here mama." I grab her hand and yank it back with a gasp. It's hard. Cold. Like she's already dead and long gone.

"No," I whisper, my chest caving in. I force myself to look at her face, but what's staring back at me makes my stomach turn.

Her eyes are glazed and lifeless, fixed on something just beyond me.

"No!" My hands fly to my mouth to hold back the sob threatening to tear me in half. I grab her hand again, patting it like I can warm it back to life. "Mama, please—"

"It's time to go." Jonathan is suddenly right next to me. His grip on my wrist is like iron, dragging me backward.

"Let me go!" I scream, swinging at him with my free hand. My fist connects with his arm, his chest, anywhere I can reach. No matter how hard I hit, it feels like I'm hitting nothing. "I need to say goodbye to her! *Let me say goodbye!*"

He doesn't look at me. Doesn't even blink. His jaw is locked, eyes straight ahead, face carved from stone.

"Please, Jonathan." My feet skid along the floor as he hauls me away, the bed—her—getting smaller, and smaller—

We're almost to the doorway when he finally turns. His voice is sharp, cutting through me.

"Wake up, Cricket."

The tone shifts mid-syllable, Jonathan's voice dissolving into Jaxon's.

"Wake up, Cricket."

I jerk upright, gasping. The hospital room is gone. The shadows rearrange into Jaxon's face, inches from mine, his near-black eyes locked on me with that same fierce intensity he always has when something's wrong.

"It's okay," he murmurs, his voice a lifeline in the dark.

Tears spill before I can stop them. "She died," I choke out. "She was dead."

"Oh. No, baby." He doesn't hesitate—just pulls me against him like he can physically shield me from the dream. His chest is warm, his scent grounding me as he tucks my head under his chin. His leg hooks over mine, his arms tightening until I'm wrapped in him completely, hidden away from the world.

"I've got you," he whispers, stroking my hair. "She's okay. You're okay. I'm right here."

And I let myself sink into that safety, sobbing into his skin until the ache in my chest is the only thing left keeping me awake.

Chapter 28

Jaxon

The tray's heavy in my hands, but the smell makes it worth it—biscuits and gravy, eggs, crispy tater tots, coffee still steaming, and a single white lily in a bud vase. I nudge the door open with my shoulder and pause in the doorway.

She's still asleep.

Raven-black hair spilled across the dark satin pillowcase, lips parted just slightly, face soft without the usual guarded edge. Yeah... I could get used to this. Waking up to her and this view every damn day.

She stirs, a small stretch under the covers, and I step in.

"Hey," She says sleepily.

"Don't worry... I didn't blow up the kitchen," I say, keeping my voice low, teasing.

She pushes up on one elbow and rubs her eye.

"Jaxon, you didn't have to—"

"I didn't," I cut in. "My chef's here prepping some meals, so I put in a special request."

I set the tray on her lap, and she immediately notices the flower, brushing her fingertips over the white petals. I lean down, kiss the side of her head, then move to the other side of the bed and slide in under the covers with her.

She reaches for the coffee first, but her eyes are already darting to the food.

"Ooh, it's my favorite."

"I know."

Her grin widens as she lifts the lid. "Even eggs and tater tots?"

"And sausage biscuits with gravy a little spice the way you like," I say.

She gets her silverware, building her *perfect bite*—something she is very insistent on for select meals. A bit of egg on the biscuit, then a tater tot, then a generous scoop of sausage gravy to crown it.

"Mmm." She closes her eyes on the first chew, sighing like she just bit into heaven. "This is the best biscuits and gravy I've ever had."

I try to keep my face neutral, but inside I'm doing cartwheels. She likes my breakfast the most.

She feeds me a bite, and, yeah—it's fucking good. I steal a sip of her coffee, and we fall into a rhythm of sharing the plate between us. I talk about one of my companies—a new datacenter that's coming online—and she shows me pictures Big Ben sent of Saving Grace and Dominion.

"Not bad," I say, studying the shots. "He's actually got a good eye for photography. Would've never guessed it."

She nudges me with her knee under the blanket, mock-offended.

I wait until the moment feels right before I ask, careful with my tone, "Speaking of very talented artists... will you let me sit with you in your studio while you paint?"

She freezes, coffee cup halfway to her mouth, and I can see the flicker of nerves in her eyes. I let her sit with it, no pressure, just quiet between us for a moment.

"I can even throw in this last tater tot as a bribe." I tease, spearing the last one and holding out the fork to her.

Finally she smiles a little and says, "Okay."

***

The art room I made for her doesn't look like my space anymore. Hell, it doesn't even look like a room I'm letting her borrow. It's hers—solely and completely hers. The easel's set just so, a scattering of brushes and tubes of paint on the table, one of her sweaters draped over the back of the stool like it lives here.

I brought my laptop, but I'm not sitting at the desk. Instead, I drop down onto a floor pillow, lean my back against the wall, legs stretched out with one ankle crossed over the other. I keep my posture lazy, like I've got work to focus on, even though we both know I'm watching her.

She puts on some low music and stands in front of a blank canvas, just staring at it. I think maybe she's nervous with me here. Not everyone wants an audience while they work, and I can be... a lot.

But then she moves, grabbing a brush and a few other tools, and I realize she wasn't stalling—she was deciding.

And then... it's beautiful. Not just the painting, but the

way her mind works. How she sees things. She mixes paint with pastels, works in bold strokes and delicate touches, adds gold leaf in places like she's hiding treasure in plain sight. Sometimes she dilutes the paint, letting it drip down in chaotic streams that somehow make the whole thing more balanced.

I don't even realize how much time passes until I'm pulling out my phone and snapping a few shots of her. She doesn't notice—she's too deep in whatever world she's creating.

One picture in particular stops me. She's bent forward slightly, face tilted in concentration, hair falling loose around her cheeks, brush poised on the canvas. She looks... peaceful.

I turn it black and white, and the light catches her just right, softening the edges while still showing that fire in her expression. Yeah... this one's perfect.

I set it as my lock screen, glance at it one more time, and slide my phone into my pocket, a smile tugging at my mouth.

She's stepped back, one arm folded over her chest, the other holding the tip of a paintbrush between her teeth. She tilts her head one way, then the other, studying the canvas like she's weighing its worth.

I push up from the floor and come up behind her, wrapping my arms around her waist. I press a kiss to the side of her head, breathing in the floral scent of her shampoo.

"It's beautiful," I murmur against her ear.

She leans back into me, her head resting against my chest, and from here I can see the whole thing better. It's her

—painted in deep, layered shades of green, surrounded by abstract lilies that seem to bloom right out of the canvas.

"Thanks," she says softly. "I thought my mom would like to have it in her room."

I pull her tighter against me. "She'll love it," I promise, kissing her again. "We can take it to her when it's dry."

She nods and turns in my arms, looping her hands around my neck.

"What are your paintings, really?" I ask, curious.

She plays it off with a shrug. "Just... silly paintings."

"I know they're not," I tell her, but she just smiles like she's not ready to give me more, and leans in to kiss me.

Fuck, I could kiss her all day. Her soft lips, the slow sweep of her tongue—it pulls my stomach tight, and my cock's getting harder by the second. My hands roam over her, gripping her ass and pulling her flush against me.

She breaks the kiss, lips plump, cheeks pink. She looks like sin wrapped in innocence, and it's mine—at least right now.

She bites her lip and holds her breath, eyes darting away. I narrow mine.

"What?" I ask, suspicion edging my tone.

She hesitates, like she's fighting herself. "C-can..." Her voice falters, then steadies. "...Can we go sit outside for a minute?"

The way she says it—quiet, careful—puts a weight in my chest. Something's coming, and I'm not going to like it.

Still, I nod. "Yeah." I lace my fingers through hers and lead her toward the terrace, the sinking feeling growing heavier with every step.

Chapter 29
Cassidy

Outside on his private balcony, it's warm—sunlight spilling across the wood planks, the faint scent of the ocean drifting in from somewhere beyond the city. The breeze is light enough to ruffle my hair but not enough to steal the heat from the day. Puffy clouds drift lazily overhead, moving slower than my heart is beating.

Jaxon sits back in one of the chairs, lounging like he's got all the time in the world, while I pace the length of the balcony like a caged animal. My stomach twists tighter every time I glance his way.

He's watching me—waiting. His knee bounces like it's trying to burn a hole through the floor.

"Jesus, Cassidy," he says finally, voice edged with impatience. "You're killing me."

"I'm sorry..." My voice cracks, my eyes dart anywhere but him. "I'm just... nervous."

I bite down on a nail without thinking, and that's when he starts to rise out of the chair.

"No." I hold my hand out quickly, stopping him. "I need you sitting."

His brow furrows. "Christ."

I suck in a breath. This is it. Now or never. My brain is screaming at me to just spit it out, but my body's moving before I can think it through. I grab a cushion from the empty chair beside him and set it on the floor in front of him. His eyes narrow slightly, surprise flickering there.

Then I kneel.

My hands find his thighs, fingers splayed against the firm muscle, but I keep my eyes down. If I look at him too soon, I'll lose my nerve.

His voice drops low, dark, and smooth enough to roll down my spine. "What are we doing, Cricket?"

A shiver races through me. My thumbs trace the seams of his jeans before sliding higher. I'm still staring at my hands, but every inch of me is hyperaware of him—his heat, his size, the weight of his focus pressing into me.

"It's just…" My throat feels like it's closing. "I've never…"

I swallow hard, forcing the rest out.

One of his large hands cups my jaw, tilting my face up until I'm trapped in the molten steel of his gaze. His thumb brushes over my lower lip, slow and deliberate. "Tell me."

I lean into his touch, eyes fluttering closed for a second before I open them again. Deep breath.

"I've never seen a… penis," I whisper, cheeks flaming, "like… up close."

The grin that spreads over his face nearly melts my bones—and my panties.

I rush to clarify, words tumbling over themselves because we both know I've seen his—from across a room—with *two* women *obstructing* the view.

"I mean, you know I've seen... and I've watched porn before. On my phone. You know. But... not up close."

He leans back, his grin turning wicked. Then he sinks lower in the chair, legs spreading wider. "You want to look at my cock, baby? Have at it."

My breath catches.

He laces his fingers together and rests them behind his head like he's settling in for a show and I simultaneously want to slap him and climb him like a tree.

But with a deep breath I reach for the button of his jeans, hands trembling. I glance up at him for one last second before flicking it open. The zipper slides down slow, the sound far too loud in the quiet between us.

He lifts his hips just enough to help me tug them down a few inches, and I see the unmistakable outline straining against the fabric of his boxers.

I can't help it—I run my palm over him. Solid. Hot.

His breath escapes in a deep, satisfied sound—like my touch is something he's been waiting for. Or maybe it's the fact that I'm finally giving it.

My fingers trace the outline again, slower this time, feeling every ridge and curve through the thin fabric. I glance up at him, but he's watching me through half-lidded eyes, jaw tight, a muscle ticking there like he's fighting to stay still.

I hook my fingers over the waistband of his boxers, hesitating just long enough to feel my pulse in my ears. Then I tug them down and his cock thumps on his stomach.

"Oh,"

He's thick. Heavy. Hard in a way that makes my mouth go dry and my heart trip over itself. My fingers hover for a second, uncertain, before I wrap one hand around him.

God, he's so hot—literally hot—in my palm. Smooth skin stretched over steel.

He exhales through his nose, slow but sharp, like he's trying not to give me too much. That makes me bolder. I run my hand from the base to the tip, my thumb brushing over the bead of slick at the crown.

His breath catches, and it shoots straight through me, low and electric.

I try again, a little firmer this time, and his hips shift just barely toward my hand. A small, involuntary movement, but I feel it—and I like it. I grip him a little tighter, moving in a slow rhythm.

"Yeah," he murmurs, voice deep and rough, eyes locked on mine now. "Just like that, Cricket."

I lick my lips without thinking, my gaze flicking between my hand and his face. His head tips back just a little, the muscles in his neck going taut, and watching him fight for control does something to me.

My thumb circles over the head again, and his breath shudders. "Fuck…"

That word, from him, makes me squeeze just a little harder, experimenting. His hips shift again, like he can't help it, and my stomach flips. I'm turning him on. I'm making him squirm.

And I don't want to stop.

I keep my pace slow but deliberate, my other hand bracing against his thigh. The more I touch him, the more I feel my own body heat rising, this strange ache blooming low in my belly. It's intoxicating—the weight of him in my hand, the way he's letting me explore, the way every reaction feels like a reward.

"Look at you," he says, voice low and dark, his eyes dragging over my face. "First time touching a cock and you're already killing me."

I don't answer. I just tighten my grip a little, sliding my hand down again, watching the way his stomach muscles tighten.

And now I'm wondering what other sounds I can pull out of him.

I lick my lips again, heat crawling up my neck.

"Can I..."

"I don't care what you do," he says, voice low and rough, "as long as you get your mouth around my dick."

A slow grin tugs at my lips. I slide closer, both hands wrapping around him, and he grips the armrest like it's the only thing keeping him from losing it. His head dips back as I start stroking, twisting my wrists in opposite directions the way I've seen in videos.

"You'll tell me what to do?" I ask, needing to hear it.

His hand threads along my jaw and into my hair, his fingers curling at the base of my skull. "Yeah, baby. I got you."

The reassurance makes my stomach tighten. I lean forward, running my tongue along the underside of him, tasting salt and heat. I circle the head once, a second time, and he lets out this low groan that makes me want to hear it again.

"Swirl your tongue around the head," he murmurs, voice almost breaking.

I do it, slow and deliberate, and his mouth drops open.

"Oh, god... baby, that's perfect."

The praise makes me bolder. I close my lips around him, taking him into my mouth inch by inch, feeling the weight and heat fill me. I pull back and go again, a little deeper this time.

"That's it," he breathes, his fingers tightening in my hair. "You're a natural."

I keep moving, slow at first, then finding a rhythm as he guides me gently. "Add your hand. Squeeze and slide it with your mouth."

I follow his lead without hesitation, wrapping my fingers around the base and stroking in time with each pass of my lips. His hips shift just slightly, like he's fighting to keep still, and I know he's close.

"Slow down," he warns, voice strained. "I'm not gonna last like this..."

But I like that—knowing I'm the reason he's losing control. I go faster instead, sucking harder, taking him deeper until my throat flutters.

"Fuck—Cassidy," he groans, swearing and praising in the same breath. "God, you're so beautiful... messy for me like this... look at you."

Both of his hands are in my hair now, holding it back so he can watch every second. His eyes are dark, locked on my mouth, and the way he looks at me makes my thighs press together.

"I'm gonna come," he says, his voice almost pleading. "You wanna swallow it?"

I shake my head, not stopping.

"Okay, baby... keep your hand on me," he says, his own hand sliding down to wrap over mine. "God. Almost, Cricket. Keep going."

This is making me so wet. I didn't think I would like it this much. Maybe it's him though and I love unraveling him.

My spit is running down his shaft and I'm sucking faster, sliding my hand quicker and he looks like he's about to combust.

"Oh, fuck me." He's panting, eyes never looking away from me. "Fuck, baby. Yes."

I don't mean to moan but I do because the way he sounds is making my pussy clinch.

"Ah, that's it. Okay, watch baby."

Together we stroke him, my mouth pulling back so I can take him all in.

"God damn Cassidy."

His whole body goes tense, and then hot, thick spurts spill over our fingers. My eyes flick between his face—jaw clenched, mouth open, eyes half shut—and his cock as his release oozes down our hands.

He's panting, cursing under his breath. I'm still curious.

Before I can second-guess it, I lean in and give him a slow lick.

"Fuck," he groans, head tipping back like I just broke him.

I taste him—salty, warm—and it's not bad at all. I like it. I lick again, slower this time, just to watch him shudder.

I let go of him and make a point to drag my tongue from the base all the way to the tip, my eyes never leaving his.

The way he looks at me—like I just became his entire religion—sets me on fire. I'm so close to asking him to fuck me. I want it... God, I want it.

But the words stop in my throat. My nerves choke them back.

I know he wants it too—he's been holding back for me.

"Come on, beautiful," he says softly.

He takes my hands and helps me stand. From the side table, he grabs a towel and hands it to me for my mouth and fingers. By the time I've wiped away the evidence, he's already put himself away.

Then he's in front of me, standing tall, taking my face in both hands and kissing me like I just gave him something priceless.

"That was fucking incredible," he says against my lips.

"Really? It was... okay?"

"Better than okay. That was the best blow job of my life."

My lips curve into a smile, and I let him kiss me again, welcoming the slow slide of his tongue in my mouth.

"You hungry?" he asks.

I nod, still smiling.

"I have an idea," he says, that glint in his eyes that means trouble. "The chef left pizza dough. I have a pizza oven."

I give him a cautious look. "Is that really safe?"

He laughs. "Yeah, this I can actually cook. It's just ingredients... and it's already on fire."

I snort, and he wraps his arms around me. "So... pizza?"

"Pizza," I agree.

"And Glee?"

My smile grows wider. "Glee."

"And each time they sing," he says, voice dropping wickedly low, "I get to eat your pussy."

"Jaxon!" I smack his chest, but I'm laughing.

"You'll have a tongue cramp before the first episode is over," I tease.

"I'm fine with that," he says, dead serious as he bends down and lifts me over his shoulder.

"Jaxon Kane!" I smack his ass and he smacks mine back.

"I can survive a tongue cramp as you sit that sweet cunt on my face a few times tonight."

Chapter 30

Jaxon

I'm in love with her.

I haven't fully said it to myself—not out loud, not even in my own head without qualifiers—but it's been there for a long time. Maybe forever.

I've danced around it. Convinced myself it was too soon, too messy, too dangerous. But the truth? There's no one else. There never has been.

I know I need to tell her everything. About that night at the party six years ago. Why I did what I did. That I love her. That I don't want these thirty days to end.

I don't give a damn about the contract. I never have. I just want her.

So tonight, I've planned something. A night out, and a surprise.

I texted her earlier: *Be ready at 8 p.m.*

She immediately tried to pry for details, but I didn't give an inch.

When she pushed harder, I teased her: *Tell me the secret ingredient, and I'll tell you the surprise.*

Of course, she stayed stubborn, refusing to cave.

Fine, I told her. *I'll send something to the penthouse for you.*

The dress arrived less than an hour later—a deep emerald that will make her eyes burn brighter than the city lights. The cut will hug every curve I can't stop thinking about, like it was sewn for her and only her.

Now I'm waiting on the rooftop of Ember and Ash, a swanky, exclusive steakhouse tucked inside a lavish hotel one of my buddies owns. The whole space is lit in a soft golden glow—overhead fixtures humming low and steady, fire torches flickering against the warm summer night.

My phone buzzes from my driver with a text they've arrived.

A few moments later, the hotel's maître d' leads her through the glass doors and into the rooftop's open air.

And fuck... I wasn't ready for her.

She's a vision.

More beautiful than I even let myself imagine.

She steps out onto the rooftop, the soft light catching on every glimmer of that dress, and I have to remind myself to breathe.

"Jesus, Cricket... you're beautiful." My voice is low, reverent. "More than beautiful."

Her lips curl into a smile. "You clean up nice yourself, Kane. All black, huh?" Her gaze slides down me, slow and deliberate. "Trying to look dangerous?"

I smirk. "No trying necessary."

She laughs, and I take her hand, bringing her knuckles to

my lips. "I've been staring at this dress all day in my head. You managed to make it look better."

She rolls her eyes, but her cheeks flush. The maître d' appears with perfect timing, and I release her hand only long enough to pull out her chair.

The first course arrives—plated like art, flavors that hit like fireworks. I expect nothing less from one of Manhattan's richest men... after me, of course.

Dinner flows easily. No pretense, no roles, no games. Just her and me. We talk, we laugh—easier than I thought possible—and somewhere between her biting into a perfectly seared steak and me stealing the last roasted carrot from her plate, I know it with certainty.

She's it.

I need to make her mine. Forever.

But every time I think about starting the conversation— about telling her what happened six years ago and why I did it—the words get stuck. I tell myself I'll wait for the right moment.

After dessert, the low hum of music drifts through the rooftop speakers. I know the playlist by heart—I made it. Which is why I'm already grinning before she even tilts her head and says, "Is this... the *Glee* soundtrack?"

I shrug. "Might be."

She laughs, shaking her head, but then *Marry You* starts, and I can't resist. I catch her wrist and pull her to her feet before she can protest.

"I don't dance," she says, already trying to dig her heels in.

"Good thing I do." I spin her once, then pull her close,

while I sing along. She's stiff at first, hesitant, but a few steps later she's laughing, letting me twirl her again.

When the song slows toward the end, I pull her back in, lowering my voice.

"'Cause it's a beautiful night. We're looking for something dumb to do. Hey baby…"

She's smiling at me, waiting for me to say the line.

I think I wanna marry you.

But I don't. I lean in and kiss her instead.

The city stretches out below us, lights glittering like spilled diamonds. She leans on the railing, catching her breath as the wind teases her hair, and I can't stop watching her.

When the last sip of wine is gone and the night air has cooled just enough to make her shiver, I take her hand and lead her toward the exit.

Her heels click against the stone until we reach the street. My driver waits beside the limo.

I open the door, but instead of letting her in, I spin her around and pin her gently against the sleek black frame. Her breath catches, eyes wide, right before I kiss her—slow and deep, tasting wine and something far sweeter.

When I pull back, my voice is rough. "Let's get going, beautiful."

She turns to climb in, but I can't resist. My hand slides over the curve of her ass, giving it a deliberate squeeze. She squeals, swatting at me as she ducks into the car.

I follow, grinning like a man who knows exactly what he's doing.

God, I hope I don't fuck this up.

The limo slows, pulling up in front of an old brick building wedged between a taller one that's just as aged and a sleek glass-front structure on the other side. No signage. No flashing lights. Just brick, shadows, and curiosity tightening her features.

I step out first, offering my hand to help her down. "It's an art gallery," I tell her. "There's a special artist being featured tonight."

Her brows lift slightly, and I guide her toward the door where Clara waits, sharp as ever in a fitted black dress. Clara's work fills the front of the exhibit—bold, unapologetic pieces that demand attention.

Clara's a former Ledger Companion, retired and on fire in the art world now, with Lucian as one of her biggest contributors.

"Cassidy, meet Clara," I say, watching their hands clasp.

"It's a pleasure," Clara says warmly. "Enjoy the featured works in the back. They're... worth it."

Cassidy drifts inside like the space belongs to her, eyes catching on every canvas. She walks slow, studying each piece, taking in the brushstrokes, the layers, the texture. I can see the gears turning—how she'd paint it, how she'd mix the colors.

I've been waiting all night for what's coming.

We round the corner into the back gallery, and she's talking to me about the last painting's technique, her hands gesturing as she explains.

Then she sees them.

Her paintings.

Her mouth parts, eyes wide, her gaze locking on the display like she's seeing ghosts.

"I had some help from Shanae picking a few out," I say, stepping closer, ready to watch her light up.

But she doesn't.

She's not amazed—she's... horrified.

Her eyes fix on the largest canvas. The one she's been hiding away, working on in the studio I set up for her.

Tears pool instantly, shimmering in the gallery light. "Why would you do this?"

"Baby, what—" My confusion hits like a brick. This is not how I saw tonight going.

Her gaze darts to the people milling about, glancing at her work. Her hand clamps over her mouth like she's holding in a sob, and the tears break free, sliding down her cheeks.

Fuck.

"Cassidy, I'm sorry—"

"How could you do this to me?" Her voice is soft but laced with a gut punch that nearly knocks the air from my lungs.

She turns, moving fast, and I'm right on her heels.

She bursts outside into the cooler night air, but I catch her arm, turning her toward me. "Talk to me."

Her arms fold across her chest, her whole body curling in like she's bracing against something. "Those are private, Jaxon."

The words slice clean. She looks so much smaller like

this, and I hate it—hate that I put that expression on her face.

"Cass, I'm sorry," I say, reaching to smooth my hands down her arms, desperate to pull her back into me—into the warmth we had all night.

But she flinches like my touch burns. Turns away, hugging herself. Shutting me out.

"Can we just go home?"

The words are quiet, but they gut me.

I stand there for a beat too long, trying to process how the hell this all went sideways. I'd pictured her lighting up when she saw the walls filled with her work—beaming, proud, maybe even a little overwhelmed, but in a good way. I wanted tonight to be special. Something she'd never forget.

I guess I got the unforgettable part right. Just not the way I intended.

"Is this about... I know there is something you're not telling me, baby."

I search her face for a crack in her armor, for any sign that maybe this is just initial shock and I can explain. But her expression is locked down tight—hurt, angry, something deeper I can't put my finger on.

"Cass..." My voice comes out lower than I mean it to, almost pleading. "It wasn't about showing them off to anyone else. It was about showing *you* what I see when I look at you. What you're capable of. You don't know how fucking good you are—"

Her head shakes once, sharp. "Please, Jaxon. Just... take me home."

That please isn't soft. It's a wall slamming shut.

My jaw tightens until my teeth ache. My hands curl at my sides because if I touch her again and she pulls away, I'm not sure I can take it. I swallow the hundred things I want to say—explanations, apologies, the truth about why I wanted this night, about how long I've loved her. None of it will land right now.

I give her one last look, committing every detail of her to memory in this moment—not the one I wanted, but the one I've got—then I nod.

"Yeah," I say quietly.

I open the limo door for her, letting her slide inside first. The driver catches my eye in the rearview, but I shut the door on whatever question he's got sitting on his tongue.

Tonight was supposed to be hers.

And now I'm terrified it still is—just for all the wrong reasons.

Chapter 31

Cassidy

The studio is dark except for the silver wash of moonlight spilling through the windows. It paints the floor in long, cold streaks, glinting off the jars of brushes and the edges of my easel.

Some of the canvases are gone.

The big one—the one I'd shoved behind other pieces so no one, *especially him*, would see it—it's gone. And not just gone but on display. Hanging on a wall for anyone to look at.

The others too. The pieces I paint when I can't breathe. When the air feels thick and heavy, and I need somewhere to put the memories before they eat me alive. The ones that bleed my pain in color and shadow. My prison, my invisible scars.

My brother never left a mark that would last on the outside. He was too smart for that. A bruise here and there, gone in days. But inside... inside they never faded.

These paintings—they're my only way to bleed without

breaking skin. And Jaxon just... took them. Put them up like they were trophies.

Tears sting my eyes and slide down my cheeks before I can stop them.

Tonight was so perfect. *He* was so perfect. The way he looked at me at dinner, the way his touch lingered like it meant something more.

It feels like it's more than the contract. And it can't be.

I want it to be. God, I *want* it. But there's something he doesn't know. The reason I keep refusing him, no matter how badly I want to give in. The reason I started this whole thing in the first place.

And then there were his words, out on the street.

"It was about showing you what I see when I look at you."

He didn't see the jagged, ugly pain in those strokes. He didn't see the bruises that never made it to skin. He saw *me*. And maybe—just maybe—he was trying to show me that it isn't ugly. That it's worth something. Worth showing. Worth being proud of. Even if he doesn't know the truth of it all.

And now I feel... stupid. Like I was so wrapped up in my fear that I couldn't see his intention until it was too late.

Like a jerk, because he did all of this for me. Every bit of tonight. Not as part of some deal to get me into his bed, not as leverage, not for the contract.

Just because he cares about me.

And I didn't let myself realize it until now.

It just feels like this is all too much. My mom's treatment. The possibility of what may be out there... I don't know if I can risk it.

But what if he can fix this. What I need fixed. What if he can do it?

If I only told him.

"Jaxon?"

My voice echoes into the stillness, but the penthouse stays quiet—too quiet. The city hums faintly beyond the floor-to-ceiling windows, but in here, it feels like everything's holding its breath.

I'm still in the dress. My heels are abandoned at the elevator door where I bolted away from him, like a coward. Barefoot, I pad over the polished floors, each step a soft whisper in the dark.

The kitchen counter catches my eye—a single sheet of paper sitting in the middle like it's been waiting for me.

I'll be back later. I'm sorry.

That last line makes my chest tighten. I trace the words with my fingertips, slow, like maybe I can feel what he was feeling when he wrote them. My throat burns. One tear escapes and slides down my cheek before I can stop it.

I don't even know how to tell him everything I'm holding inside. But I need to.

I almost want to.

The thought of it knots my stomach. Not yet... but soon. I have to find him first. I have to tell him I'm sorry.

Slipping my heels back on, I call the elevator. The metallic doors glide open, and I step inside, pressing the lobby button. Maybe he's downstairs—at the building's restaurant or the bar. It's late, but it's Friday night in New York City. People will still be out.

I check both places, scanning for his tall frame, but he's nowhere. I text him as I walk, my thumb flying over the screen, but there's no reply.

Then I see his driver standing near the concierge desk and he spots me immediately.

"Miss Hayes," he says politely. "Did you need some help?"

I fidget with my hands, embarrassed. He saw me earlier, red-faced and trembling. He knows we fought—if that's even what this was. No... it was just me being ridiculous. Now I have to make it right.

"Where would Jaxon go if he needed to... decompress?"

The corner of his mouth tips up. "He only goes one place, ma'am. He'll be at The Gym."

I exhale, relief mixing with nerves.

"Would you like me to take you there?"

"Yes, please."

It's only a fifteen-minute drive before we pull into a small lot beside a two-story brick building. The words *The Gym* are painted in block lettering across the front windows—but the place looks dead. No neon, no flicker of light from inside.

The driver comes around to open my door and tilts his head toward a narrow side entrance where light spills out into the dark.

My eyes sweep the lot—and there's his bike. Relief floods me so fast I feel weak for a second.

"Thanks," I tell him quietly.

"You want me to wait here?"

I shake my head. "No, thanks."

He gives me a look, half protective, half wary. "Okay. You look out in there. It can be a rowdy crowd."

I nod, murmuring another thank you before making my way toward the side door.

The closer I get, the louder it is—a roar of sound spilling out into the night. Music. Shouting. The thump of energy that bumps against you.

Inside, the space opens up to a crowd pressed around a fighting ring, the air thick with sweat and adrenaline. Two men circle each other inside the ropes.

And one of them is Jaxon.

His skin glistens under the harsh overhead lights, muscles coiled and moving with precision. He's in shorts, knuckles wrapped, fists high. His opponent lunges, but Jaxon's quicker—slipping aside, driving a hit into the man's ribs.

I edge closer, drawn in, when someone suddenly presses up beside me. I shift a few inches away without taking my eyes off Jaxon. He doesn't see me. He's locked in, all sharp focus and quiet violence.

"You need a drink, sugar?"

The voice is too close, too loud, and reeks of cigarette smoke. I glance over—a tall man, bald, with a long beard and a worn leather jacket. Definitely the Harley Davidson type.

"No. Thank you."

I turn back toward the ring, hoping the hint is clear.

Jaxon looks incredible. Efficient. Lethal. My chest tightens when his opponent's fist connects with his cheek, snapping his head to the side.

The bearded man sidesteps, appearing on my other side. "What's your name, sweetheart?"

"I'm not interested." I meet his eyes when I say it, flat and direct, before looking back to Jaxon.

"See, that's where we have a problem."

He moves in front of me, blocking my view of the ring completely. If Jaxon were looking this way, he probably couldn't see me at all.

"Because I *am* interested," he says, crowding me. I take a step back, but he matches it, closing the distance again.

Now I'm closer to the door than I want to be, the cold edge of night air licking in from outside. My pulse spikes. I try to angle around him. "I'm sure you can work out your confusion in therapy, but I said no."

"Maybe I don't care what you said."

He pushes forward again, forcing me to keep retreating, his size cutting off my line of sight to the ring. A knot of real fear starts to form low in my stomach.

And then there's a heat behind me. A presence so solid, it steals the air from the room.

"I care very much what she says."

Jaxon slides an arm around my waist, pulling me back into him. His rich, dark voice sends relief rushing through me.

"And she said fuck off." he growls.

He steps fully in front of me, chest to chest with the guy, who's suddenly looking a lot less sure of himself. Jaxon's taller, broader, and still slick with sweat from the fight he clearly abandoned—the other man still standing in the ring watching this unfold.

The bearded man throws up his hands. "My bad."

Jaxon doesn't move until the guy turns away, melting into the crowd. Then his head whips back but he doesn't look at me and keeps his eyes dark and unreadable.

He catches my hand, sharp and sure, and whistles toward the door. A man near it nods.

"Let's go," Jaxon says.

At the door, the man hands him his helmet, a black backpack, and his shoes. Jaxon makes quick work of pulling on his black jeans and sneakers, still shirtless, hair damp, adrenaline radiating off him in waves.

Then he tugs me outside into the night, not loosening his grip once.

Someone hollers after him as we step into the cool night.

"What about the fight, Kane?"

"I'm done," Jaxon calls back without slowing.

"That's a hundred grand you're walking away from!"

"Keep it."

"Jaxon!" My voice comes out sharper than I mean it to, but he doesn't stop. He's moving fast, his hand locked around mine, practically dragging me. I have to half-jog in my heels to keep up.

"Jaxon—your fight—"

He stops so abruptly I almost crash into him. He's shaking, and not just from the fight. Full-body, bone-deep tremors. The helmet and bag drop to the asphalt with a dull thud before he turns on me.

"I don't care about a fucking fight, Cassidy. I care about you." His voice is rough, almost breaking as he rips the tape from his hands. "Did he touch you? Are you okay?"

He looks like he's unraveling right in front of me, and my mind flashes back to the barn. The horses. The men he saved me from. His desperate plea in the dark—*Don't let me go, Cass. Don't let me go or I'll go kill them.*

And right then, I know I never want to let him go. I let myself finally admit it and I'm not going to.

He hastily tugs his black tee over his head, and I step into him, my arms looping around his neck as I rise on my toes.

"Hey. I'm okay." My nose brushes his, and he fists the fabric of my dress at my hips like it physically hurts him to touch me. His eyes squeeze shut.

"What if I didn't see you?" His voice is low but jagged. "He was pushing you toward the door, Cassidy. What if he took away from me? Where I couldn't find you?"

"Shh." I stroke the back of his neck, threading my fingers into damp hair. "I'm right here. Touch me."

I need to pull him back from whatever edge he's standing on. I know exactly what's running through his mind—how easily I could have been hurt. I want to strip that thought away from him, even if only for a moment.

"Kiss me, Kane."

I whisper it against his lips, and he does.

The world narrows to the heat between us as our mouths part, tongues sliding together. His hand curves to the back of my head, pulling me deeper into him. He tugs my hair, angling my face so he can take more, and I give it willingly.

He steps forward, and the hard edge of his motorcycle presses into me. His palms smooth down over my ass, fingers tracing bare skin at my thigh before he hooks my leg up over his hip. The slow, deliberate grind of his body into mine makes my breath catch.

"I want you so fucking bad, baby," he growls against my skin. His mouth trails from my neck to my collarbone, down the line of my chest. My fingers tangle in his hair, holding him close.

If I weren't a virgin, I'd let him take me right here, in the shadows, with the fight still raging next door. But I know he wouldn't—not my first time, not like this.

"If anything ever happened to you…" His gaze locks with mine, so intense it steals my breath. His hand cups my jaw. "It would be the end of me. Cassidy, I—"

"I'm okay," I cut in. "I'm right here. And I'm not going anywhere." I press my lips to his again, softer this time. "I don't ever want to go anywhere."

Something in his expression shifts, and I think he gets what I'm saying because his arms lock tighter around me, his face buried in my neck.

"Jaxon," I murmur.

He pulls back, and I can feel a smile curve my lips.

"Take me home and fuck me."

I run my tongue along his lower lip before he can reply, but he fists my dress again and leans his forehead against mine.

"Say that again."

My smile grows. "I want you to fuck me."

"No... the first part."

I can't stop grinning now and my eyes bounce back and forth between his. "Take me home."

She said it so easily—*take me home.*

Not *your* home. Not *my* home. Just... home.

And I swear to God, I almost choke on it.

Because with her, that's exactly what it feels like. Like home is wherever the hell she's standing.

There's only one problem.

I drove my bike.

And I've only got one helmet.

I glance around the lot. If I spot another helmet, I'll steal the damn thing without thinking twice.

"We could call your driver," she suggests, pulling me back to her.

I shake my head instantly. "There is no fucking way I'm waiting a second longer than necessary to get you in my bed."

My gaze drags down the length of her, lingering on that dress, the way it clings to every curve. "Come on."

I scoop her up bridal style, and she makes a soft sound

that shoots straight to my cock. Setting her gently on the back of my bike, I hold out my hand. "Give me your heels."

She blinks at me but slips them off. I shove them into my backpack, sling the strap over her shoulders, and pull my helmet on her head, clipping it under her chin.

"What about you?" she asks, voice muffled under the visor.

"I'll be fine." I say quickly, tucking the tag on my bike out of view.

Her dress rides up as she adjusts, and fuck—her creamy thighs and black lace panties are like a goddamn invitation.

I climb onto the bike in front of her, and she slides up close, her chest pressing against my back. Her hands lock around my waist.

"Hold on, baby," I tell her, starting the engine. The bike rumbles to life under us, vibrating through both our bodies.

And then we're gone.

It doesn't even take five minutes before I see flashing red and blue in my mirrors.

Perfect. Just what I fucking need.

I'm in no mood to sit through a lecture or a ticket for not wearing a helmet, not tonight.

I glance back over my shoulder at the cop car gaining on us. "You trust me?" I holler over the roar of the engine.

Cassidy doesn't hesitate. She shifts even closer, her chest flush to my back, her arms locking tighter around me.

"I'm ready," she says, and the firmness in her voice hits me low in the gut.

That's my girl.

I face forward again, and everything sharpens. Every

turn, every lane shift, every set of brake lights ahead—mapped in my head before we even reach them.

I gun it.

The bike surges forward, the engine snarling under us as I thread between two cars with inches to spare. The wind roars in my ears, and Cassidy lets out a breathless laugh that's half thrill, half disbelief.

A second set of flashing lights appears in the side mirror—a second patrol car joining in.

"Hang on," I call back, and I feel her grip tighten.

We weave hard left, shooting down a narrow side street. I dodge a parked delivery truck by leaning the bike just enough to skim past its mirror. A horn blares. The cops are still with us, but we've got distance.

Cassidy laughs again, louder this time. She's having the time of her life. I can feel it in the way she clings to me—not scared, not tense—just... alive.

I shake my head, chuckling despite myself. This is ridiculous. Absolutely insane. And somehow, it's perfect.

Another sharp right. I know exactly where I'm going.

I cut down an alley I've used before, braking hard at the end and angling us between two massive dumpsters. The stench hits instantly, but it's worth it. I kill the engine, and the bike goes still.

Cassidy's breathing fast against my back. My hand goes to her thigh like gravity drew me to her. I rub my palms up her leg feeling how smooth and soft she is.

The cop cars scream past the mouth of the alley, lights blazing, sirens wailing.

I give it another ten seconds before I turn the key again.

The engine rumbles to life, low and steady. I back us out of our hiding spot and head the opposite way, slow at first, then faster as the city opens back up in front of us.

Every time I open up the throttle, she presses closer, her thighs hugging mine, her nails digging lightly into my stomach. My head's full of her—her laugh, her scent, the way her dress rode up when I put her on this bike.

The city blurs by in streaks of yellow light and shadow, every turn pulling us closer to my building. I don't slow until I have to, coasting us into my private garage.

I glance back at her, and she lifts the visor, her eyes bright, cheeks flushed from the wind. She looks... wrecked in the best way.

"Fun?" I ask, knowing the answer.

Her lips curve into a slow smile. "More than fun."

I swing off the bike, unfasten the helmet from her head, and set it aside. She starts to slide off, but I catch her around the waist and lift her down myself. Another glimpse of black lace again nearly breaks my last shred of patience.

I sling the backpack to the ground and pin her against the bike, my palms braced on either side of her. My mouth is on hers in an instant, swallowing her moan.

"Upstairs. Now."

She doesn't tease. Just nods, like she wants it as badly as I do.

The second I hit the button for the penthouse, we collide —mouths crashing together, hands everywhere. Her nails bite through my shirt, my palms gripping her hips, sliding over the curve of her ass to pull her in tight.

"You have no idea what you've just done to me, Cricket,"

I growl against her lips. "And when I'm done with you, you'll never want anyone else touching you again."

She makes a sound in the back of her throat that damn near undoes me.

The elevator hums upward, but I don't even register the floors passing. It's just her—her scent, her heat, the way she moves against me like we've been doing this for years.

The doors slide open, and I don't waste a second. I hook an arm under her thighs, lifting her effortlessly. She gasps and clings to my neck, kissing me like she's afraid to stop.

I carry her straight into my bedroom, dropping my keys somewhere along the way. The city lights spill through the massive windows, washing her in silver.

I set her down on the edge of the bed but keep my hands on her, my forehead pressed to hers. "Tell me to slow down, and I will. Tell me to stop, and I'll stop."

"Don't stop." Her fingers trace my jaw, her voice soft but certain. "Don't ever stop."

I kiss her again—slower now—tasting her, savoring every sigh. My hands skim the outside of her thighs, up over her hips, tracing the line of her waist.

The zipper of her dress slides down beneath my fingers, the sound loud in the quiet room. She shivers, and I push the fabric off her shoulders, letting it pool at her waist.

"You're so fucking beautiful," I murmur, brushing my knuckles over the swell of her breast.

Her hands find the hem of my shirt, and I pull it over my head. Her eyes roam my chest, my shoulders, my arms like she's committing them to memory.

I ease her back onto the bed, my weight braced on one

arm so I'm not crushing her. My free hand strokes down her side, learning her curves, mapping out every inch.

"I'm going to take my time with you," I tell her. "You deserve that. Your first time should be... perfect."

Her breath catches, and I press my lips to her collarbone, trailing kisses down to the edge of her bra. I look up at her once, and when she nods, I slip the strap down her arm, kissing the skin I reveal.

Her body arches toward me, and I tell myself to slow down. Tonight, isn't about me. It's about her. Making her feel safe. Worshiped. Completely undone in my hands.

And I plan to make sure she enjoys every damn second.

Her mouth is warm and open under mine, kissing me like she needs me to breathe. My hand slides down, under the lace, between her thighs—finding heat and slickness that makes my cock throb instantly.

"Fuck, Crick..." I groan against her lips, my fingers barely parting her folds. "Already wet for me? We've barely started."

A small gasp escapes her, and her hips roll instinctively into my touch. I let one finger trace up her pussy, slow, teasing, until it circles her clit. Her whole body shivers under me.

"You're wet..." I drag the pad of my finger through her again, gathering more of her arousal. "...but I want you dripping for me."

I pull my hand away and hold the glistening finger between us. Her eyes lock on it, wide, pupils blown. I lick it clean, groaning low in my throat. "Always so fucking sweet for me."

Before she can even catch her breath, I lean in and kiss her hard, sliding my tongue into her mouth. "Taste yourself, baby," I murmur against her lips. "That's mine."

She whimpers into the kiss, and I can feel her thighs pressing together like she's already desperate for more.

I start my descent—kissing down her throat, her sternum, the curve of her breast. My hands push the lace bra up, baring her completely to me. "Perfect tits," I mutter, dragging my mouth over the soft swell. "I'm going to make you come just from this."

Her breath hitches, and I wrap my lips around one nipple, sucking slow and deep while my thumb teases the other. She arches hard into my mouth.

"Jaxon…" Her voice is already strained, needy. "God, that feels so good."

"That's it," I growl, alternating between sucking and flicking her with my tongue. "Let me hear you. I want every person in this building to know how good I'm making you feel."

Her hands bury in my hair, holding me there, and I grin against her skin before biting lightly—just enough to make her gasp. I soothe the spot with my tongue, feeling her tremble.

"Right there," she pants. "Don't stop. Oh my god, don't—"

"I'm not stopping until you're shaking for me," I promise, moving to her other nipple and giving it the same slow torture. Her back lifts from the bed, her thighs squeezing together as if she can trap the pleasure inside.

Her breathing turns erratic, and I feel the change in her

body—the way she tenses, the soft cry building in her throat. I press harder with my mouth, rolling the sensitive peak between my teeth just as she breaks apart.

"Oh, fuck—Jaxon!"

She comes in a rush, her nails clawing at my shoulders, chest heaving as waves of pleasure roll through her. I keep my mouth on her until every last shiver fades, licking her softly as she tries to catch her breath.

When her eyes finally open, they're glazed, dazed, and entirely mine.

"First orgasm of the night. My sweet Cricket." I murmur, trailing a hand down her stomach. "You're going to give me more."

Chapter 33

Cassidy

axon's mouth leaves my breasts, and I'm already aching for wherever he's going next.

He kisses down my stomach, slow and deliberate, like he's savoring every inch of me. Each press of his lips sends a fresh wave of heat through me. By the time he reaches the waistband of my panties, I'm squirming, my fingers tangled in the sheets.

He glances up at me from between my legs, eyes dark and dangerous, and hooks his thumbs under the lace. "These are coming off."

My hips lift without me even thinking about it, and he slides them down my legs, tossing them aside. The cool air hits me, and I shiver—not from cold, but from the way he's looking at me, like I'm the only thing in the world worth his attention.

He kisses the inside of my thigh first. Then, the other. Soft, lingering presses that have me biting my lip and rocking my hips, silently begging for more.

"Patience," he murmurs, his breath warm against my skin. "I told you I'm going to take my time with you."

When his mouth finally reaches me, I gasp. His tongue traces a slow line through my cunt, the sensation so sharp and new it steals my breath.

"Jaxon..." My voice is already shaky, my fingers gripping the sheets tighter.

He groans low in his throat, the vibration making me twitch, and then he licks me again—slower, deeper. "You're heaven," he says against me. "So fucking delicious."

His hands slide under my thighs, lifting and spreading me wider as his mouth works me over. Every flick of his tongue sends a shiver up my spine, every gentle suck pulling me closer to something I can't stop.

When he circles my clit, my back arches off the bed. "God, yes—right there—"

"That's it, baby. Let me have it," he says before sealing his mouth over me, sucking hard enough to make my vision blur.

I can't think, can't breathe—just feel. His tongue moves in perfect rhythm, his grip on me firm but gentle, keeping me exactly where he wants me. The pressure builds so fast it's almost overwhelming, pleasure curling low in my stomach until it's too much to hold.

"Oh, Jaxon—" My voice breaks as I come, the world fracturing into pulsing waves that leave me shaking.

He doesn't let up, licking me through it, dragging out every last tremor until I collapse back against the bed, panting.

When he finally looks up at me, his mouth is wet, his smile pure sin. "Two down, beautiful. We're just getting started."

Before I can fully catch my breath, his mouth is on me again.

It's softer this time, a gentle sweep of his tongue that makes me twitch because I'm still so sensitive. I try to close my legs, but his hands keep me open, holding me exactly where he wants me.

"Easy, baby," he murmurs, his lips brushing over me. "I'm not done tasting you yet."

The slow, teasing licks start to build again, and I'm barely able to contain the sounds spilling from my mouth. My hands find his hair, tugging, and he groans against me like he loves it.

Then he pulls back just enough to speak, his voice low and dark. "I'm going to slide a finger in. Just a little."

"Yes—please," I breathe, my hips lifting in pure need.

He groans again, the sound vibrating through me, and then I feel it—his tongue circling my clit while one finger slowly presses inside, shallow, careful. He doesn't go deep, just enough for me to feel the stretch, the delicious pressure mixing with the rhythm of his mouth.

"Holy shit, that feel's so good." My voice breaks as the pleasure coils tight, my body clenching around his finger.

"Keep your legs open for me, baby," he growls against me. "Come for me again."

I couldn't stop it if I tried. A few more flicks on his tongue timed with the movements of his fingers is all it takes. My back arches, a sharp cry escaping as another orgasm crashes over me, pulsing through every nerve. My thighs shake against his hold, and I swear the world tilts for a second.

When it finally ebbs, I fall back against the bed, trembling, my chest heaving.

Jaxon lifts his head, his eyes locked on mine like I just gave him something priceless. "Three," he says, voice thick. "You've got more in you."

Jaxon sits back on his heels, wiping his mouth with the back of his hand, grinning down at me like he just conquered the world.

"Fuck, you're perfect, Cricket," he says, voice still rough from the last thing he pulled out of me. "So... so good for me."

He stands, and my eyes follow him up—up the lines of his abs, the curve of his shoulders—until his hands go to his waistband. He peels his pants and boxers down in one smooth motion, and suddenly, he's as bare as I am.

My gaze drops, and my breath catches. He's big. Thick. Hard enough that the tip glistens, and then he wraps his hand around himself and strokes slowly.

I can't stop staring at that hand—how large it is. How easily it grips him. And all I can think is how that same length and thickness is supposed to fit inside me. My mouth goes dry.

He crooks his finger at me once. Twice. "Come here... crawl to me, Cricket."

The sound of that name in his voice makes my whole

body hum. I move toward him on my hands and knees, my pulse pounding in my ears. By the time I'm kneeling in front of him, my face is already hot.

"Now," he says, looking down at me with something dark in his eyes, "get that smart mouth on my cock."

I grin, full of mischief knowing he loves it when I push him.

I lean in and take him into my mouth, bolder than the first time—sinking down further, my hand wrapping around the base.

The taste of him hits my tongue, salt and heat, the slick of his pre-cum making it easier to glide my lips over him. My pussy clenches hard just from the feel of him against my tongue, from the groan that rumbles out of his chest.

"That's it," he rasps. "Look at you—on your knees for me. Getting my cock nice and wet so I can fuck that tight little virgin pussy."

A whimper slips out before I can stop it, my thighs pressing together.

"You like that, baby? You like me telling you what I'm going to do to you?" His hand slides into my hair, not pushing, just holding me there while I swirl my tongue over him. "Mouth so pretty around me… getting ready to take me where I really want to be."

I moan against him, and he hisses in a breath.

"Good girl. Deep as you can, Cricket. I want to see those lips stretch for me before I stretch your pretty cunt and make it mine."

Every word sends another shiver through me, my core

clenching tighter, the ache between my legs almost unbearable.

After another moment, Jaxon's hand slides into my hair and tugs me off him.

"Turn around," he says, his voice deep and steady in that way that makes my knees weak.

I shift, facing the bed.

"Spread your legs wider."

I do.

"Lay your tits on the bed, ass up... let me look at you."

Heat rushes to my cheeks, but I follow every word. My chest sinks into the mattress, my hips still high.

"Higher," he orders, his tone rougher now. "And spread just a little more."

I part my thighs another inch, feeling the cool air kiss my bare skin.

His big hands cup my ass, kneading once before he bends down to press his lips to one cheek. Then both hands spread me open, and the groan that rumbles out of him makes my pussy clench hard.

"Fuck, baby. You are dripping."

Before I can even catch my breath, he drops to one knee behind me and licks a slow, deliberate line up my cunt. My head falls forward with a strangled sound.

The first flick of his tongue over my clit nearly unravels me. My hand flies to my breast, pinching my nipple, my body twitching under the sensation.

"Jaxon—please," I gasp. "Please lick me. Make me come again."

I roll my hips against the air, desperate for more contact.

"Still, baby," he growls, one big hand pressing gently against my lower back to keep me in place.

Then he seals his mouth over my clit and sucks—hard.

The pleasure detonates instantly, ripping through me so fast my scream bounces off the walls. My legs tremble violently, my arms giving out so I collapse onto the bed.

I'm shaking too much to hold myself up, and he notices. He eases me over onto my back, his weight shifting as he climbs up my body.

His mouth meets mine in a deep, consuming kiss, and I wrap my legs around him automatically. His cock slides between my pussy lips, hot and heavy, the friction making me gasp.

"You ready for me, Cricket?" His voice is low, but I hear the edge in it—like he's barely holding on.

"Yes." My answer is immediate, certain. "I'm ready for you to fuck me."

He moves to reach for the nightstand, but I grab his wrist.

"Bare," I whisper. "I'm on birth control. I want to feel *just you* for my first time."

His jaw clenches, his eyes searching mine, and I see the exact moment he decides he's not going to argue.

His gaze holds mine as he settles between my thighs, his hands braced on either side of me.

"You sure, baby?" he murmurs, his voice rough but steady.

I nod, my chest rising and falling fast. "I'm sure."

He lowers his head, kissing me slow—nothing rushed, nothing greedy—like he's telling me without words that he's here, that I'm safe. His cock slides along my slit again, hotter now, heavier, the blunt head catching at my entrance.

"This is going to feel... different," he says against my lips. "But I'm going to make it good for you."

I shiver. "I know you will."

He pushes just enough for the tip to breach me, and I gasp, my nails digging into his shoulders.

"That's it," he whispers. "You're doing so good for me, Cricket." He kisses my cheek, the corner of my mouth, my throat—peppering me with warmth as his hips shift forward another inch.

The stretch is sharp, unfamiliar, but the way he's looking at me—like I'm the only thing in the world that matters—keeps me grounded.

"You're perfect," he murmurs, brushing his nose against mine. "Tight, warm... made for me."

Another slow push, and I can feel my body stretching around him, yielding bit by bit. My breath catches with every small movement, but the pain dulls under the constant stream of kisses and praises he gives me.

"Almost there, my sweet Cricket," he says, voice tight with control. "Just a little more. Let me in."

I exhale, my legs tightening around his waist, and he slides the last inch home until he's fully seated inside me.

He doesn't move right away, just stays there, his forehead resting against mine, his breathing ragged.

"You've got all of me now," he says softly. "Every inch. You feel so fucking good."

And in that moment, with him fully inside me and his

lips brushing mine, I know—I'll never forget this for the rest of my life.

He stays still inside me, kissing me slow, letting me breathe through the stretch. His lips trail from my mouth to my jaw, down my neck, before coming back to press against mine again.

"You okay?" he murmurs, his voice low and deep.

I nod, my hands gripping his shoulders. "Yeah."

"Okay." He rests his forehead against mine, eyes squeezed shut, and for a moment I think he's just gathering himself. Then...

"Grandma's... abandoned kittens... toenail fungus..."

I blink at him. "What are you doing?"

"I'm trying to last longer than twenty-three seconds," he says, dead serious. "It's been a while, okay."

I laugh—can't help it—and he lets out a strangled breath, gripping my hip like he's hanging on for dear life. "I'm *serious*, Cassidy. Just give me a second."

He whispers under his breath, "Don't come, don't come, don't come..."

That just makes me laugh harder, and he groans like I'm torturing him.

"Cricket," he growls.

I bite my lip, trying to hold it in, and he kisses me—hard—before rocking his hips just enough to make me gasp. "You feel too fucking good, little Cricket."

The slow roll turns into something deeper, heavier, and my breath stutters.

"That's it," he says, his voice dropping even lower.

"Open for me. Take me. You're mine now—aren't you baby? No one else gets this pussy but me."

"Yes." I pant out.

"Tell me, beautiful." He kisses my lips so tenderly. "I need to hear it."

Heat floods my face, but I can't stop the truth from spilling out. "I've always been yours."

"Say it." His thrusts get a little rougher, the bed creaking beneath us.

"I'm yours," I gasp. "I belong to you."

His eyes flash with something primal, and he fucks me harder, deeper, like my words broke something in him. "That's right, Cricket. This virgin cunt is mine. You were made to take my cock. Say it again."

"I'm yours, Jaxon—oh God—"

"Again," he demands, his pace relentless now.

"I'm yours!"

I feel myself teetering on the edge, and he must feel it too because his hand slides between us, his thumb finding my clit. "Come on my cock, Cricket. Let me feel you squeeze me."

It hits so hard I cry out, my back arching, nails clawing at him. He groans, pounding into me through it, muttering filth between kisses—how tight I am, how good I taste, how no one will ever fuck me like this.

He gives me all of his focus. Intent on giving me another orgasm, and then another, until I've lost track of how many times I've shattered around him in nearly every position.

"Fuck—Cassidy—" His thrusts turn erratic, his voice raw. "Gonna come—gonna fill you up—"

"Yes," I gasp. "Come in me, Jaxon. I want it so fucking bad." I can't help the tear that rolls out of my eye.

He groans my name, burying himself deep as he finally lets go, spilling inside me in hot, pulsing waves as I grind against him screaming out one last orgasm. Our bodies locking together in a desperate, breathless tangle.

When it's over, he stays inside me, kissing me softly like the rest of the world doesn't exist.

Chapter 34

It's late. Hours past when the city outside should have quieted, but I don't hear a thing but her breathing.

We're lying on our sides, facing each other, her head on my pillow, my hand lazily tracing the inside of her arm. She's already given me three times tonight, and I'm still thinking about being inside her again. Hell, I'm *always* going to be thinking about it now.

I can't get enough of her.

"You okay?" I ask softly. "Sore?"

She shakes her head and scoots closer, pressing her naked body against mine. "I'm perfect."

I smile. "Yeah. Me too."

The way she's looking at me right now, fuck. I want to remember it forever.

"Can I ask you something?" I kiss the tip of her nose gently. She nods with a pleased smile.

"Why did you wait? Why didn't you...with that cock-sucker baseball dick?"

Cassidy laughs, hiding her face in my neck.

"You want me to tell you the truth?"

"No, I prefer a lie little Cricket." I tease her.

"I never wanted to. I was never over you." She rests her head on her hand and her words shoot into me. The other stroking along my chest. "And then I caught Bree and Matt fucking in my dorm room."

"Fuck."

"Yeah." She lays back down. "He blamed me because I wouldn't put out for him. *Men have needs.*" She mocks his voice.

"He's a cock wipe." I move a piece of hair behind her ear. "I"m sorry they hurt you."

She takes a deep breath like she's working up to something but stays quiet. I give her a second. Then she tries again.

"Can I ask you something?"

My hand slides over her back, slow and reassuring. "By now I'd hope you know you can tell me anything, Cricket."

She dips her head, hiding her face against my chest. "You said... it had been a while?"

I can't help the small smile that tugs at my mouth.

"So how long... is a while?" she asks, her voice muffled.

She's still not looking at me, so I hook a finger under her chin and tilt her face up. "Look at me."

"Six years."

Her mouth parts in disbelief, her breathing picking up, and I know exactly where her mind's gone. That night. The party. The frat house.

"Why?" she whispers. "Why haven't you had sex in six years?"

I don't even hesitate. "Because the girl I wanted hated me."

She sits up, clutching the sheet to her chest, her eyes shining. "Why? Why didn't you want me then?"

Her voice cracks, and the tears follow.

"No," I murmur, reaching for her. "Shhh, Cricket." I pull her back down, wrapping her tight against me. My hand strokes her hair until I feel her breathing steady, even if her body is still trembling.

I press my lips to her temple. "I wanted you so fucking bad, baby. And that was the problem."

I can still see it like it was yesterday—her weaving through that crowded house, searching every corner, every face.

"I watched you looking for me," I say quietly. "I knew I should've left before you found me, but I couldn't. I just had to look into your eyes one time."

Her breath catches, her lashes lowering.

"Then you were talking to that asshole at the party," I mutter. "I'm the one who called the coach and told him his players were out getting drunk." Sitting up a little to look at her.

She lets out a shocked laugh and smacks my chest. "You didn't."

I grin faintly. "I did. And I'm not sorry."

Her smile softens, but it fades when I say, "Then you wanted to kiss me... and fuck, Cricket, I wanted to kiss you too. But Jonathan saw us. Thought something happened. And he reminded me why I needed to leave you alone."

Her brows draw together. "Why?"

"Because I'm broken. Because I'd already fucked enough women and didn't need to add my best friend's sister to the list. Because I didn't know what love looked like without someone punching you."

She flinches at that. "That's not true."

I shake my head. "But I believed it, Cricket. Jon knew what my life was like before."

I take her hand and guide her fingers to one of my tattoos, letting her trace it slowly. "He knew I covered cigarette burns my dad gave me with ink."

Her voice is barely a whisper. "Jaxon..."

It breaks something in me.

"I didn't want to love you the wrong way and ruin you," I say. "I haven't slept around like people think. I just don't correct them because I don't give a shit what they think."

I turn my head so I can see her clearly, even in the low light. "But I care what you think, baby."

Her eyes glisten, and she swallows hard.

"I wouldn't have been strong enough to stay away from you if you'd kept coming around. And you were only seven-teen. I wanted to give you a chance to let someone love you the right way, so I had to make you hate me."

Her grip on me tightens.

"After you saw me with those girls... when I watched your heart break... I threw them out. I scrubbed myself raw in the shower and threw up." My voice goes rough, heavy. "I hated myself for years. Maybe even hated myself until that auction."

I cup her cheek, my thumb brushing over damp skin. "I'm sorry for what you saw. I hate that you saw it. I hate that day. I wish it never fucking happened."

Her eyes are shining, her lips trembling, and she presses her forehead to mine like she's trying to make up for every second we lost.

I cup her face in both hands, my thumbs brushing over damp cheeks. "I thought I couldn't love you right," I admit, my voice low and raw. "Because I was broken. Because all I knew was the kind of love that hurt. But I was wrong, Cricket."

Her breath catches, her eyes shining in the low light.

"I *can* love you. I *do* love you. And no one—no one—will ever love you the way I do. No one will see you the way I see you. Every stubborn, smart, beautiful inch of you. You're it for me. Always have been."

Her lips tremble, and the tears come faster, sliding warm over my fingers. But she's smiling through them, the kind of smile that steals my air.

"Don't say it back," I murmur, pressing my forehead to hers. "Not after tonight. Not after your first time. I don't want tonight to confuse you. I just need you to know."

Her chin wobbles, and I kiss her before she can answer —slow and deep, letting it linger until the ache between us shifts from heavy to hungry.

The kiss changes, turns sharper, needier. Closure blurs into passion until she's tugging at me, urging me over her. I brace my weight on one arm, looking down at her, and she gives me that sly little smile.

"How many times can you go in a day?" she teases, her hand sliding between us.

The second her fingers wrap around me, I'm swelling in her palm, my cock hardening fast.

I smirk, my voice low. "I don't know... but I'm more than happy to find out with you."

Her laugh melts into a soft gasp when I kiss her again, my hips shifting until the head of my cock glides through her folds, hot and slick from the night we've already had.

Then I sink into her in one slow, steady push, her warmth pulling me under until I'm home.

Until she's mine.

I lean against the bathroom doorway, arms crossed, watching Cassidy in the shower.

Whoever decided on this clear-glass design deserves a medal. I've got an unobstructed view of *all* of her—wet skin, curves I can trace in my sleep, water streaming down her back.

She tips her head back under the spray, lathering her dark hair, and my eyes catch on the hickey I left on the side of her breast. It makes my chest tighten in a way I'm not used to.

I've never been happier in my life.

And then it hits me—loud and sharp in my brain, like a bell. *I'm going to marry this woman.*

No question. No hesitation. I'm going to put a ring on her finger and make her mine in every way. A smile pulls at my mouth as I think about picking it out. I've already got something else for her, sitting on the bed—a black gift box with a bow that I can't wait to see her open.

My phone rings.

Jonathan.

That fucker is *just now* calling me back? I called him last week about the horse catastrophe and never got a response.

I answer. "Well, look who's not dead after all."

"Sorry, man. Things have been busy."

"What do you need?"

"Have you seen Cass? I can't reach her."

Shit.

I'm going to tell him about me and Cass—but not like this. I need to talk to her first. Make sure she's okay with it. So I play it off.

"I'm sure she's just in her studio."

"She needs to get out of there and do something useful."

That makes my jaw flex. But I'm not starting shit with him right now—not before I've cleared it with her.

"What did you need, man? I've got something going on here."

Right on cue, Cassidy notices me watching. Her lips curl into a slow smile as she starts lathering up her body, soap suds sliding over every perfect inch. My dick nearly springs out of my pants.

"Can you tell Cass I'm on my way back early? Tomorrow morning," Jonathan says.

Inside the shower, one of her hands slides between her legs while the other pinches her breast. God, she's a fucking siren.

"Earth to Jax," Jonathan says, irritation creeping in.

"Yeah... sorry."

"So, you'll tell her?"

"Yeah, I can pass that message along."

She turns and bends at the waist, giving me a perfect view of her ass. I nearly have to bite my knuckles to keep from groaning.

"Yeah, I'll tell her—but I've gotta go."

I hang up before he can answer, tossing my phone and the gift box onto the bed. Then I head straight for the shower.

If my little siren wants to play, I'll be more than happy to give her a hand.

***

After I've made Cassidy fall apart twice in the shower —once with my hands, once with my mouth—I hand her a towel and tell her, "Get dressed. We're going out. I've got a surprise for you."

Suspicion flickers in her eyes, but she wraps up and heads for the bedroom. The black gift box is waiting on the bed.

She lifts the lid, pulls out the contents, and stares. "Leather pants?"

"A very special pair of pants," I say, walking over to her. I turn them in her hands so she sees the zipper that runs a lot longer than normal. All the way to the back so they'll open up and let me see her sweet cunt and perfect ass.

Her jaw drops. "You're not serious."

"Dead serious." I lean in, brushing my mouth against her ear. "We're making one of my fantasies come true tonight. So get dressed. We're going for a ride."

Thirty minutes later, we're on my bike, the city rolling by in a blur. She's pressed tight against me, arms locked around my waist, helmet tucked against my back. I can feel her curiosity in the way she keeps shifting, probably dying to ask where we're going.

When I finally make the turn and pull up to the taco truck—the same one from the night before the auction—she grabs my sides and I feel her wiggling back and forth like she's doing a little happy dance back there. I laugh under my breath, cutting the engine.

She practically bounces off the bike the second I lower the kickstand, tugging off her helmet with a look that says she's *way* too happy to see a food truck.

We order and sit at one of the rickety little tables off to the side, this time next to each other instead of across.

We can't stop touching.

We hold hands. I rub her thigh. She wraps her arm around my elbow and rests her head on my bicep. When our food gets here, she rests her leg over mine.

I love it.

Fuck. I love *her*.

These past three weeks have been the best of my life—chaos, heat, laughter, and more than I ever thought I'd have.

I wipe a bit of salsa from the corner of her mouth and chase it with a quick peck on the lips.

"I'm glad I bought you, Cricket."

Her fork stills. The smile she'd been wearing softens, just a touch. Those green eyes find mine, and for a second, there's no teasing in them—just something darker, deeper.

"Yeah," she murmurs, voice low. "Me too."

That's the answer I've been waiting for.

We toss our trash, climb back on the bike, and I feel her arms wrap around me like she never wants to let go. The highway opens up in front of us, dark and endless. I tap her leg twice—our silent signal—and she squeezes me tighter just before I gun it, pushing as fast as I dare with her holding on like I'm the only thing keeping her tethered.

When I ease off the throttle, she loosens her grip and spreads her arms out wide behind me, hair whipping in the wind.

"I love it here," she calls over the roar of the bike. "I feel so free."

I take the long way around the airport, pulling into a spot I know by muscle memory—where the planes fly low enough to rattle your chest, and I've spent more than a few nights filming myself tearing down this stretch.

I kill the engine. Cassidy swings off, but I stay put, watching her. Helmets come off. Mine hits the ground. She follows suit.

"Get your ass up here," I tell her, patting the space in front of me.

She climbs on, straddling the bike, and *fuck*. Those leather pants hug her like they were painted on. In this position, her ass is flush against my lap, and she knows exactly what she's doing when she arches and grabs the handlebars, glancing back over her shoulder.

My hands slide over her cheeks, giving them a firm squeeze. "Goddamn, baby." I drag one palm up her spine, the other locking on her hip.

"Let me take a picture of that."

She smirks, nodding, then glances at me over her shoulder as I snap the shot. It's obscene how good she looks.

"I've got a surprise for you too," she says, mischief curling in her voice.

Curious, I help her turn to face me. She scoots forward, settling on the gas tank, boots braced on my knees so her legs are wide open. My hands are halfway to that zipper when she reaches for her jacket.

And unzips it.

No shirt. No bra. Just bare, perfect tits staring me in the face.

"Holy shit," I breathe.

It's all I can say. She's rendered me fucking speechless.

My hands come up automatically, cupping her. My thumbs brush over her nipples, and she tips her head back with a low moan. "It feels so good when you do that."

I lean in, swirl my tongue around one tight peak, kissing and sucking until she's arching into me.

"Let me take your picture like this," I say, reaching for my phone.

She gives me a look that's pure challenge.

"If you think I'd let anyone else see you like this, you're fucking crazy."

Her lips curve. "Well... I suppose." She shifts, posing just enough to make my pulse spike.

Black leather pants. Black jacket. Dark hair tumbling loose. And then those tits—creamy, full, perfect—above a body that looks like sin itself. Her green eyes are locked on me like she's already imagining me inside her.

She poses for me and I snap every one. Her hands braced

on the tank pushing those full breasts together like a fucking invitation. Then biting her finger. Slipping the jacket down one shoulder, then both. Wrapping her arms around herself and perching those perfect tits on her forearms.

My cock leaks the whole time begging to slide between them and mark her with my cum.

I pinch her nipple and roll it between my finger and thumb, making her gasp. "You ready to test out these pants?"

She bites her lip and nods.

I find the zipper, and pull. The leather parts, revealing her slick, glistening pussy—and *fuck*, it's even better than I imagined.

She rests her hands behind her, opening her legs wider.

"You want to take another picture, baby?" she teases.

"Fuck. Yes." I snap a few more and groan when she slides her finger between her pussy lips and plays with herself, then sucks her arousal clean.

I can't wait another second to get my hands on her—and my cock in her.

I grip her hips and pull her forward until her ass is right at the edge of the gas tank.

"Put your legs up here," I tell her, tapping my shoulders.

Her eyes flare with heat, but she obeys—slow, deliberate—like she knows exactly what she's doing to me. Her boots hook over my shoulders, the leather creaking softly, and I can smell her now. Hot. Sweet. Already wet for me.

She wraps her fingers around the handlebars like I told her, chest rising and falling faster. "Jax..."

"Hold on tight, Cricket."

I drag my palms up the backs of her thighs, spreading her wider until the zipper's gaping open and I've got an unobstructed view of heaven. One long lick from base to clit and she's already trembling. I hold her steady, tongue circling her clit before sucking it into my mouth.

Her head tips back with a gasp, the night air catching in her moan. "Oh, fuck—"

"Eyes on me," I order, looking up at her from between her legs.

Her gaze drops, locking with mine, and it's like pouring gasoline on an open flame. I eat her like I've been starving, my tongue flicking, my mouth sealing over her until her hips start rocking against my face. She's holding the bars like she's riding me instead of my bike, knuckles white.

Every sound she makes goes straight to my cock. I grip her ass, pulling her closer so I can bury myself deeper between her thighs, tasting every drop.

"Jax... I'm—"

I hum against her clit, and that's all it takes. She shudders, thighs clamping around my head, her orgasm hitting hard while I keep licking her through it.

When she finally slumps forward, breathing like she just ran a marathon, I kiss the inside of her thigh and grin up at her. "I'm getting you three more pair of these pants."

I straighten up, wiping my mouth with the back of my hand.

"Take my cock out," I tell her, voice low and rough.

Her lips part, and she swallows like she knows exactly what's about to happen. With slow, teasing hands, she unbuttons my jeans, the metal teeth of the zipper catching on the night air as she drags it down.

Her hand slips inside, warm fingers brushing over me, and I feel my whole body tighten. She finds the head and traces her thumb over it, spreading the bead of precum.

"Tease me again, Cricket, and I'll make you ride home naked."

She smirks but obeys, pulling me free, her hand wrapping around the base. "You're so hard," she murmurs.

"Yeah," I rasp, pushing her back slightly. "And you're going to fix that."

I line myself up, sliding the head through her slick entrance before pushing inside. The position's awkward at first with her perched on the gas tank, but when I stand, lifting her just enough to fit against me, it's like she was made for this.

Her legs wrap around my waist, boots pressing into my back as I drive deeper. She leans back, one hand gripping the handlebar behind her, the other braced against the tank.

"Fuck—Jax..." she gasps, her head tipping back as I set the pace.

The bike rocks slightly beneath us with every thrust, the engine long dead but the metal humming with the echo of movement. Her jacket slides down further, the sight of her tits bouncing with each snap of my hips making me want to ruin her right here under the floodlights of the airport lot.

Fuck I want to record this and watch her over and over.

I slide one hand between us, finding her clit. My thumb circles once, twice—her whole body jerks.

"Oh, God—"

"That's it," I growl, keeping the pressure steady, my other hand gripping her ass to pull her down harder on me. Those beautiful, bare tits bouncing with each thrust. "Come for me again."

Her nails bite into my shoulders as her hips start to shake. She's close—I can feel it in the way her walls tighten around me.

"Look at me, Cricket."

She forces her eyes open, green and glassy, and that's when it hits her. Her second orgasm tears through her, thighs trembling, a cry breaking free as I keep working her clit until she's practically begging me to stop.

I don't give her time to catch her breath. My hands wrap around her hips, lifting her enough to slide out before I turn her around on the tank.

"Face forward," I tell her.

She obeys, swinging her leg over so her ass is back against my lap. The leather jacket slips from her shoulders and drops to the ground, forgotten. She plants her boots on the pegs, both hands gripping the handlebars like she's bracing for impact.

I lean in, my mouth finding the soft skin of her neck, teeth scraping before I suck hard enough to make her gasp. One hand fists in her hair, pulling her head back as I line myself up again and push into her in one movement.

"Fuck..." she breathes, arching her back, offering herself to me.

I lock an arm around her waist and set a brutal rhythm, my hips slamming into hers, the slap of skin on skin echoing in the quiet night. My free hand comes up to her chest, squeezing one perfect breast hard enough to make her cry out.

"You like that?" I growl against her ear.

"Yes—Jax—oh, God—"

"I'm going to take a picture of this tight pussy swallowing my cock, baby."

"Yes.,"

I open my camera and point it at her ass. I spread her cheek with my free hand and groan at the sight of my dick disappearing into her. Coming out slick with her juices coating me.

Fuck, I could live here.

"Look at me."

She turns back as I move into her. Leaning back so I can capture the space where we connect. Up the curve of her bare back. Capturing her just right to see her gorgeous face and full tits pressed against my bike.

I drop my camera into my helmet and squeeze her ass with both hands, sliding into her as she braces her feet against my bike's pegs, using them to ride me.

"You feel so good inside me, Jax." She pants, face tilted to the heavens as she moves.

Her walls flutter around me, that telltale clench that means she's on the edge again. I take her hair tight in my grip, forcing her to feel every deep, punishing thrust until she's shaking, her knuckles white on the handlebars and I'm about to lose it.

"Come with me, Cricket," I command, my own release building fast.

Her body goes tight, and she shatters around me, crying

out as I fuck her through it. I slam into her one last time, burying myself deep and groaning as I spill into her, the heat of it spilling down between us.

Above, the deafening roar of a plane tears through the night sky, lights sweeping over us as it descends toward the runway. The timing's perfect—her body still spasming around me while the sound drowns out everything but the pounding in my chest.

I don't pull out right away. I just hold her there, her back to my chest, both of us breathing hard, the echo of the moment burned into my head.

I pull the zipper up slow, sealing her in those damn pants like I'm locking away something only I get to touch. My fingers come away wet, and I taste her without shame, letting the flavor linger before I reach for my helmet.

She tips her head, a little smirk tugging at her lips. "So... did it live up to your imagination?"

I grin, leaning in just enough that my words brush her ear. "No, Cricket." I press a kiss to her jaw. "It was better."

Chapter 36

Cassidy

I wake before Jaxon does.

The early light through the curtains makes him look even more handsome, his jaw relaxed, lashes dark against his skin.

I scoot closer, throwing a leg over his and tucking myself into his warmth. He doesn't budge. Just sleeps like a rock while I snuggle in, breathing in that clean, masculine scent of his skin.

I try to drift back off, but it's useless. My naked body is pressed against his, and the heat building low in my stomach refuses to be ignored.

I place a kiss on his chest but, nothing. He's out like a light.

A few more gentle pecks on his chest, his abs, working myself lower. His cock hardens and my pulse spikes. I glance up at him, but he's still completely out.

Biting my lip, I slide my hand under the covers, wrapping my fingers around him. I give him a gentle squeeze and stroke.

He groans, low and deep, but doesn't open his eyes.

A slow smile curls my lips.

If he's not going to wake up, I guess I'll have to wake him.

Carefully, I shift down between his legs, dragging the covers with me until they drape over my head like a tent. I take him in hand, licking from base to tip, and his cock jerks in response.

I tease the swollen head with my tongue, swirling around it before taking him in, slow at first... then deeper, until I can't anymore without gagging. I pull back, suck harder, then dive in again, letting my tongue work every inch.

He's moaning now, but still on the edge of sleep. I can feel the exact moment he starts to wake—the subtle shift of his legs, the slow thrust of his hips toward my mouth.

"Fuck, baby..." His voice is rough, wrecked from sleep.

The covers are tossed back, and he moves my hair out of my face so he can watch. "Look at you—waking me up with your slut mouth around my dick."

God, I love it when he talks like that.

"My beautiful Cricket couldn't even wait for me to wake up? You needed my cock that bad?"

I hum around him in answer, still sucking, still taking him as deep as I can.

I keep going until his breathing turns ragged and his thighs tense under my hands.

"God you feel so fucking good." I suck harder, faster, moaning around him wanting him to lose it.

"Fuck—Cassidy—" He holds my hair tight, as he tenses his abs and there is a slight arch in his back. "Holy shit, you're going to make me come."

God this makes me so wet.

I feel him lean up watching his cock slide in and out of my mouth. He pulses his hips with my movements. Cussing praises and gives me everything. "Fuck baby," He pulls on my hair slightly still holding it, thrusting deeper as I take every drop, licking and swallowing until he's shuddering.

When he finally slumps back, I let him slip free and run my tongue along him again, catching the few stray beads I missed.

I climb back up to him, grinning. "Good morning."

He catches my chin and kisses me—slow, lazy, the kind of kiss that says he's in no rush to start the day.

"Morning," he murmurs against my lips, one hand sliding down my back.

I snuggle into him, leg thrown back over his hip, my cheek pressed to the warm skin of his chest. His heartbeat is steady beneath my ear, his arm heavy and protective around me. For a few blissful minutes, we just breathe together, the world outside this bed feeling so far away.

It's perfect.

And then my phone rings.

I groan, reaching blindly toward the nightstand, but the second I see the name on the screen, my stomach twists and I sit up.

It's my brother.

Jaxon glances over, frowning. "Fuck. I forgot to tell you."

My fingers tremble as I swipe to accept the call. "Hello?"

"Where the *fuck* are you?" His voice roars through the line, all rage and accusation. Jaxon sits up hearing the tone.

My blood runs cold. "Are you... back?"

"I'm back. And I want you here. *Now.*"

The call ends before I can reply. My hands feel clammy, my chest tight. My perfect morning crumbles like it was never real.

"Cass?" Jaxon scans my face and knows somethings wrong. "What is it?"

I force a shaky breath, pulling the sheet tighter around me. I shouldn't have let this go so long. I should have told him.

But I need to do this. Me. Alone.

"It's... something I have to handle. My brother."

He studies me, jaw flexing, like he already knows he's not going to like whatever comes next.

"Cassidy—"

"I can't tell you. Not yet." My voice cracks. "Please... just trust me. I'll tell you everything when I get back. But right now... this is between him and me."

His breathing is picking up, likes he's struggling with how much to push.

"Does this have anything to do with why you put yourself up for auction?"

It makes my throat burn and my eyes water. I grit my teeth and nod. Suddenly, not touching him is making it hard to breathe so I climb on his lap. My arms are around his neck, and he buries his face in mine. I love it when he does this. He takes a deep inhale like he can bury my scent into him.

"Hey," He pulls back cupping my jaw. Concern etched into every dark rivet of his eyes. "You don't have to do this alone." He whispers against my lips but doesn't kiss me.

"I do though." I kiss him. "Just trust me."

His eyes are hard, but he nods once. "You come back to me."

"I will." *Forever.*

By the time I reach the house, my pulse is pounding so hard I can hear it in my ears.

"Mom?" "Shanae?"

This will be easier if they're here in the house. Jonathan acts tough unless someone else is there. Because he's actually a coward. An insecure asshole who's trying to be more important than he really is.

"She's at the doctor." He comes out of the kitchen wiping his hands and finishing a bite of something.

Shit. I forgot—they had that follow-up doctor's appointment today.

Which means it's just me and him.

"It's time to go."

"No." I drop my purse on the table, trying to sound steady even though my stomach's twisting itself into knots.

His eyes narrow. "Excuse me?"

"I said no. I'm not going. I'm not going through with it." My hands are shaking, but I don't let him see. "I'm in love with Jaxon. And I'm going to be with him. We can... we can work something else out."

His expression morphs from disbelief to fury in a blink. "You're in love with him? Are you fucking insane?" He steps closer, voice rising. "Did you fuck him?"

"That's none of your business."

"Oh but it is my fucking business. You were supposed to be a virgin, Cassidy. That was the whole deal, you stupid fucking bitch. He already saw your doctors exam confirming that slut cunt of yours was—shockingly—untouched."

I cross my arms, forcing the words out before I lose my nerve. "Then *you* go marry the English lord. Take it up the ass if he needs a virgin hole to fuck... unless yours has already been claimed by someone before."

The slap comes so fast I barely see his hand move. My head snaps to the side, skin stinging, eyes watering.

"You ungrateful little whore." His breath is hot, sour with rage. "I've done everything for this family—"

"No. You've done everything for yourself." I'm backing away and reaching into my back pocket for my phone when he shoves me hard, my back hitting the wall with a thud. The edge of a picture frame digs into my shoulder.

I make a break for the door—I can run to Ben—but Jonathan catches my hair and yanks me back. My knee buckles, and the phone skids across the floor, clattering against the baseboard just as the doorbell rings.

Before I can move, he's yanking me upright until my

scalp burns. "We're leaving," he growls, dragging me toward the door. "You're doing what you agreed to."

"No, I'm not."

I try to activate my phones voice command. "Call Jaxon." God I hope it does.

I kick at his shins, nails raking at whatever skin I can find, but it only makes him yank my hair harder until white-hot pain shoots across my scalp. His other hand clamps around my face, fingers digging into my cheeks so hard I can taste blood from where my teeth cut the inside.

"You think this is a choice? You already agreed." His voice is low and poisonous. "If you don't cooperate, I'll sell this house right out from under her. I'll sell the horses—separately. And I'll tell her it's your fault. I'll make her hate you."

Hot tears spill down my cheeks. "You're a monster."

"No." His smile is pure venom. "You're the monster. Lord Greville is offering to get her better treatment—a shot at a real cure. All you had to do was marry him and let him fuck your virgin cunt." His grip tightens, and I can't even cry out. "But no... you had to go be a whore. For Jaxon."

The doorbell rings again, shrill and jarring.

"Coming!" his voice booms at my back. Then, he returns to me in a hiss: "You want our mother to die and have it be your fault?"

"Don't act like you're doing this for her." There is venom in my voice and tears running down my face.

"You think she can survive the cancer, losing the house, the horses? Knowing her daughter did it to her?" He leans in close, his breath a hot whisper against my ear. "No. She'll die of a broken heart. And you'll be the one who killed her."

He drags me to the door by my hair, my scalp screaming. The door swings open.

A sleek black limo idles in the driveway. The man standing beside it—dressed in a tailored suit and wearing the coldest expression I've ever seen—doesn't even blink at the sight of my brother manhandling me.

Before I can think, I'm shoved inside. I scramble for the opposite door, but the handle doesn't budge. Of course it's locked.

My brother slides in beside me, pushing me to the floorboard. The door shuts, sealing us in as he lands a kick right to my thigh. "Get the fuck away from me. Fucking pathetic."

The engine hums, and the limo glides away from the house, from safety, from everything.

And I'm trapped inside with the devil.

I try reasoning with him again, pleading for him to just think about another way, but Jonathan's eyes flash—and then he snatches a crystal glass from the limo bar and hurls it at me.

I brace for the hit and it thumps hard on my knee. It doesn't break, just falls to the carpeted floor. I cover my knee with my hand, swallowing back the cry of pain.

"Shut the fuck up," he snarls. "And practice closing your fucking legs. Maybe the lord can be fooled on your wedding night when he fucks you."

My stomach churns and I close my eyes. I should have brought Jaxon. I should have listened when he tried to help me. I should have been honest with him.

My eyes scan the limo for something—anything—to help me. A phone. A pen. A weapon. There's nothing.

The car slows, pulling onto a stretch of tarmac that gleams under the afternoon sun. My heart plummets when I see the sleek jet waiting at the end. A coat of arms glints on the fuselage, the same one stamped on the box Jonathan gave me. The shirt. The necklace.

The symbol of the prison he was preparing for me.

The driver opens our door. Jonathan doesn't wait to see if I'll cooperate—he yanks me out by the arm, hard enough to wrench my shoulder.

A man descends the jet's stairs, buttoning a navy blazer over a too-slender frame. Older than I expected. His balding head catches the light, and his beady eyes rake over me like I'm meat on display.

"Even more lovely than the pictures," he says.

Jonathan shoves me forward, and Lord Greville steadies me—but only for a moment. I snap, kicking at him, trying to tear away, but he spins me around with frightening speed, fisting my hair and clamping a hand around my throat. His grip tightens, choking me until spots burst in my vision.

"I take it you trust my discretion on the manner best to make my fiancée heel," he says over my head.

"She belongs to you. Do as you see fit," Jonathan replies without hesitation. Then he turns back toward the limo... and stops. "And Cassidy?"

I glare at him, tears of pure rage and hatred burning tracks down my cheeks.

"An early congratulations on your marriage."

He smiles like it's the cruelest joke in the world, then walks away.

Greville's fingers bite into my neck as he pushes me toward the plane. He's not as physically strong as Jonathan, but the clammy malice in his grip makes my skin crawl. I fight for breath with every step.

Inside, he shoves me so hard I stumble across the plush cabin and hit the floor. I scramble on my hands and knees toward the narrow hallway, then stand and sprint. Desperate to find a door I can lock. But I slam into a wall of solid muscle.

A large man—built like a boulder—looks down at me without expression.

"Sit down, my bride." His words slither down my back and make me shiver.

Greville doesn't even glance at me, already lowering himself into a leather seat and buckling in. "We're taking off immediately."

The wall of muscle hauls me up and throws me into a chair so hard the air leaves my lungs. "Put on your fucking seatbelt. Now."

I glare at him, but my hands obey, knowing in my bones this man wouldn't hesitate to break me in half. Jonathan's abuse was cruel, but cowardly. This man... he's killed before. I can feel it radiating off him.

The only saving grace—the one thin thread I cling to—is

that the lord wants a virgin bride. He plans to wait until the wedding night to consummate.

That buys me time. At least a week.

I just need to make it to London. From there, I'll find my way out.

I'll keep my promise to Jaxon.

I will come back to him.

Chapter 37

It's been hours since she left.

I've tried to distract myself—answered a few work emails, reviewed technical contracts, even took a few laps in my pool—but every time I stop moving, the same thought comes back.

I should've gone with her.

I lean back against the couch, my phone in my hand like it's an extension of my own damn body. Cassidy's bitmoji still hovers over her parents' house on Snap Map. That's the only thing keeping me from grabbing my keys and showing up uninvited. At least she's still there.

I'm kicking myself for not pushing harder this morning. For not making her tell me whatever the hell she's been holding back. I saw it in her eyes—the secret she wasn't ready to share. I thought giving her space would help. That she'd come to me on her own, trust me enough to tell me the truth.

That she'd believe me when I say I would do *anything* for her.

The city skyline spreads out past my floor-to-ceiling windows, the glass gleaming with the fading orange light of early evening. I can't seem to take it in tonight—the view's wasted on me. My chest feels tight, my pulse a steady drumbeat in my ears.

I type out a quick message.

> JAXON: You okay?

My thumb hovers over the screen, wondering if that sounds too clipped, too impersonal. I hit send anyway.

One minute passes. Then two.

Nothing.

I stand, pacing toward the glass, the reflection of my own restless shadow moving with me. My hand tightens around my phone until my knuckles ache. I tell myself she's just busy. Talking with her mom. Sorting out whatever she went there for.

A few minutes later, my phone buzzes in my hand.

Fuck. Finally.

Relief lasts exactly half a second—until I read the message.

> CASSIDY: I made a mistake getting involved with you. I shouldn't have strung you along, but I was using you. It's better if we go our separate ways.

What the fuck?

My lungs forget how to work. The room seems too quiet, the kind of silence that presses in on you until you can hear your own pulse.

I was using you.

The words echo in my head, ugly and sharp, carving through every moment we've shared until they don't even look real anymore. No laughter. No heat. No soft mornings with her curled into me. Just a con, start to finish.

No. No, she wouldn't—

I dial her number and it rings twice—then voicemail.

She fucking sent me to her voicemail. I call again. Same thing. My call is rejected.

The third time it goes straight to voicemail. Again when I call back.

Did she fucking block me?

> JAXON: Cass, what's going on?

Nothing. No delivered notice. She's cut me off.

My grip tightens around the phone until my knuckles ache, until I'm seconds from crushing it in my palm. The urge to throw it into the wall claws at me, to hear it shatter and see it die so I can go back. Back three minutes ago, when she was still mine—

Except she was never mine.

Apparently, I was just a pawn in whatever game she was playing.

The burn in my chest ignites into something else— something sharper. Anger. At her. At myself for letting her in, for thinking I could keep her.

My breath is coming in too fast. Taking in too much of the air around me. The air that smells like her. Sweet and warm and fucking everywhere, clinging to my sheets, the couch, my skin. It's suffocating.

I can't fucking breathe here. I've gotta get out of here.

I grab my helmet and keys, not giving a shit where I'm going, just knowing I can't stay.

I don't even realize where I'm going until I'm pulling into the back lot of *The Gym*.

Lucian's already here, hands wrapped, sweat darkening his shirt. He glances up when I walk in, eyebrows lifting like I'm the last person he expected. "Didn't think I'd see you today."

I don't answer. Can't. The storm in my chest doesn't leave room for words.

"Get taped up," he says, nodding toward the counter. "You're getting in the ring."

Fine.

It's muscle memory—wrapping my hands, stepping through the ropes—while my head is still stuck on her text. Lucian's posture is loose, ready for a warm-up. Mine isn't.

I swing. Hard.

He dodges, surprise flashing across his face.

"What the hell, Kane?"

I don't answer—I just swing again. Then again.

"Jesus—" He blocks, but my fists keep coming faster, harder, heat burning through my veins. A kick follows, then another punch—this one cracks against his guard and slips through, landing solid.

That's all it takes.

The gate blows open, and everything I've been holding back comes pouring out. "Come on," I growl, another strike flying. "Move!"

Anger. Hurt. Betrayal. I'm hitting harder than I should, moving like I'm trying to break something—anything—that isn't me. Swing. Miss. Connect. Again.

Lucian's throwing shots back now, his voice clipped between blows. "What—" *block* "—is—" *counter* "—your —" *jab* "—problem?"

I barely hear him. My pulse is a roar, drowning out everything but the need to keep going.

Then he catches me—one hit that rattles my fucking skull, and before I can recover, he's behind me. My feet leave the mat as he locks me into a hold and takes me down hard.

"What the fuck is your problem, Kane?" His voice is sharp, controlled.

I thrash against him, teeth gritted, adrenaline still driving me. My fists are trapped, my chest heaving.

"Let me go," I snap.

"Not until you stop swinging at me like you've lost your damn mind." His tone is level, but there's steel under it.

I shove again, jerking against his hold. "I *have* lost my mind."

"What happened?" His grip only tightens. "Is it Cassidy?"

Her name coming out of his mouth hits harder than any

punch he's thrown tonight. I grit my teeth, my anger renewed. "Don't say her fucking name."

"Jax." He shakes me once, sharp enough to snap my focus to him. "What. The fuck. Happened?"

He lets me go, pushing me away to give us both some space. I know it's in case he needs to hold me back again.

"It wasn't real." I bite out.

But the words make the fight drain out of me in pieces— anger first, then the strength to keep pretending I'm fine. My shoulders sag, my hands go slack. "None of it was real," I manage, voice low, raw.

My steps falter backwards until I hit the post behind me. I slide down it, sitting on the floor and letting the weight of her dismissal crush me.

Lucian waits only a second before he's kneeling next to me. "Tell me what happened."

"It wasn't fucking real," I bite out, and then it's like everything I've been holding together unravels at once. My breath catches hard. "None of it was. She—" I cut myself off, my throat tight, "—I thought she felt the same. I told her I loved her."

My eyes burn and tears fall heavy down my cheeks.

"She was only using me and I'm the fucking idiot who didn't see it."

"Jaxon." He says my name the way you'd talk to someone standing on a ledge.

"She fucking told me to go fuck myself and then she blocked me." My vision blurs, and I hate it. I look at my hands, red and shaking, then I ball them into fists and cover my eyes.

"How did I get this so wrong?"

Lucian doesn't say anything for a while. After a moment, he sits next to me. I cry. The pain leaking out of me with no way to stop it.

"I don't think that's true, buddy." Lucian's voice is low. Either uncomfortable or unsure if I'm still a bomb ready to explode. "Any idiot could see she was in love with you the night of the auction. And you were in love with her."

He places a hand on my shoulder. My tears are beginning to slow and I wipe my nose on the back of my hand.

"I *am* in love with her." I nearly whisper it.

"Then figure it out." He says it like it's so simple. "You said there was something she wasn't telling you. Maybe there is more to that than you know."

My heart is pounding. My mind starting to rush back to me.

"You really going to tell me you're going to let one little blocked number stop you?"

That makes me look at him. He cocks half a grin but it's not out of humor. It's a challenge.

"Step back," he says evenly. "Look at it again when your head's clear. You'll find what you missed."

I swallow hard trying to ease whatever is making my throat constrict.

"Then what?"

"Then you go get your fucking girl." He pauses a beat. "And you tear the whole goddamn world apart if you have to."

The wind is screaming in my ears, the roar of the bike swallowing everything else. I'm not even sure how long I've been riding—just gunning it down the open stretch, leaning into the curves, letting the speed strip me bare. The faster I go, the less room there is in my head for her words.

I don't mean to end up here.

The bike idles to a stop at the edge of the old airport, the place I brought her. Our spot. The one I've never shared with anyone else. The one where, for a little while, I thought I'd found something I didn't even realize I was missing.

My chest feels like it's going to split right down the middle.

It couldn't have been fake.

You can't fake that.

You can't fake heat so sharp it burns through you, or the kind of fire that makes you forget the rest of the world exists. You can't fake the quiet after, when her head was on my shoulder and I finally—finally—felt like I wasn't just existing anymore. I felt whole. Whole, after years of being nothing but splintered pieces.

My phone chimes.

The sound snaps me out of it, my gaze dragging to the screen.

> CLARA - GALLERY: Let me know when you're coming to pick up Cassidy's pieces.

> They're amazing.

I blink, the words taking a second to register. The paintings. I almost forgot about those.

Another message pings before I can reply.

> CLARA - GALLERY: If she's interested, there's a few buyers lined up.

My thumb hovers over the screen. I don't know if I'm doing this for her or for me. Maybe both. Maybe I just need some part of her that isn't poisoned by whatever the hell happened today.

Finally, I type back.

> JAXON: I'll be there in a few.

I pocket the phone, fire up the bike again, and pull away from the airstrip. But the truth is, no matter how far I ride, I'm still there—with her—in that moment when everything felt like it was ours.

And I'm not ready to let it go.

The bell over the door gives a soft chime as I step inside the gallery. The smell of fresh varnish and coffee hits me first, the air too still, too clean.

Clara's behind the counter, bright smile already forming. "That was quick."

I force something that might pass for a smile. "Yeah. Just...figured I'd get it done."

She chats as she walks me through, telling me she'll wrap everything carefully, that Cassidy's work has gotten a lot of attention. I nod at the right places, pretending I'm listening, pretending I'm alive.

When she disappears into the back, the pretense falls away.

The room feels cavernous without anyone in it. I head for the space where her pieces were displayed—where I'd planned to surprise her. It had been perfect in my head. It ended in disaster.

The largest one is still hanging, dominating the wall. I drop onto the bench in front of it, my elbows braced on my knees.

Cassidy downplays her art. Calls them silly paintings, nothing serious. But they're not. They're her. The parts she hides. The beauty, the chaos, the raw, unfiltered emotion she locks away from the world.

I stare until my eyes blur. And then something starts to feel...off.

Not wrong. Not bad. Just...not right.

I tilt my head. The composition looks strange, unbalanced. Then it hits me—the damn thing is upside down.

I'm on my feet before I can think, fingers finding the frame. I ease it off the wall, careful not to damage it, and rotate it.

And the second it's upright, it slams into me like a train.

It's Cassidy. No doubt in my mind.

A bride, bleeding out on the steps of a cathedral. Her white veil dissolves into a river of red that snakes down the stairs.

It's not abstract. It's not open to interpretation. It's intentional. Specific.

The air gets sucked right out of the room. My lungs forget how to work.

I take out my phone, snap a picture, and run it through my AI engine. I don't build the most powerful tech on the planet for nothing.

I isolate the chapel windows—tall, ornate, stained glass. Restrict the search to New York. Nothing.

Expand to the US. Still nothing.

Then it clicks—Jon's been in the UK.

I run it again and... bingo.

There it is. Clear as day.

My knees hit the floor in front of the painting before I realize I've moved, like I'm praying to it.

Her brother sold her off to be someone's bride... so she sold off a piece of herself first. On her terms.

That's it. That has to be it.

The rage comes fast, soldering the cracks in my heartbreak into something solid. Unshakable.

I stand and hit Lucian's number.

"Well, that was quick," he answers.

"How fast can you have someone in London?" My voice is steady. Deadly.

"Send me an address. They'll be there before dinner."

"I'll have an address soon."

"I'll be waiting."

I hang up, already calling my senior engineer.

"Get the interns into a war room and spin up a bridge," I order as I push out of the gallery, the door swinging shut behind me. I swing a leg over my bike, and it rumbles to life under me.

"We're going hunting,"

I keep my face still, my stomach turning.

If I don't find a way to escape before the wedding next week—or if Jaxon doesn't come looking for me before then—I know I'll vanish. He'll never find me.

Lunch on the flight was some dainty salad I ignored. Hours later, a hot dinner was served—beef in some rich-smelling sauce that made my stomach cramp with hunger —but I refused again. The thought of eating at *his* table made my throat close.

By the time we land, it's well into the night. London time puts it close to midnight, the city wrapped in a damp, chilly darkness. The car waiting for us is sleek and silent, its tinted windows shutting me off from everything beyond the glass.

Minutes later, we roll to a stop at what looks like a boutique. From the street, it's all dark windows and polished brass handles—the kind of place where women shop for something special. But I don't get anywhere near the front.

The muscle opens my door and steers me down a narrow alley to the rear of the building. An unmarked service door waits between two loading docks, propped open by a woman who looks like she was carved from old stone—sharp nose, thin lips, and a permanent frown. She's holding the door like she's been expecting us.

Inside it smells of fabric and steam, like freshly pressed dresses. There's no chatter of customers here. No music. Just the sound of my own pulse thudding in my ears as they lead me deeper inside.

The lord takes a seat and behind him, the wall of muscle shifts. Big. Mean. Silent.

There's a platform in the center of the room, surrounded by racks of white. Wedding dresses. So many they look like ghosts lining the walls.

A woman enters—haughty, narrow-faced, beady eyes that match his. She doesn't smile.

"Strip," he says, as if it's nothing.

My arms fold over my chest. "No."

The woman's tone is deceptively gentle. "Just remove your clothes, dear. Undergarments remain on."

I start to shake.

The muscle clears his throat, and it's not a polite sound —it's a warning.

"I'll do it for you if you refuse to comply."

I stare at him, just long enough to know he means it. Then I turn my back. My shirt comes off. My jeans follow. I look only at my own reflection in the mirror, closing myself off to everything else.

"Mmm," the lord hums, eyes crawling over me. "Very lovely."

"She is," the muscle agrees, gaze openly raking my body.

I close my eyes. I am anywhere else. Anywhere but here.

The woman steps in, tape measure snapping between her fingers. She works quickly, efficiently—like I'm nothing but fabric to her. It's only when she calls out a number that I notice another girl in the room. Young. My age, maybe younger. She slips into the racks, silent, returns with several gowns draped over her arms.

The woman sifts through them, plucks one. "Try this one."

I glance at the muscle in the mirror, then take the dress and step into it. The fabric is heavy, suffocating.

"Yes. This one," the woman says, her voice clipped.

The lord stands like the decision is final. "Have it ready by tomorrow."

My stomach drops. "Tomorrow?" I spin to face him.

He takes slow, deliberate steps toward me. "Yes. Tomorrow. No need to draw things out. I'm eager for an heir." His gaze drags down my body. "I'm eager to *put* an heir *in* you... as well."

The back of his finger runs down my breast. Instinct takes over—I smack it away.

His smile disappears. His hand shoots down, grabbing the hem of the dress and yanking me toward him. "We'll have none of that once you are my wife. You will learn that lesson quickly." He releases me, smooths his jacket like nothing happened. "Best not make the punishment worse on yourself."

He heads for the door, the muscle following with a smirk that makes my skin crawl.

"I will take you every way I want you tomorrow night, my bride," the lord says without looking back. "It will hurt less if you behave."

They're gone, but the air feels no lighter.

The woman and the young girl remain. The muscle stands at the door, watching me with a stare that feels like hands on my skin. I can see it in his eyes—he's already imagining things he'd do to me if the lord allowed it. And I'm betting, eventually, he will.

"Turn around. We'll pin the adjustments." The woman's voice is cold. Detached. As if she doesn't know—or doesn't care—that I'm here against my will.

I turn. Stand still as she works.

The first pin bites my side and the tears come, hot and silent, falling down my face as she fits me for the dress I'll be married in.

And possibly destroyed in.

Chapter 40

I slide to a stop so hard the back tire skids. Kickstand down, kill switch flicked, helmet off—done in seconds.

I take the steps to her front door three at a time and don't bother knocking. Don't bother breathing. I shoulder the door open like I own the place.

Jon's in the foyer with a concerned-looking Shanae.

"This doesn't sit right," she says, her voice tight.

Jon turns toward me just in time for me to rear back and drive my helmet straight into his face. The crack is sickening, satisfying.

"You're right, Shanae," I say, calm as steel.

Jon staggers back, cursing, blood already running. I swing the helmet again, harder this time, and feel his nose break under it. He drops like a sack of bricks, head bouncing off the hardwood. Dazed. Moaning.

I look at Shanae. "She's not here, is she?"

Her lip trembles. Then she shakes her head, tears welling. "No. I found her phone on the floor—broken." She points to the foyer table where it sits, dead and useless. "Her purse is here. And look—" She points to the wall. A divot in the drywall, right at Cassidy's height. Like someone slammed her into it.

The sight makes the edges of my vision burn.

I kneel down in front of Jon, forearms resting on my knees, staring at him like the snake he is.

"He knows where she is," I tell Shanae, my voice low.

She gasps.

"Because he's the one that sent her there."

I fist his shirt and haul him up until his feet barely touch the floor. "And he's going to tell me everything."

Jon's still half out of it, but his mouth twists into something ugly. Blood covers his teeth when he grins. "I don't know what you're talking about."

I don't take my eyes off him when I ask Shanae, "Where's Lilly?"

"In her room. Resting," Shanae says quietly.

Now I look at her. "Don't tell her what's going on. And don't worry." My voice hardens as I glance back to Jon. "I'm going to get her."

Jon chuckles wetly. "You'll be too late."

I lean in, close enough he can smell the threat on my breath.

"For your sake," I murmur, "you better hope I'm not."

I half drag Jon down the path, gravel crunching under my boots. He's stumbling, mumbling, too dazed to fight back. His shoes slip in the dirt when we hit the stables.

Big Ben's inside, brushing down one of the mares. He glances up, that big, calm frame filling the space.

"You may want to take a walk," I tell him, shoving Jon forward. "Close the doors behind you."

Ben's brows lift, but I'm already dropping Jon onto the dirt floor. The bastard groans, clutching at his ribs. I cross to the corner, grab a chair—the same one Mrs. Hayes had to sit in while Jon's hired trash tried to take the horses. The memory only tightens the coil in my chest.

I haul Jon upright and slam him into the seat. He nearly folds sideways. I have to set him straight before I head for the workbench, scanning for rope.

Behind me, the heavy stall doors thud shut. I glance over my shoulder. Ben's still here.

"This is about Cass?" His deep voice doesn't need to rise above a murmur.

"Yes. He sent her somewhere." My tone is flat, deadly. "And I'm going to get it out of him any way I have to. You don't need to be part of this."

Ben doesn't leave. Instead, he turns to his own bench and starts going through his tools—slow, methodical. The sound of metal shifting, clinking, setting down on wood.

"I wasn't always a horse master," he says, voice gone darker. He lays out a few pieces—old farrier tools, pliers, something with a hooked end I don't recognize. "If it helps find Miss Cassidy faster, I'll help."

I loop the rope around Jon's legs, pulling tight, binding his wrists behind the chair. I look up at Ben. "As long as you know what you're getting into."

His eyes meet mine, steady and cold. "I know. Do you?"

"I'll do whatever it takes."

Jon's head lolls forward, blood dripping from his nose to the dirt. I grab a bucket from the corner, slosh water into it from the pump, and toss the whole thing in his face.

He jerks like a fish on a hook, sputtering, eyes wild. I slap him hard across the cheek. "Wake the fuck up."

He groans, twisting against the rope.

"Where is she?" I demand.

"I don't—"

I backhand him. "Don't start with that."

He smirks through the blood. "You've got nothing, Kane. I made sure of it. No calls, no cards, no GPS. You won't find her."

He's not wrong—there wasn't much of an electronic trail. Jon knows I'd tear through his life in minutes if he left one.

I glance at Ben. "You ever get information out of someone before?"

Ben's mouth curves in something that's not quite a smile. "I have. And I was very good at it."

"What do you suggest to get him talking fastest?"

Ben doesn't hesitate. "A finger."

I hold out my hand. Ben drops a pair of cutters into it. The weight is cold, solid.

I drag the sharp point down Jon's cheek, slow enough for him to feel every inch of it. The tip bites into his skin, a deep gash that oozes bright red blood.

"I know you sold her to Lord Greville," I say, voice steady. "I just need to know which property. He's got too many to waste time guessing—and I'm eager to get my future wife back where she belongs."

Jon's eyes flare with something ugly. "Fuck you." Then he spits—right in my face.

I wipe it off, calm as a priest at confession. "Underestimating the lengths, I'll go for her is a mistake you won't make twice."

Before he can say another word, I take the cutters and snip.

The sound is wet, sharp, final.

Jon screams like an animal caught in a trap. Blood pours over his hand, onto the dirt.

I grab the severed pinky, shove into his mouth, and clamp my hand over his jaw. "Swallow." I growl, tightening my grip until his teeth sink in.

His eyes roll back as he gags it down, the sound echoing in the stables.

"Now," I say, leaning close enough for him to feel every word, "let's try this again. Where the fuck is she?"

He put up a fight—longer than I expected.

Two more fingers—both currently digesting—and a meat hook to the thigh before he finally broke. The moment Ben started pulling it down his leg, tearing through skin, muscle, and tendon like he was dressing out a deer, Jonathan's resolve crumbled and the words spilled out.

He gave me the location, and I sent it straight to Lucian.

His reply came within seconds:

LUCIAN: He's on the way.

But I wasn't done with my old friend.

I wanted the truth.

And what came out made my stomach turn.

Jonathan inherited his father's business and burned through the money with a coke habit. He'd started running drugs through the operation, and for a while it worked—until greed pushed him into deeper waters he couldn't swim in. When the walls started closing in, he needed a bailout.

Lord Greville wanted a wife and an heir. Jonathan had a sister. Done deal.

He told Cassidy it was for their mother's cancer treatment, that when she was well again, she could divorce him and be free.

But that was never his plan. He intended to let the house go, sell the horses, and pocket the cash. The payout from Greville would line his own pockets. Once Cassidy was gone, he would have walked away from his mother without a second thought, leaving her to spend whatever time she had left alone in a hospital bed.

Greville would own the Hayes' enterprise and run whatever the fuck he is into through it.

My phone buzzes with more information about Greville from my senior engineer. He's got a lot. Drugs. Strip clubs. Entertains the scum of the world so his property is a fortress and has round the clock security.

I've heard enough from this piece of shit, and I want my girl.

I look at Ben. "Keep him tied up. I'm going to get her."

Ben moves toward Jonathan with a slow, deliberate stride, like he's approaching a dangerous stallion. He hooks his tool beneath Jonathan's chin, applying just enough pressure to lift his head. "I'll keep an eye on him," he says, his voice a low rumble. "And if she's hurt, boy, you won't die quick."

I find a rag on the workbench, soak it in the bucket, and scrub the blood from my hands and arms before pulling my phone again. *May need a few more guys,* I text Lucian, attaching everything we've gathered on Greville.

His reply is immediate:

> LUCIAN: I'll tell my guy to hold and we'll regroup.

> JAXON: She can't get hurt.

> LUCIAN: We'll get her out of there.

I pocket my phone and head for the barn doors, feeling sharp gratitude for having a friend like Lucian Vale in my corner. I've just pulled them closed when a piercing shriek cuts through the air.

Shanae bursts out onto the porch, panic written across every line of her face—

"It's Lilly," Shanae gasps, her voice breaking. "She tried to go to the bathroom on her own and fell—hit her head on the sink. She's hurt bad. She's not... she's not responding."

I'm already running and take the porch steps two at a time before I even process what she said.

I bolt up the staircase, my feet pounding the same path I ran a thousand times as a kid, straight to Cassidy's mom's bedroom where I'd never been allowed in but always knew.

She's there, sprawled on the cold tile of the ensuite bathroom, her skin pale as porcelain, a dark pool of blood blooming around her.

"Call an ambulance," I snap.

"I already did," Shanae says, her voice shaking so hard the words almost don't make it out. "If she dies while Cassidy is gone—"

"She's not going to die."

I kneel beside her just in time to hear the faintest moan. Her head shifts toward me, and I finally breathe for the first time since I heard the scream.

"I'm cold," she whispers.

Against every rule in my head about head injuries, I slide my arms under her and lift. She's so light and I can feel her trembling. "We'll take you outside, wait for the ambulance."

But the ambulance doesn't come.

Shanae's pacing, phone clutched tight to her ear. "There was an accident," she says, eyes wide with panic. "Multiple fatalities and all services are being rerouted, They'll send someone when they can."

I look toward the drive, cursing under my breath. My bike's useless for this. But Shanae's SUV is parked by the fence.

"Get your keys," I tell her.

She nods, takes off toward the house.

I glance down at Lilly, keeping my voice steady for her sake. "You're going to be okay."

"Where's my baby girl?" She asks with a voice too frail.

"I'll go get her." I promise. "I just need to get you to the hospital, and I'll go get her."

I look at the night sky. The full moon moving across it and send up a prayer.

Please, please don't let me be too late.

Chapter 41

Cassidy

It's somewhere around two in the morning when the muscle shoves me into the back of another car. He takes the front passenger seat beside the driver, shutting me in like I'm precious cargo—or a prisoner.

The door handle gives a metallic clunk when I try it. Locked.

Of course.

I lean into the window switch next, pressing it down hard. Nothing. The glass doesn't so much as twitch.

In the rearview mirror, the muscle's eyes meet mine. He's grinning—like he knows exactly what I'm doing and finds it adorable. My skin crawls. I shift my stare to the blur of streetlights instead, counting the seconds in my head as we drive.

We leave the city behind in a slow bleed of darkened suburbs and winding country roads. When the car finally turns, it's onto a long, tree-lined drive that swallows us whole.

The estate rises out of the black like something obscene—too big, too loud in its wealth to be hidden, and yet here it is, tucked away from the world. The grounds sprawl so far in every direction I can't make out the edges. All I can see are the scattered glows of security lights strung along the perimeter fence and the harsh wash of flood lamps at the main gate.

Two armed guards stand on either side of the car, rifles slung over their shoulders. They scan us like they're looking for an excuse to pull the trigger.

The gates swing open slowly, deliberately, the kind of delay that says *We could kill you before you ever make it to the house.*

The car glides forward, swallowed by the shadows beyond.

Perfect. Armed security.

Looks like hatching an escape plan won't be easy... or quick.

The room they shove me into is big, old, and cold—like everything in this place was made to impress, not comfort. The muscle hangs my dress on a hook just inside the door, his beefy hand smoothing it like I'm going to thank him for the favor.

"Be ready to leave by eight," he says flatly. "I'll be stationed outside your door all night. Don't try anything."

The door shuts with a finality that makes my stomach turn.

I try everything. Every window—locked and sealed tight. I press my fingers along the edges, check for hidden latches, anything. Nothing gives. I even knock on the walls, praying for one of those secret passages old houses have in movies. No luck.

Sheer curtains sway in the occasional draft, and beyond them I catch flashes of lightning.

I stand in the center and look around the room trying to think. How am I supposed to sleep when I'll apparently be a bride in a few hours?

There are footsteps outside. I press my ear to the door, straining to hear, but the sound is muffled.

I crack it open—only to jolt back. I expected the muscle, but it's someone else. Just as big. Dressed head-to-toe in black. He doesn't face me fully, just turns his head enough for me to catch the edge of his profile.

"Oh... um..." My voice comes out awkward, unsure.

Maybe I can trick him. Maybe he's easier to get past.

"Did you need something?" His American accent catches me off guard.

"I'm... a little hungry," I say, quieter than I mean to.

He nods once. "I'll send for something."

"Can I go myself?"

"No. It's not safe in the halls. You need to stay in the room."

Not safe in the halls? That does nothing to settle my nerves.

"My name's Killian," he adds, gesturing for me to step back. "If you need anything, ask for me."

The door shuts, sealing me in again. I slide down the wall, hugging my stomach until my arms ache. And then I cry. Quiet at first, then harder, until my chest hurts.

Several minutes later, maybe more, a knock at the door pulls me back. "It's Killian."

I scrub at my face and open the door. He's holding a tray—scrambled eggs, toast, and a bottle of water.

The sight of the eggs hits harder than I expect. I think of Jaxon in his kitchen that first morning, nearly burning down the penthouse trying to make breakfast for me. My throat tightens, and I start crying all over again.

I pick at the food but can't eat more than a few bites. My stomach is knotted too tight. I drink most of the water, saving the rest for later. For when the clock strikes eight and they come to take me—to a chapel, to marry a beady-eyed devil whose name I don't even want to say out loud.

I have three, maybe four hours to figure this out.

I have to find a way out of here... before it's too late.

***

I barely sleep. When I finally do drift off, it feels like I've just closed my eyes before there's a knock at the door. "One hour."

The voice is American—probably Killian from last night. At least it's not the muscle. I hope I don't have to see him again before... before whatever this day is supposed to be.

Every part of me aches—my shoulders from the fight with Jonathan, my back from hours in that cramped plane seat, my jaw from keeping it clenched the entire seven-hour flight. I feel like my body has been wound too tight for too long.

The shower is a small mercy. I stay under the hot spray

longer than I should, letting it burn away the outside world for a few stolen minutes. Steam curls around me, and for a moment I can almost pretend I'm home.

When I finally step out, I find a bra and panties folded neatly in the drawer. My size. The thought makes my stomach twist. The gremlin had these brought here for me —prepared for me like I'm an object he's purchased, not a person.

I blow-dry my hair, more for something to do with my hands than for vanity. The mirror shows the faint smudge of a bruise on my neck from his slimy grip yesterday. I don't cover it. Let everyone see. Let it be a silent declaration: I'm here against my will.

Back in the bedroom, a new breakfast waits under a silver cloche. I lift it—biscuits and gravy. My throat closes. I slam the lid back down before I can start crying, but it's too late. All I can think about is Jaxon in his bedroom, that lazy smirk on his face while he brought me a breakfast tray.

Everything makes me think of him—the way he smells, his smile, the way he drives me insane in ten different ways and still manages to make me feel safe.

Just one choice. That's all it would have taken to stop all this. If I'd told him the truth from the start, maybe I wouldn't be here. Maybe I wouldn't be walking toward something I can't escape.

Another knock. "Five minutes."

My heart kicks into overdrive. I blink away the tears, forcing my hands to steady as I pull the dress over my head. Then the shoes. Then, the stupid, mile-long veil.

One look in the mirror and I hardly recognize myself. I look exactly how I feel—tired, worn down, trapped.

The door opens. Killian's there, all black and broad shoulders, eyes unreadable.

"Time to go."

The drive to the cathedral takes twenty minutes. I watch the clock in the front of the car like it's counting down to my execution. Every minute ticks away another piece of hope.

A bouquet is on the seat next to me as we drive—lilies. My mother's favorite. For a split second, I want to hug them to my chest, like if I hold them tightly enough she'll appear and make this nightmare stop.

Killian opens my door, scanning the street like he's part of the Secret Service. The place is deserted—no cars, no photographers, no crowd. My feet root to the ground. I don't want to go inside. I don't want to walk down an aisle in front of strangers to give my life away.

His hand is gentle but firm on my arm, urging me forward. Inside, the sunlight from behind us fades, replaced by the dim glow of chandeliers. My eyes adjust, focusing on the set of heavy double doors ahead. Closed, hiding what's waiting for me behind them

A tear slips down my cheek before I can stop it.

Music starts.

I close my eyes, swallowing hard. But then... I *hear* it. Really hear it.

It's a beautiful night, we're looking for something dumb to do...

My chest tightens, breath hitching.

"No," I whisper.

One step. Then another.

Hey baby...

I shove the double doors open, my heart in my throat.

I think I wanna marry you.

The church is empty. Not a single soul—except one.

At the end of the aisle stands the most beautiful sight I've ever seen.

Jaxon. Dark jeans. Black T-shirt stretched tight across his chest.

For a split second, pain flickers across his face. Then relief takes over.

"Hey, Cricket."

Chapter 42

The second those doors open and she's there it's like I can finally breathe.

For a heartbeat, neither of us moves. She stands frozen in the threshold, the veil trailing behind her like a shroud, white silk pooling around her feet. Her eyes are wide and glassy, like she doesn't trust what she's seeing. Like she's afraid if she blinks, I'll disappear.

Then the flowers slip from her hands. They hit the stone floor with a dull thud, petals scattering in every direction. She gathers her dress in trembling fists and starts toward me—stumbling at first, her heels catching on the fabric, but pushing forward anyway.

I don't wait for her to reach me. My body moves before my mind catches up, closing the distance in long, unbroken strides.

She all but collides with me. I catch her before she can lose her balance, her arms locking around my neck with a desperation that claws at my chest. She's shaking—so hard I can feel it in my bones—and I pull her in tighter, crushing her against me until I'm not sure where she ends and I begin.

Her breath hitches against my throat, and then the dam breaks. The sobs are violent, wracking through her small frame, each one tearing something out of me. I press my mouth to her hair, inhaling her scent like I need proof she's real.

"I thought I'd never see you again," she whispers, the words splintering apart in the middle. "I thought—God, Jaxon, I thought you'd never find me."

"I've got you," I murmur, over and over, holding her like the world might try to rip her away if I loosen my grip. "You're safe now. I've got you, baby. I'm here."

"I'm sorry," she says, the confession rushing out on a breath. "I should've told you everything sooner. I should've trusted you. I—"

"Shh." I slide a hand to her jaw, tipping her face up until her tear-streaked eyes meet mine. They're red-rimmed and shining, but they're still Cassidy—still the girl who's been under my skin from the second I saw her on that stage.

Fuck. Since the moment a little boy with ghosts in his eyes stepped foot on Emerald Ridge Farm.

"None of that matters. Not now. You're here with me. That's all I care about."

"I love you," she says, almost like she's afraid she won't get another chance to say it. Her voice trembles but doesn't break. "I've loved you forever, Jaxon. Since before I even knew what love really was. I wanted to say it that night—when you said it to me—but I was scared. I didn't want to risk losing what little I had of you. And then everything happened so fast and I thought…" She swallows hard, her voice dropping to a whisper. "I thought I'd never get to tell you at all."

The sound of it tears me apart and puts me back together in the same breath.

"Baby." My thumb brushes the damp track of a tear from her cheek. "I love you too," I tell her, my voice low, rough. "More than you'll ever know. And I swear to you— no one will ever touch you again. Not while I'm breathing."

"Jonathan is *never* going to touch you again." At some point I'm going to have to admit what I did to find her.

That I called Big Ben and told him Jonathan did in fact hurt her. And Ben assured me he'd keep true to his promise.

But I'm not bringing her monster into our moment.

She makes a small, broken sound and leans in. I meet her halfway, my mouth finding hers in a kiss that's as much a vow as it is a claim. There's salt from her tears, the faint hitch of her breath, the way she clings to me like I'm the only solid thing in a collapsing world.

When we break apart, I keep my forehead against hers, breathing her in, grounding myself in the only thing that matters—she's here. She's alive. She's mine.

And I'm never letting her go.

Her lips find mine again.

The first kiss was relief—proof we'd made it back to each other.

This one… this one is different.

It's a vow.

A promise sealed in the press of her mouth against mine, in the way she clings to me like letting go isn't an option.

When we part, she keeps her eyes on mine, voice no louder than a breath.

"You found me."

I rest my forehead to hers, my hands still framing her face.

"The world wouldn't have survived my heartbreak if I had lost you."

She lets out something between a sob and a laugh, and I can't stand the distance anymore. I kiss her again, slow and certain, like I can brand her with the truth.

"Run away with me," I tell her, my voice low but steady. "You belong with me—back home with your horses and your paintings. Let me give you a good life. Take care of you. Love you." My thumb brushes her cheek, and I see fresh tears fill her eyes. "Let me ask your mom for permission to marry you. Let me buy you the biggest ring I can find and get down on one knee and beg you to be my wife."

She laughs through the tears now, shaking her head like she's not sure if she should believe this is happening.

"And when you walk down the aisle, in the wedding dress of your dreams, let it be me you walk to."

I take her hand and press my lips to her knuckles.

"So run away with me, Cricket... because I don't have a life if you're not in it."

"Yes. Forever yes."

She smiles through tears, kissing me again—pressing her whole body against mine, her fingers curling into my hair like she never wants to let go.

When I pull her closer, I swallow the little sound she makes, and it goes straight to my chest—and lower.

The kiss deepens, turns hotter, until her hands slide under my shirt like she needs my skin. Hell, I need hers too.

"I'm tired of seeing you in a dress another man picked out," I growl.

Before she can respond, I fist the fabric at her front and tear it two.

"Jaxon!" she gasps, clutching the ruined edges. "Someone could walk in. And we're in a church!"

"Killian won't let anyone past those doors." My mouth finds her neck, tasting, marking.

"You sent him?" Her voice cracks, almost a sob.

"I did. I sent him."

Kiss.

"I send biscuits and gravy."

Kiss.

"I sent a bouquet of lilies."

Kiss.

"I sent a goddamn army to fight a war all night for daring take my girl."

She sobs.

"I needed to know you were safe until I could get here." I press more kisses along her jaw, her collarbone. "And Lucian owes me. I cashed in a few favors."

Her hands grip my face, pulling me back to her mouth. "Thank you."

I kiss her hard, my voice rough against her lips. "You never have to thank me for protecting what's mine."

She trembles, and I can't tell if it's from relief or the way I'm looking at her. Probably both.

I slip my hand past the waistband of her panties feeling how fucking wet she is.

"Fuck."

She gasps when I drag my mouth up her throat, when my fingers run through her wet cunt and I slide two inside her. "We're in a church."

"You think this is wrong?" I murmur, my lips brushing her ear. "I don't fucking care. Let them damn us for it."

Her breath hitches, a smile tugging at her mouth. "We're going to hell for this."

I smirk against her skin as I move my fingers in and out of her. "Sounds like fun… as long as you go with me."

I pull my fingers from her and slip them into my mouth, groaning as her taste coats my tongue.

"Fuck…" I savor it, dragging my teeth over my knuckles before letting them go. "I need to taste you, baby."

Chapter 43

Jaxon

I kiss her—hard, filthy—so she can taste herself on my lips, and walk her backward until the back of her thighs hit the first pew. Her gaze drops to my mouth, and I see it—the hunger, the way her pupils blow wide when she knows what I'm about to do.

"I have an idea," I murmur, my grin slow and deliberate.

I reach up, pulling the comb from her hair, letting the veil slip to the floor. It pools around her heels like a surrender flag. She's standing there in only her bra, panties, and those fucking heels that make my blood run hot.

I make quick work of the bra, then hook my fingers into her panties and drag them down her legs, tossing them aside.

Lowering myself to the ground, I lean back until my head rests against the polished wood of the pew. I spread my knees, patting the space between them.

"Get that pussy up here and let me worship you."

Her breath catches, but she does as she's told—one knee

on the pew beside my head, then the other. I wrap my hands around her thighs, pulling her down until she's hovering right where I want her.

The first taste hits my tongue like a drug. I groan against her, holding her in place as I drag my mouth over her, slow at first, then deeper, hungrier.

She braces herself on the back of the pew, hips rocking, head tipped back as a cry tears from her throat. The sound bounces off the high ceiling, echoing through the empty church like a confession.

I tighten my grip and bury my face in her, determined to wring every moan from her until she forgets where we are, who we are, and why this should be a sin.

Every filthy word that falls from her lips makes my cock throb harder. Praise drips from her like sin, her voice breaking on moans that spike straight through my chest and settle low in my gut.

When she starts to come, she grinds against my mouth, rocking hard, yanking on my hair like she's trying to fuse me to her. My name tears from her throat, loud, desperate—like I'm the god she's been praying to.

I ride it out with her, sucking her clit until she trembles and shudders against me, tasting every ounce of her pleasure.

"I need you in me," she pants, breathless, voice wrecked. "Now."

I'm on my feet in a second, my chest heaving. "Don't move."

My fingers fly to my belt, yanking it open, pushing my pants down just enough to free my cock. I wrap a hand around it, nudging the head through her slick folds, coating myself in her wetness before plunging in—one deep, punishing thrust to the hilt.

She arches hard, her head tipping back, a cry tearing from her lips that sounds like angels singing. My own groan rumbles through the space, mixing with hers.

"Fuck... you feel so good," I grit out, my hands gripping her hips. "You're my home, Cass. Exactly where I'm meant to be—inside you. Loving you."

I drive into her, my pace hard and relentless, the sound of our bodies colliding filling the room. I spread her ass cheeks apart, watching myself slide into her, over and over, and it's so fucking beautiful I almost lose it right there.

"Look at you," I rasp, thrusting deeper. "Look how perfect you take me."

She cries out, her voice breaking as she comes again, clenching tight around me.

"Play with your beautiful tits," I order, my voice dark, rough. "Pinch those pink nipples until they are red for me."

She obeys, fingers toying with those perfect peaks, and I drop one hand to rub her clit, working her through it. She shatters beneath me, her cry ringing out like the sweetest blasphemy I've ever heard.

"Listen how beautiful my whore comes for me."

But I'm not done with her. Not even close. I want to feel her squeeze my cock again—tight, desperate—while she comes apart in my arms.

I grip her hips and lift her clean off the pew, her legs wrapping around my waist in an instant. Her tongue is down my throat before I've even taken a step, her nails raking over my shoulders like she's trying to mark me all over again.

I cross the space to the altar, pressing her back against it. She gasps when I lift her higher and slide back into her, slow at first, just to feel that perfect stretch again. Then I hook her legs over my arms, spreading her wide for me like an offering.

Her arms brace on the altar behind her, head tipped back, her hair spilling over her shoulders as I fuck into her. Her full breasts bounce with every snap of my hips against hers, the sound of skin on skin echoing in the hollow quiet of the church.

"Look at me, baby." My voice is rough, commanding. "Let me see those green eyes when you choke my dick with your tight pussy."

Her gaze locks on mine, wild and glassy, and it's all I need. "Rub your clit. Come with me."

She does, circling that spot with frantic fingers, her breaths coming in jagged bursts as I pound into her. We break together, my hips slamming into hers as I spill into her, her body milking me for every last drop.

But she doesn't stop. Even after I've emptied inside her, she's still rubbing her clit, pinching her nipples, her voice breaking on a cry. "I'm—oh, fuck—I'm about to come again—"

I shift, setting her down just enough to move us, then sit on the altar steps with her straddling me. My hands grip her hips. "Ride me."

There's no hesitation, no build-up—she sinks down onto me in one smooth motion and starts riding me hard, taking exactly what she wants from me. The slap of her hips against mine is filthy, perfect.

"Lean back," I order, my voice low. "Let me see how pretty you look taking my fat cock in your tight cunt."

She braces her hands behind her on my thighs, leaning back so I can watch every stroke, every stretch. I reach up, pinching and tugging at her nipples, watching her chest rise and fall with ragged breaths.

"Fuck, baby... you're gonna make me come again."

The cum from earlier slides down her thighs, coating my lap, oozing down my balls and dripping to the floor beneath us. It's so filthy I almost lose my mind.

"I'm—oh—" she gasps, voice breaking. "I'm coming again—"

"So am I."

I hook my arms under hers, locking my grip on her shoulders and pulling her down as I thrust up hard, meeting her stroke for stroke until we shatter together. Her body clamps down around me, and I let go, groaning against her mouth as the world narrows to the heat, the squeeze, and the way she says my name like a prayer I'll never stop answering.

We stay locked together, kissing, rubbing, moving slow. Every brush of skin makes us both shudder—too sensitive, too raw, too full of each other to stop.

"I love you," she whispers against my mouth.

"I love you too, Cricket." My voice is rough, but it's the truth in its purest form. "I went fucking crazy when I thought you were gone. I haven't rested a second since you left my sight in New York."

Her hands slide up my neck, her eyes shining. "I'm here now."

Eventually, our breathing evens out, and she glances toward the door with a smirk. "How exactly am I supposed to walk out of a church in just panties and heels?"

I chuckle against her neck, nodding past her shoulder. "I brought you some clothes."

We finally separate, and I grab the torn wedding dress from the floor. I wipe myself off, then I stare between her legs, watching my cum run down her creamy thighs.

My smirk pure sin. "I want to push that cum back inside and fuck my baby into you."

"Oh, my god." She shakes her head at me but smiles as I lick up the column of her throat and wipe between her legs with the dress. "You just came twice."

"And I could come again."

She pulls out jeans and a soft T-shirt from the bag, slipping them on while I tuck myself back in and gather her discarded "bride" costume, dumping it in a bin near a side exit.

When she's dressed, I pull her in, sliding my hands into the back pockets of her jeans as we sway together in the quiet, just looking at each other. No barriers. No chains. Just us.

"You ready to go home?" I ask.

She nods.

"I need to tell you about your mom."

Her eyes widen instantly, and I hurry to get the words out. "She had a little fall, but I took care of her. Shanae's with her—she's okay. That's why it took me a little longer to get to you, baby, but she's fine."

Her eyes water, and she breathes out a shaky, "Thank you... for taking care of her."

I brush her hair out of her face and give her a soft smile. "She's got some good news for you."

Her chin trembles. "Is it... about her cancer?"

I grin now, teasing, because I know what she doesn't. "You won't tell me the secret ingredient... so I'm not telling you."

"Sugar," she blurts out. "It's a pinch of sugar."

I blink. "Seriously?!"

"Yes. Now tell me." Her eyes are desperate, her hands curling into my shirt.

My throat gets tight before I can say it. "She beat it, baby. She's in remission."

Cassidy gasps, her mouth falling open as tears spill down her cheeks. I feel my own vision blur. "She's going to be okay."

She laughs and cries at the same time, cupping my face and kissing me before wrapping her arms tight around my neck. I hold her like I'll never let go.

"Let's go," I murmur against her hair. "I want to take you home. I fucking hate London now."

She laughs into my chest.

"After I take you to see your mom," I add, pulling back just enough to look at her, "I'm hard launching you on my biker account. We're going to record so many biker couple videos you're going to be sick of me."

Her smile is radiant. "No, I won't."

"You'll forever be my backpack?"

"I'll forever be your everything."

I smirk at her and she already knows something shit-ass is coming her way. "You're the best billion dollars I ever spent."

I full on smile at her when she narrows her eyes.

"One billion, two hundred and thirty-three dollars and seventy-four cents... to be exact." Her hand slides down and squeezes my cock. "But who's counting?"

And as she walks away from me, that round ass swaying with each step I think:

Fuck. I'm going to marry this woman.

Welcome to
The Black Ledger

Where every desire has a price...
and every contract is final.

*Love The Auction? Don't stop now.
The next Black Ledger book awaits...*

The Black Ledger
Billionaires

Check Out www.RebekahSinclairWrites.com for more!